PHOENIX & CALISTA SAGA
BOOK 1

A WORLD DIVIDED

Emily Stone & *Diana Bloom*

◆ FriesenPress

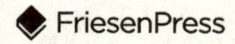

One Printers Way
Altona, MB R0G 0B0
Canada

www.friesenpress.com

Copyright © 2022 by Emily Stone & Diana Bloom
First Edition — 2022

Paul Schultz: Illustrator

Disclaimer
This book is a work of fiction.

All names, places, characters, events, and incidents are a product of the author(s) imagination or used in a fictional manner. Any resemblances to actual persons living or dead or events past or present are entirely coincidental.

All rights reserved.

No part of this publication may be reproduced in any form, or by any means, electronic or mechanical, including photocopying, recording, or any information browsing, storage, or retrieval system, without permission in writing from FriesenPress.

ISBN
978-1-03-914965-6 (Hardcover)
978-1-03-914964-9 (Paperback)
978-1-03-914966-3 (eBook)

1. FICTION, FANTASY, ROMANTIC

Distributed to the trade by The Ingram Book Company

A World Divided is a riveting drama action packed fantasy! The perfect balance of magic and technology, love and friendship and friction and tension! A must read!

-Danielle M

Do you enjoy magical fantasy that is spicy and adventurous? Then this young adult book series is for you. Emily and Diana have created a world of endless magical possibilities. The citizens whom live in West Marra and East Marra are not alike in many ways but there is a common link between the two. East Marraners love strong, fierce and have unbreakable bonds. Betrayals are rare but when they happen they are unforgivable. There are so many mysteries to uncover, with every action taken there is more to discover, more to revealed and curiosity needs answers!

A World Divided is a place where you should sync your soul into and enjoy the ride of the endless possibilities and the endless moments of happiness plus sorrow. I have enjoyed getting to know A world divided and you will as well.

Welcome to the beginning

-Simonne Rickett

Do you believe in magic? *A World Divided* transports you to such beautiful scenery and surroundings in Lamarra. It allows you to use all of your senses to enjoy the descriptive story-from flora and fauna, to foods and drink, to fancy dwellings! The map acts as useful tool and, the keys on the pages add an extra element! Many different parts of the plot allow you to make connections to your own life experiences-friendships and relationships, witty banter, adventures and travelling and the realities of life that combine both real and surreal! There are many different characters that are masterfully interwoven into the plot! The journey allows you to escape reality and enjoy laughs along the way! The stars, water and elements of nature were appreciated!

-Gen Louise

DEDICATION

To the Escapists.

ACKNOWLEDGEMENTS

This book would not have happened without the team of people who have come together to make this project possible. The team at FriesenPress has been outstanding in their commitment to the development and success of this book. Their knowledge and expertise have proven to be invaluable, and for this we thank you profoundly.

There is another support team that also needs to be recognized: our friends and family who have been there to support this endeavour from its inception. Our parents, Rocco and Tina; Carmela, our aunt; and our cousin, Lauren, have provided sobering reality checks sprinkled with outstandingly honest and constructive criticism as well as knowledgeable information about culinary artistry. Thank you for keeping us grounded in this project as with everything else you have been a part of in our lives. What would we do without you?

To the friends we have adopted as family, thank you for your endless enthusiasm, encouragement, and support. You know who you are, but for those who don't know the great depths of generosity found in your spirits, Simonne, Iola, Tracy, Melissa, Leslie, and Lena—we thank you.

I (Emily) would like to also thank my husband, Danny, who, for reasons I could never explain, has put up with my endless bombardment of weird and often uncomfortable questions in my quest to better describe a scene or a character. He thanked me for saying "yes." when he proposed, and now I need to thank him for sticking around now that he knows what he has signed up for in a marriage to me and my crazy ideas.

Finally, to you, our readers, for without your interest in our fantasy world and the characters in it, we would have no one to share our story with. For that we are eternally grateful.

 Thank you
  Emily & Diana

PREFACE
Some things are just simply better together.

This book was dreamed into existence during a time when the world was in the grip of its first pandemic in one hundred years. Isolation and the trials that came with it became a harsh pill to swallow. The contrasting worlds described in this book are a reflection on one of many views of what our society has become. More often than not, there is more to any given situation than meets the eye. Individualism is a wonderful quality to possess, and we should all wear it with confidence. However, inevitably, there comes a time when we all need someone to lean on, and in those moments when people need each other most is when we recognize the value of togetherness.

"If you want to go fast, go alone. If you want to go far, go together."
-African proverb

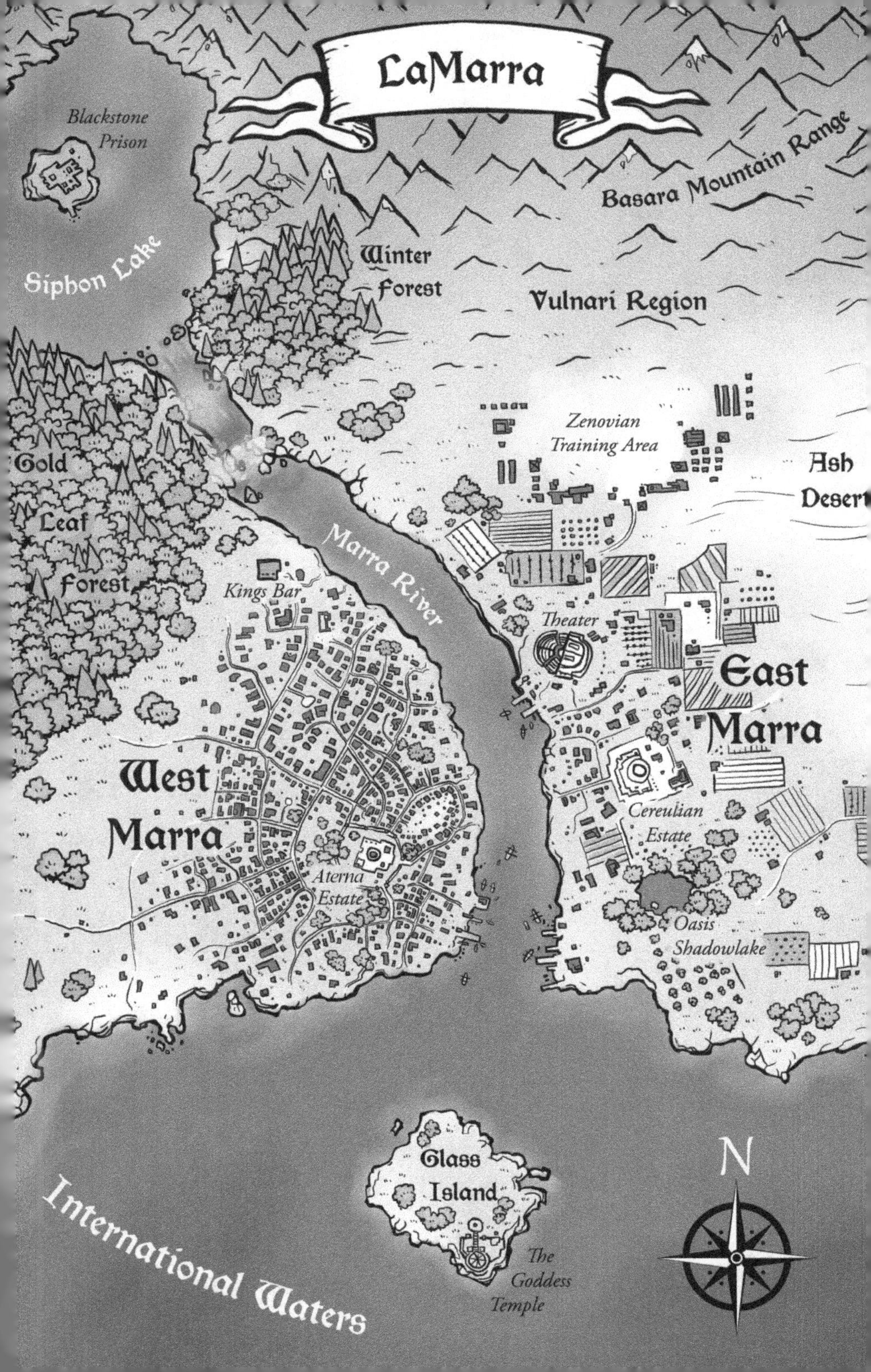
LaMarra
Blackstone Prison
Siphon Lake
Basara Mountain Range
Winter Forest
Vulnari Region
Zenovian Training Area
Ash Desert
Gold Leaf Forest
Marra River
Kings Bar
Theater
East Marra
West Marra
Cereulian Estate
Aterna Estate
Oasis Shadowlake
Glass Island
The Goddess Temple
N
International Waters

CHAPTER 1
Queen's Audience
Calista

Calista stood awestruck, gazing up toward the temple where the Goddess Marra's shrine sat. The misty air glittered and swirled in soft, translucent clouds, imbuing the surrounding area with an atmosphere of tangible, otherworldly power. The temple was situated at the peak of a gently inclining path leading up from the beach not far from the marina. Lush green tropical trees bordered the path, as did flowers with blooms so large they could create a canopy if the island gardeners didn't groom them into perfection. Calista inhaled the jasmine- and plumeria-infused air as she meandered up the path toward the temple, holding a secure case containing unblessed daggers.

A light breeze ruffled the hem of her gauzy, cream-coloured dress, making it flutter and giving her the appearance of walking on waves. She arrived at the entrance to the atrium and gently pushed aside the delicate curtains that shielded the shrine within from view and stepped inside. She glanced around the large space, then focused her attention on the sparse furnishings. In the center of the atrium sat a simple stone pedestal table and two soft but elegant wingback chairs with soft green upholstery. As she stood at the table and unpacked the unblessed blades, Phoenix entered the space and tossed his folio on the table. It knocked the case of daggers over, sending them crashing to the floor. Calista grabbed a blade and held it to Phoenix's throat. With a white-knuckled grip on the unblessed dagger's hilt, Calista eased the blade away from the pulsing vein in Phoenix's neck.

A few tense moments passed before Calista spoke. "Relax. As if I would slit your throat with an unblessed blade," she said, her warm breath brushing the side of his stubble-covered cheek.

Calista collected the daggers and rearranged them on the tray, then placed it in the centre of the table. She locked eyes with Phoenix, sending him a silent warning: *Drop these daggers again, and you will become a human pincushion.* Phoenix's brooding expression suggested he understood her meaning, but he also knew the smirk that crossed his face would enrage her. He had known since they were children, since before they became unwilling rulers of their respective territories—picking up where their parents left off, forced to assume the roles and responsibilities of opposing rulers. Roles steeped in traditions that neither of them felt entirely convinced was right to uphold.

The atrium itself overlooked the reflection pool that flowed away from the temple into a clear, sparkling pond. The calming sounds of the short waterfall just beyond the water's edge added to the temple's tranquility. The pool hummed with ancient and intrinsic magic. The shimmer of bioluminescence sparkling along the water's surface showed that magic was alive in that space. In a small alcove in the corner of the atrium stood a marble fountain that was used for ceremonial occasions and required the water from the pool. A carved statue of the Goddess Marra was situated just behind the rim, overlooking the bowl of the fountain that faced the atrium.

Calista finished arranging the daggers, then took her seat across from Phoenix, whose dark presence was at odds with the temple's calming atmosphere. He was glowering at her, his gray eyes piercing her. *If looks could kill,* she thought. He was well dressed in a black tailored jacket and dress pants with a white linen shirt open at the collar, revealing a gold chain that hung around his neck, though the pendant disappeared below the open buttons of his shirt. His clothes hugged his muscular form and accentuated his dark, occasionally dangerous mood. There was no denying his attractiveness, the strong jawline, covered by what seemed to be a permanent five o'clock shadow, was always groomed to perfection. He raked his fingers through his short dark hair and took what she could only assume was an exasperated breath. *Wonderful,* Calista thought with disdain as she watched him across the table.

In the five years since their parent's mysterious disappearance into a wicked storm that raged over Glass Island, Calista and Phoenix, both young and inexperienced, had become responsible for the fate of their countries at the tender ages of twenty and twenty-five, respectively. Within days of the horrific storm and while reconstruction was still in progress, their lives as they knew them ended. As Queen of East Marra, Calista took to heart the values instilled in her by the king and queen, keeping her people close and doing all she could to preserve the now dwindling magic that her people so depended on for their survival. Phoenix, King of West Marra, continued to fortify his lands by suppressing the chaos of magic with technological interventions.

In assuming the roles of rulers in divine power, Phoenix and Calista were forced to discuss the equitable division of the Zenovia Army, appointed in divinity by the Goddess Marra. It was not uncommon for their monthly meetings to devolve into vicious bickering matches.

"Why did you bother bringing daggers here, today of all days? What are you thinking?" Phoenix asked, his words dripping with mockery and disdain.

Calista narrowed her eyes at him. "Unlike you, your wealthy, spoiled highness, I am being resourceful. Why make a separate trip out here for the sole purpose of blessing the blades in the water of reflection pool?" Calista took a deep breath as she smoothed her dress, sitting straighter in her seat and levelling a solid stare at Phoenix across the table, challenging him to say something nasty. Phoenix broke their stare and sat up, accentuating his considerable size over her, then opened the sleek black folder in front of him and started reviewing the chicken scratch written within.

Calista laced her fingers together and set her hands on the table as a young servant walked in and placed two drinks in front of them. The server nodded nervously and then scuttled out, obviously aware of the tension in the room.

Calista started. "I think—"

"I don't want this to become another pointless argument, Cali, so let's just agree that I'll take full and complete command of the Zenovia Army moving forward," Phoenix interrupted.

Calista levelled a look of pure contempt at him, trying with every ounce of self-control she possessed to keep her boiling temper from exploding. "Nix," she said, struggling to keep her voice calm and even, "I am here to negotiate the terms of the Zenovia Army, who in case you have forgotten, pay allegiance to the Goddess Marra and protect both of our regions from potential threats. If you have no intentions of working with me, I'll command the Zenovia Army myself. As you are well aware, I possess my own blessed blade, and believe me, I am very tempted to use it right now."

"Vicious little thing, aren't you?" he murmured, then narrowed his eyes to slits as he regarded her with a slight tilt of his head. "You wouldn't dare take on the full financial responsibility of divine military protection. Your territory could never support it. Your people are practically on death's doorstep as it is, and you don't have the funds." He scoffed dismissively. "Please, spare me the drama. We both know I could buy and sell East Marra ten times over."

Calista sat back, dropping her hands from the table to her lap, so he couldn't see that she was now clenching her hands into fists. "You make a point of flaunting your wealth at every one of our meetings. I know you're rich beyond measure, but you're so broken. If you think that your precious defenses are worth anything without the trust of your people, you are delusional and pathetic."

She twisted in her seat to look at the reflection pool, crossing one leg over the other and revealing her thigh through the slit in her dress. The silence stretched between them, both Phoenix and Calista seemingly absorbed by the nasty exchange. Calista could feel Phoenix's intense stare burning a hole right through her. To stop herself from revealing her discomfort, she picked up her glass and took a long sip of the cool blue liquid, savouring the delicate bubbles as they tickled their way down her throat and the slight sweetness and tart flavour that lingered on her tongue. It reminded her of her childhood; this drink was pure happiness in a glass for her.

She must have had a slight smile on her lips as she set the glass on the table because she heard Phoenix's low chuckle. It broke her from the reverie and made her look up at him. Of course, he was smirking.

"You always did love these kiddie drinks." He pushed his own glass away from him dismissively. "I'll take you seriously when you decide to grow up." The low timber of his voice emphasized how little faith he seemed to have in her abilities.

"If it's so hard to take me seriously, why do we bother to meet each month?" she asked. "In all the years since our parents disappeared in that storm, and we were forced to take command, it feels like we haven't accomplished anything. For as long as I can remember, the West has suppressed magic. It has become weaker and weaker, and you've all but eliminated it with your stupid technologies. You can't seem to realize you will never get rid of it; our regions are so deeply intertwined. I'm not convinced we can ever successfully separate. If it hasn't happened by now will it ever? Your parents didn't understand it, and obviously, neither do you. I really thought you were serious when we first agreed to run things differently than our parents, to cast off the shackles of the past, but it's obvious to me that the only changes we have made and stuck to so far are to drop some of the over-the-top traditional formalities our parents were so keen on." The frustration in her words was evident, the air around them increasingly uncomfortable.

"Your predecessors chose to stick with magic and all the chaos it brings," he replied. "Now that it's disappearing, you're suffering the consequences of that decision, and that's no one's fault but your own."

He stood and collected his folio with an air of arrogance, accentuated by an ever-deepening brooding attitude that only he could possess. He paused and looked over his shoulder as though he had forgotten something, then returned to the table and picked up the tray of daggers, carrying them to the fountain.

"Glad you remembered we both need to be touching these daggers while they're being blessed," Calista said disdainfully.

She joined Phoenix, who stood facing the goddess statue situated above the bowl of the pedestal that used ancient magic to draw water up from the reflection pool. The bioluminescence in the water swirled softly as it was drawn up into the bowl. The shimmering neon-blue water was hypnotizing to behold. Together, Calista and Phoenix picked up each dagger by its intricately carved handle made of Vulnari steel mined from the caves in Vulnari. They dipped the blades up to the hilt into the shimmering pool of water to bestow upon them the divine blessing that allowed Zenovia warriors to take a life in battle.

The ritualistic act of blessing the blades together seemed to settle some of the tension that had been clouding the atmosphere between Phoenix and Calista. Once the last blade was blessed, they both seemed more relaxed. Phoenix inhaled deeply and looked at Calista for a moment as she arranged the blades in the case that she'd brought them in, careful to secure each blade so that they wouldn't get damaged on the choppy boat ride back to East Marra. She sensed him watching her and felt like he might reach forward to pull her hair out of the way, but he stopped short, keeping his hand tucked in his pants pocket.

"That's a beautiful key," Phoenix said softly, almost as if noticing it for the first time.

"Since when do you deliver compliments?" Calista scoffed. She picked up the key to drop it into the neckline of her dress, suddenly feeling self-conscious that he was watching her so closely.

"Never mind. And the polite thing to say is 'thank you,'" Phoenix said as he pulled back the curtain for her to pass through.

"Thank you," she replied in earnest, then caught his gaze for a few seconds before walking briskly through the curtain toward the winding stone path that led out of the shrine and to the marina where their boats awaited them.

Just before they parted ways, Phoenix caught her arm by the crook of her arm. "Make no mistake," he said. "The only reason I blessed those blades with you today is so that your region can maintain some level of protection. I see how you look at me, Cali. I'm not the ignorant tyrant you think I am, or rather you expect me to be."

"And what of West Marra then?" she asked. "You're above the protection of the Zenovian Army?"

"West Marra is fortified well enough. We'll be fine if attacked. I can't say the same for you and East Marra."

"Well enough that the renegades from the north have infiltrated your capital right under your nose? Yes, I've heard about the riots," she continued before he could even formulate the question.

Phoenix released her elbow, shoved his hands in the pockets of his trousers, and nodded toward the boat that was to take her back to the mainland.

"Your chariot awaits."

CHAPTER 2
The yacht
Phoenix

Phoenix lingered on the beach, watching as Calista walked through the sand toward the East Marra fishing docks to board the vessel that would bring her back to what he imagined was a dilapidated estate in the East Marra territory. Looking at the beat-up, weather-worn fishing vessel, he wondered if it was even safe enough to make it back across the international waters that divided the mainland from Glass Island. It looked like one rough wave would shatter the little boat. At any rate, he watched as Calista picked up the hem of her dress and climbed rather inelegantly into the boat, then greeted the captain and first mate with a firm handshake and a warm smile. She got to work straight away, helping the captain and other deckhands hoist the sails and rigging.

She looked completely out of place wearing that flowing dress and all that jewellery, and yet she looked happier at that moment than she had throughout their meeting. If he was being honest with himself, he envied that about her. She trusted people so freely. Except him; she probably didn't trust him as far as she could throw him. That was a thought that crept up on him more often than he liked to admit. He had felt that way ever since he was a boy, and his mother's creative ways of doling out discipline had caused him to develop a healthy suspicion of anyone near him, including members of family and staff. The fear of deception was forever present in his mind.

Once Calista was clearly on board and as safe as she could be on that floating death trap, he made his way along the pier toward his luxury yacht, which was fully fortified with several defensive features that would whisk him back to his equally luxurious and fortified palace in West Marra.

As Phoenix boarded the sleek, clean vessel, the staff on board greeted him formally with a bow and offered him an empty glass, which he took. "Whisky," he said.

The young wait staff moved to the onboard liquor cabinet and took out unopened bottle of aged whisky and poured Phoenix three fingers' worth. The young man who poured it left Phoenix alone in the open air of the deck to enjoy his drink while they sped off through the water toward Aterna Palace in West Marra's capital city, Phoenix's home.

His mind drifted back to Calista helping with the rigging on the boat, and he wondered when exactly they had become such adversaries. Things were not like that between them when they were children, and yet since becoming rulers they had both leaned into the narrative of mutual hatred for one another.

He recalled a moment from his adolescence, on the brink of adulthood, really, when he was on holiday with his family at Glass Island. Of course, King Calico of East Marra made every effort to be there with his family at the same time, which meant Calista would be there as well. Phoenix recalled how that completely changed his enthusiasm about going. While on holiday the rules were relaxed, and the royal families could mingle freely, including him and Calista.

At barely fifteen years old, she was already stunningly beautiful. She could have had any boy on the beach, and yet she seemed so disinterested in any of them. She was training to be ready when called upon as a Zenovia warrior in the army. It was difficult to find a moment alone with her; she was always surrounded by people.

One day she took out a small rowboat, and she got caught in an undercurrent that dragged her out farther than she was able to swim back. When Phoenix found out, he rushed to the jetty of rocks, and the tightness in his chest nearly consumed him. Without a moment's consideration for his own safety, he jumped into the water and started swimming toward her. She was fighting to keep the rowboat from capsizing by pushing and pulling the oars. The current was too strong and was dragging her into bigger swells.

By sheer luck and force of will, Phoenix reached the rowboat and, with Calista's help, he hauled himself into the boat and took one of the oars. Together, they started moving the rickety little rowboat out of the current. By the time they made it to calmer waters, they collapsed, relieved and laughing that not only had they made it near the shore, but they were alive, and no one really saw what had happened, or so he thought.

Phoenix figured he could play it off like the drama of him swimming out to her was no big deal, so he could avoid scaring her. Unfortunately, King Calico did see what happened and reported it to Phoenix's mother, Queen Opal. Since they were on holiday, neither ruler made an event of it and instead just agreed to never speak of the incident. Phoenix was given the threat of a lifetime for risking his life to save that of the opposing ruler's daughter. Queen Opal was a shrewd woman, keen to preserve her position and power and always on the prowl to acquire more. No one, not even her adult son, was going to jeopardize her ambitions.

On the evening they returned to Aterna, after spending several weeks on the island after the boat incident, Queen Opal arranged to have Phoenix's dinner sent to his private chambers, where she ordered him to stay until she came for him later that evening. This was not unusual behaviour on her part; she was obviously segregating him to punish him for what happened on Glass Island.

With caution Phoenix inspected his food. The last time this happened he had woken up in a dark windowless cell. He spent days there alone, and not for the first time. It was his mother's choice punishment for him from the time he could walk. He shoved away the food. No amount of hunger would land him in that cell again. He poured himself a glass of whisky, which he kept at his bedside, instead, dropped a few ice cubes in the glass, and settled in for the night. The booze took effect slowly. Just as he began to let the comfort of unconsciousness overtake him, the thickness that invaded his senses felt familiar . . . too familiar. Seconds later, he realized the ice had been tampered with.

Phoenix recalled waking up and rubbing the sleep from his eyes, scrubbing the palms of his hands on his face as he realized he was waking up once again huddled against the wall in the cell. Sheer frustration had him slamming his fist into the stone wall until his knuckles were broken and bleeding. There was no indication of time or day or how long he would be in there this time. Eventually, his parents would let him out . . . Eventually.

Such memories crept into his thoughts frequently enough to keep him vigilant. His own mother had cultivated his deeply embedded mistrust in people. If he couldn't trust his own mother, who could he trust?

Calista was significantly different. He always felt like he shared an unspoken connection with her. Due to circumstances beyond his control, they never explored what that connection could be or if it was anything of importance.

The whisky bottle was half empty when they docked in the West Marra marina. Phoenix dumped the remaining whiskey over the side of the boat and then set the bottle on the bar by the liquor cabinet. Then sauntered off the boat and into the car that was waiting to drive him home.

He hesitated for a moment before climbing into the vehicle's backseat and absentmindedly fingered the Aquavass that was tucked into his shirt. It was a habit from his youth that never left him. The water in the vial that was ensconced in the gold pendant was from the reflection pool, a reminder of his divinity and his connection to his people. Everyone in LaMarra possessed a pendant with water from the reflection pool. It was gifted upon birth, protected throughout their lifetime, and used as a communication bond with loved ones when in the presence of water. On the ride back home, he couldn't help but wonder where Calista's pendant was. His thoughts returned to the key she wore so prominently. It looked vaguely familiar, but he couldn't place it. As the car pulled up the tree-lined driveway toward the front of his house, he let those thoughts fade away, resolving not to think about Calista until their next meeting the following month.

CHAPTER 3
Explosion
Calista

Calista enjoyed helping with the rigging. It was more entertaining than just sitting aboard a boat. She enjoyed the views on the voyage back to the East Marra marina, but she also enjoyed the camaraderie of the fishermen exchanging lively stories about their latest adventure at sea.

Phoenix's fancy yacht did not escape her notice, however. Although she wondered what living with that kind of luxury all the time was like, she couldn't help but notice how lonely he looked. She figured he probably liked it that way. She also couldn't stop considering what it might be like to know what was really going on in the deep recesses of his mind, what made him so closed off to those around him. Regardless of his attitude, there was no shortage of attention paid to him from young, attractive, and eligible young women from both sides of the river. A brief and unexpected pang of jealousy swept through her as she lingered on the notion of *other young women*.

Just as Calista began to relax and settle in for the beautiful albeit slightly choppy ride across the water, the radio started to emit a frantic SOS signal. As the captain looked about and asked for coordinates, in the distance they heard what sounded like an explosion and saw another vessel burst into flames. The captain quickly changed course and began heading toward the distressed vessel. The wake of the other boats racing toward it caused water to slosh onto the boat. Cold, salty water whipped at Calista's face as she helped where she could to adjust the rigging and throw flotation devices and rope to the men who had fallen overboard.

As the remains of the exploded fishing vessel floated past, pieces of what appeared to be fishing nets bearing the West Marra insignia bobbed in the water. They were poaching East Marra's fish. The realization that the dwindling supply was due to West Marra's overfishing slammed into her like a ton of bricks. A heaviness settled into the pit of her stomach, and she decided she would confront Phoenix personally. Her people were on the brink of starvation. They depended so heavily on what the fishermen brought in to sustain them that this felt like a personal attack. Calista felt any attack on her people in an acute way. Rage built up inside her to the point that she no longer saw reason.

The moment the fishing boat docked, Calista disembarked and made her way toward Luxx, her advisor, protection officer, and friend. Luxx's small stature was deceiving as she stood by the vehicle intended to bring them back to Cerulean Estate. Her bright blonde hair was woven into a thick braid that hung down over her shoulder. It contrasted with her black battle leathers, which was her preferred attire. The hilt of her blessed blade peeked out of the primary sheath in her chest plate. The chest plate was designed for easy access to various knives and weapons but also to display the blessed blade, which identified her as an active member of the Zenovia Army. Her blue eyes widened as she watched Calista approach, outrage oozing from every step.

"What happened?" Luxx asked, recognizing the look of determination on Calista's face.

"Fucking West Marra has been poaching our fish, and one of our biggest fishing boats has been destroyed in an explosion." Calista was beyond politeness and diplomatic words; she was out for blood. Luxx understood how hard this hit home for Calista. Without needing further instruction, she directed the driver of the car she had hired to drive them from the marina back to Cerulean Estate. Calista would get changed, and then she and Luxx would take a field trip across the river into West Marra.

CHAPTER 4
Field Trip
Calista

Luxx made quick arrangements for Calista and herself to make the trek into West Marra. Going from east to west was no small task. Favours were called in and promises made. The decision to arrive unannounced was made to ensure they couldn't be turned away and denied an audience with the king, but it was also to avoid the fanfare that came with making an official visit.

A few hours or so after Calista docked, she made sure the injured sailors were being tended to by the centenary healers. Then she was whisked off to Cerulean Estate where she changed out of her feathery dress and into a relaxed version of her fighting leathers, the ones she wore when she opted to join in the training sessions conducted by the Zenovia senior warriors for new recruits. It was also Luxx's preferred attire. The battle leathers' sleek yet subdued design was intended for ease of movement, unlike the ceremonial attire, which was more ostentatious, and the full battle garments, which sported more weapons holsters and a generally more protective look.

"I know you hate going into West Marra, but is that really necessary?" Calista asked as she tightened the wide belt around her waist.

"The real question is, where is your blade?" Luxx retorted without looking up and without an ounce of hesitation. "Are you going to go with the thigh strap or chest band?"

"Neither. I'm mad, but I don't want to kill him." Despite her words, Calista couldn't help but feel undressed without her dagger at her side. *I don't have to use the blade,* she reasoned with herself, especially since it looked like Luxx was gearing up to fight off an army of rabid giant Savarras, lizard-like creatures with ridged backs that reside in the waterways and among the foliage throughout LaMarra. Pests to some and pets to others, they appeared in a variety of colours and sizes. The rarest of which was the gold Savarra, which ancient legend said could produce prophecies, none of which had been recounted in recent history.

Luxx waited impatiently at the door of Calista's private chamber as Calista made a few final adjustments to her attire, putting the finishing touches on her long braid. When Calista finally approached her, she paused. Luxx relaxed slightly and looked at Calista. Calista leaned forward, and Luxx did the same. They touched foreheads for a moment before pulling apart and making their way down to the palace's front courtyard, where a beat-up pickup truck was waiting to bring them to the riverbank on the south side of Shadow Lake, which was located outside of the bank of trees that separated Shadow Lake from the surrounding landscape.

Once they arrived, Luxx sent the driver back while Calista made her way toward the man in the boat. She paid him in trade, offering a bundle of prepared food for him and his family in exchange for passage across the widest part of the River Marra. After a quick inspection of the food she offered, the man smiled broadly and welcomed the women into his boat.

It was a slower ride than necessary. Not only was the boat old, in an effort to conserve fuel, the seasoned sailor used wind power and his expert navigational skills to propel them across the water.

It was nearly dusk when they docked and disembarked. West Marra was humming with activity. The riverbank was filled with people bustling about, finishing up the day's errands, eating at restaurants, shopping, and generally enjoying the waterfront atmosphere. It was a world of difference from the East Marra from which they had departed.

Luxx kept Calista focused and reminded her constantly to stay aware, not to trust anyone, and most of all to stay mad, remembering what Phoenix did. Because of him her people had suffered, and some had died.

Calista had always been committed to her people, just like her parents before her. She was tired of being wronged. She felt for her people and suffered alongside them.

Luxx pulled the sides of her jacket tightly around her and pulled her hood up to cover her blonde locks. She instructed Calista to do the same to better obscure her face and clothing, so she could hail a wave vehicle. Wave taxis were always cruising the crowded streets, available for hire. It was a fantastic service, one that Calista often wished she could have in East Marra, but the number of cars and fuel necessary to run such a service was well beyond the means of even the wealthiest merchants and business owners in East Marra.

Calista has only ever seen Aurum, the capital of West Marra, a handful of times before she became Queen, and always in the company of her parents. Aterna Estate was a stunning building. Modern. Massive. Sleek. Windows and water features everywhere. It was a beautiful palace, one that was completely at odds with its occupant. The place left nothing to the imagination, its airy and seemingly endless rooms flowing elegantly into each other. Calista remembered the gardens the most from the events she attended with her parents. She never really had the opportunity to explore the rest of the palace.

The wave ride pulled up at the property's giant gate. The women got out and paid the driver, then waited for him to speed off down the road before Calista dared to lower her hood and take a breath of the city's thick, fuel-scented air.

Luxx grasped the bars of the wrought-iron gate and gave it a shake. "This was your plan to get us inside unannounced?" Calista asked as she watched Luxx fuss with the lock.

"Do you have a better idea?" Luxx asked, her voice dripping with annoyance.

"Look at this place. It's fortified digitally, Luxx!" Calista said. Luxx was more than an adviser to Calista; they were close friends. Together, they had gotten into plenty of late-night shenanigans when they were younger. This was different though. Especially since Calista's regency, they couldn't afford to make silly mistakes. Luxx's sworn duty now was to advise and protect Calista.

Calista surveyed the gate and all its fortifications, trying to recall the last time she came with her family to an event hosted by Phoenix's parents, King Marlon and Queen Opal. She and Phoenix were young then and got up to a fair bit of nonsense, running around the grounds trying to trip the security system to watch the guards go mad looking for intruders. There was a spot along the tree-lined street that created a border around the estate that the laser system could not fully cover. Calista began walking along close to the trees, listening carefully for the hum of power that indicated the invisible security beams were active. She arrived at a corner where the trees met, but the branches between them were bare of leaves.

"Pass me your mister," Calista said, reaching her hand expectantly toward Luxx.

"What for?" Luxx asked as she reached into one of the pockets of her training leathers and pulled out a one-ounce bottle containing water from Shadow Lake. It allowed the user to spray a puff of the water on a wound to promote healing. "Are you trying to heal the tree's naked branches?"

Calista spritzed once where she expected the invisible beams to be and saw a puff of bioluminescence when the water made contact with the laser. She moved a bit farther along the gap and spritzed again. No shimmer of bioluminescence revealing the presence of magic. She had found the weak link in the fence. A sly smile spread across Calista's face as she grabbed Luxx's hand and pulled her through the slim opening of the trees and into the back garden of Aterna Estate.

They hugged the tree line until they reached the stone path that led to the far end of the manicured flower garden. All of the flowers there were stunningly beautiful—but deadly poisonous. Yet another layer to the security that protected the estate.

Conscious of the fact that guards regularly patrolled the palace grounds, Calista and Luxx quickly found an open door that would grant them access to Aterna's inner sanctum. The doors that opened onto the back garden were obscured by a waterfall that appeared to be coming from the edge of an infinity pool above, but when opened, they pushed aside the water that cascaded over them.

"Of course he would have a fancy pool filled with no one using it just for the sake of having one," Calista muttered. Luxx cast her gaze upwards, taking in the sight before her. Calista could see she was taken aback by the sheer frivolity of the water use and the palace's overall sense of opulence.

"Come on," Calista said, urging Luxx forward. "The water will part for us as we approach. It's part of the estate's magic."

"Wait. Won't that alert security though?" Luxx cautioned.

"Yes, it will, but it will take a moment before they get to the doors, and they will be alerted to another royal being in the building as soon as I pass the threshold because of this." Calista reached into the neckline of her battle leathers and pulled out her Aquavass necklace. "The water in the vial is uniquely connected to my parents and me. It's known to be associated with royalty. Security will realize that." Calista realized Luxx was well out of her comfort zone now and fearing she would not be able to protect Calista if necessary.

Luxx steeled herself and tried to focus all of her energy on the task at hand. "So, what exactly is the plan here? Run inside, security finds us, and hauls us out on our ass?" This assessment of the "plan" made Calista chuckle, so she felt an explanation was in order.

"We'll approach the doors. I'll make sure the vial on my necklace comes into contact with the water. If we're quick, we can get through even if we get soaked. It won't keep out a recognized royal. It's a weak security feature that I'm sure he is working on.

"Once inside, we need to find Phoenix. I suggest a top-down approach. I'll go up the right side, and you can take the left. Use our bond if you get into trouble. That's why we mixed the water in our vials in the first place." As Calista explained the break-and-enter plan, the knowledge that it could all be avoided was not lost on her. However, she didn't want to risk being declined an invitation or waste time making proper diplomatic arrangements to visit. Phoenix's advisor, Knoxx, was known to make visits difficult to obtain. Calista often felt like he was trying to prevent her and Phoenix from interacting.

Luxx reached into her battle leathers and pulled out her necklace. She wrapped her hand around the pendant that contained her vial of water and squeezed it tightly. Luxx had an ancient pendant that protected her water vial. It was an antique, a strong steel piece of jewellery that was made in the Vulnari people's distinctive style. It was beautifully crafted and intricate yet very different from the gold and diamond swirls that protected Calista's vial.

As they approached the doors, they passed a large fountain with cascading water sparkling with plumes of bioluminescence as it flowed down into the pool below. The centrepiece of the fountain was a stunningly carved marble statue of a shapely, half-naked woman with wings holding what looked like a birdcage above her head as if it were a fruit basket. Calista didn't pause to take in all the details, even though something drew her to that fountain. That was not a distraction she could afford at the moment. She needed to find Phoenix.

Once inside the estate, Luxx gave Calista a sharp nod and then squeezed her upper arm reassuringly before jogging up the stars on the left-hand side into that wing of the palace. Calista tore up the right-hand staircase—and crashed directly into a large, bald man with dark eyes wearing a black suit and an earpiece.

Calista lowered her hood and stood at her full height, refusing to be intimidated by the man. She cleared her throat and lifted her chin. "Knoxx, I'm here to see Phoenix," she said with as much authority as she could muster. "You can take me to him now. Please and thank you." In the distance, she could hear Luxx opening and closing doors as she worked her way through the hallway until she reached the balcony overlooking the rotunda.

Luxx came up beside Calista, who was in the most awkward staring contest with Knoxx, who was not budging. She was eye level with his chest and, coincidentally, staring directly at his Aquavass. It looked oddly familiar to her. In fact, it was exactly like Luxx's pendant, but his had been modified to incorporate diamond detailing around the vial and the insignia of West Marra.

"Well," Luxx said expectantly, subtly angling herself in a way that would allow her to swiftly defend Calista if necessary. She discreetly hovered her hand over the hilt of the blade strapped to her thigh.

"It's OK," Calista said, chancing a glance at Luxx. "I have already announced the reason for our presence." With the quickest shift of her eyes Luxx confirmed that she understood the assignment. An instant later, Calista darted off down the hallway, leaving Luxx to distract and engage Knoxx in a brief scuffle. He tapped his earpiece and shouted instructions to other members of the security staff seconds before he was winded by a swift kick to the groin that dropped him to his knees. That allowed Luxx to manoeuvre behind him with her hands braced on either side of his head, ready to twist. Knoxx cursed. It was an old language, one that he reverted to when he was bested.

"Calm down," Luxx said as she released him. "I know better than to take your life that way."

Knoxx overpowered her as he stood up, pinning Luxx up against the railing and threatening to toss her over into the rotunda. "Don't do that again," he growled. He let her down and tied her wrists behind her back, then marched her down the hall toward the waiting area that led to Phoenix's office.

Meanwhile, Calista was opening and slamming every door she came across, poking her head into each room and calling for Phoenix, taunting him to come out.

"Where the hell are you?" she said as much to herself as anyone around who was in earshot.

The second door from the end of the hallway opened, and Phoenix poked his head out, his face twisted with annoyance and budding rage. "What the fuck?" he shouted. He looked around and then his gaze landed on Calista, who was coming at him fast, clad in black leather and with her hair braided.

She planted a hand on his chest and shoved him back into the room, then slammed the door behind her.

"Funny way to say hello," she said. "What the fuck? I should be asking you the same question!"

Ignoring her, Phoenix went to the intercom and called for his security team. When there was no immediate response, he dipped his finger into a shallow decorative dish of water mounted on the wall and drew two diagonal lines on his forearm.

"Seriously!" Calista shouted, on the verge of rage. "You're using your bond to call your advisor here? You've got to be kidding me," she said, scoffing and shaking her head in disbelief. "The awful chaos of magic you hate so much and yet here you are using your water bond," she muttered as she shook her head and rolled her eyes.

Her behaviour seemed to grate on his nerves, putting him on edge. "How did you even get in here undetected, Cali?" he said, the anger that infused his words unmistakable.

"Wouldn't you like to know," she shot back.

"I knew palace security was breached, but . . . never mind." He clearly didn't want to give away any information about his obviously lacking security system.

The room Calista found him in looked more like a study than a library or an office. The room had a small bar in the corner, a sleek and modern marble-ensconced fireplace that divided the room into what appeared to be a receiving area, and a more private area toward the back.

The bar area had chairs and low tables while the back had a large, expansive sofa and ottoman and a frame with all manner of moving pictures mounted on the wall. Calista chalked it up to the magic of the estate and didn't give it a second thought. She was still raging over what had happened to her fleet of fishermen.

There was a gentle tapping on the door. Phoenix moved to open it, careful not to turn his back on Calista. She noticed his defensive stance as he backed toward the door, never taking his eyes off her. She couldn't help but feel like he was looking at her like she was psychotic. He opened the door to find Knoxx with Luxx beside him. She was furious, her hands trussed together.

With a discreet nod, Knoxx reluctantly released Luxx's arm. She shrugged away from him and held her bound wrists out, so he could snip the tie that held them together. Once her wrists were freed, she made a show of smoothing her hair and the front of her battle leathers, checking and securing her various daggers, went to stand beside Calista.

They exchanged the briefest of nods to ensure they were both unharmed. Then Calista turned on Phoenix, praying her rage wouldn't seep through and cause her to act irrationally. "Explain yourself," she said.

Knoxx and Phoenix exchanged a glance. There was an unmistakable smirk on Phoenix's face that matched the one threatening to break through on Knoxx's usual stony expression.

"I was trying to unwind from today's *stimulating* meeting," Phoenix said, his voice dripping with condescension.

Desperately trying to control her blood from boiling over, Calista replied as calmly and regally as she could. "Cut the shit, asshole! A third of my fishing fleet is mangled and burned beyond recognition, and some of my fishermen died today!"

Phoenix stared at her for several long moments, apparently stunned by the accusation. He didn't appear to have any idea what she was talking about.

Phoenix gestured to Knoxx to leave them. Calista urged Luxx to leave as well, "I'll be fine," Calista assured her. As Luxx crossed the threshold of the doorway, she glanced back at Calista, then narrowed her gaze on Phoenix and made a rude gesture, to which he rolled his eyes

"Thanks," he said dryly. "Try not to kill each other out here." He closed the door behind her, then walked to the bar and poured himself a glass of amber liquid. He offered one to Calista, but she declined with a wave of her hand and a look of disgust.

"Well, why did you do it?" she asked impatiently, albeit calmer than before.

Phoenix sat in one of the overstuffed chairs and gestured for Calista to take a seat in the one across from him. Calista reluctantly accepted the offer. In the eerie silence, she was very aware of the squeaking sound she made walking across the room in her battle leathers. She sat on the edge of the comfortable chair but refused to relax, her back ramrod straight and her hands folded neatly in her lap.

Calista watched as Phoenix took a long sip. With a raised eyebrow, he lowered the glass and took in her uncomfortable and agitated form. All she could think about was tearing him a new asshole.

"Please explain why you think I'm personally responsible for mangling, burning, and killing a third of your fishing fleet," he said calmly. "Preferably without injuring me in the process," he added.

Calista took in his calm exterior and his carefully schooled features. He was sitting in the ridiculously large, soft chair with one ankle resting on his opposite knee, leaning back and holding his glass near the rim between his fingertips as she gently swirled the liquid inside. He was dressed simply but elegantly in an untucked dress shirt with the collar open and tailored gray pants, not quite formal but relaxed. His Aquavass hung on a thick gold chain down to the centre of his chest. She watched it rise and fall in time with his breathing. *Why am I watching him breathe?* she wondered as she tried to formulate a response to his question. As she watched him rake his hand through his short dark hair, she realized she was just staring at him, and he was becoming impatient.

Calista recounted the events of day in a clipped tone, then paused, as she relived the scene of destruction. Her thoughts were on her people, wanting to check in on everyone. "As we collected the injured men who had fallen overboard, there was debris everywhere. It was the remnants of your stupid fancy fishing nets, and there were buoys and floats with West Marra's insignia on them."

Calista looked down at her hands. Her fingers were interlaced, and her palms were clasped tightly together. "What were all your nets doing so deep in East Marra territory?" she asked, raising her head to look at Phoenix.

CHAPTER 5
Explanations
Phoenix

A long moment passed before Phoenix blinked and leaned forward in his chair. His expression didn't give away the confusion bubbling beneath the surface of his skin.

"All my *gear*," he said slowly and condescendingly, "is digitally monitored. If it was in your territory, we would know about it."

Calista's face was a mixture of absolute disgust and incredulity. She stood up and began pacing the room. She roamed to the other side of the fireplace, then briefly observed her surroundings before approaching where he was sitting with his legs spread wide. She stood between them and braced her hands on the armrests of his chair, causing Phoenix to lean back. "Your equipment was all over the place," she said, her voice dangerously calm. "There was a massive explosion, and my people suffered because of your carelessness."

Calista leaned in so close that he could feel her breath on his face as she spoke. "Fix it," she said before shoving herself back from him.

Phoenix fought the sudden urge to grasp the backs of her legs and hold her in place. *She thinks she's intimidating me,* he thought. *Cute.*

Phoenix watched as Calista stepped back from him, giving him some space. She looked so different than she had that morning. He considered her for a few moments while he mulled over her version of events. She had mentioned that there was an SOS call from a distressed vessel. He was on the water as well and hadn't heard or seen anything. He wondered if any of his citizens were injured in the mess. She had been right there and saw the whole thing, so why was he completely unaware? Something else had to be going on to make her so unhinged that she felt she needed to break in and come at him. *Not that I would ever be unwelcoming toward a woman dressed in leather who sought me out*, he thought. Then he chastised himself. *Mind out of the gutter. man. Stay focused. She wants me to fix this problem. She thinks I orchestrated it. Knoxx. I need to talk to Knoxx. The asshole could have mentioned this to me.* Before Phoenix could let his thoughts run away from him, he had to get to the bottom of this whole mess, one of many that he had the privilege of dealing with.

"OK." He stood up, face to face with Calista. "I'll have Knoxx investigate what happened. As soon as we find out, we'll see what needs to be done to prevent it from happening again."

He watched Calista for her reaction. She stood stock still, staring up into his face.

"Fine. Figure it out," she spat. "Fast."

Phoenix couldn't help but admire her at that moment. *She's not the frivolous child she used to be. When did that happen?* he wondered.

Calista moved toward the door, but Phoenix caught her by the crook of her arm. "Where are you going?" he demanded in a low voice.

"I'm getting Luxx and going home," she replied sharply, then pulled free of his grasp.

"Like hell you're going back across that river tonight. You and Luxx are staying here tonight. I'll have Knoxx make all the necessary arrangements."

Phoenix walked past Calista toward the intercom and pressed a button. Barely a moment passed, and Knoxx was at the door.

"Nix!" Calista shouted, causing Phoenix to turn around. She slammed her forearm and fist into his chest. "I'm going home! You can't keep me hostage here1" Knoxx tried—and failed—to hide his amusement at her outburst.

Phoenix rubbed the spot on his chest where she made contact and smiled crookedly as he glanced at Calista. "Have meals, baths, and rooms prepared for Calista and Luxx," he said to Knoxx. "They're staying here tonight—despite her attacking me and accusing me of holding her hostage." Barely able to conceal the amusement in his voice, he turned to face her. "You can be such a brat."

Calista stormed past both men and out of the room. She walked with Luxx toward the main rotunda, fully prepared to waltz straight out the front palace doors and hail another wave ride. She was a ruler in her own right and more than capable of getting herself home. He watched as the realization hit her that it was late, and passage across the Marra would be difficult to get, but he suspected that she and Luxx had slept on the bank of the Marra before, and they could do it again if they really wanted to.

Luxx pushed on the doors that led toward the long driveway, to no effect.

"Stupid doors aren't budging. You try," Luxx said, giving Calista better access. "It's probably some royal thing."

Calista reached forward, and the door swung open. She smiled and took one step over the threshold, only to be drenched by a waterfall of shimmering neon water. She and Luxx were forced to step back, suddenly discovering they were dry again.

"What a fun security feature!" Calista said humourlessly. "If we leave we'll be forced back by the water, and if we can get through we'll be soaked and have to spend the night drenched to the bone."

Outright belly laughs from the balcony of the upper level drew Calista and Luxx's attention away from the massive, enchanted doors in front of them. Phoenix, nearly in tears, slowly collected himself as he came down the staircase to greet them. He crossed his arms over his chest, smiling broadly. "Ladies, may I please show you to your rooms now?"

Scowling at him, Calista seemed anxious to get back home, presumably to check on everyone. She was clearly not up for a night in the lap of luxury. She looked exhausted from the day's events. It seemed like she was trying to be gracious, but her efforts left something to be desired. She stood up straight and inhaled deeply. "Fine. You win this round. We'll stay the night. It's late, and it will be inconvenient to have someone bring us across the river at this hour. But we're leaving at first light tomorrow morning."

Without a word, and barely bothering to conceal his continued amusement over the circumstances, Phoenix led the women upstairs to a pair of large guest rooms that were beautifully appointed with oversized beds and white fluffy linens. Each room had floor-to-ceiling glass doors that opened onto a stone balcony overlooking the gardens. It was a truly beautiful view and one that he hoped Calista might appreciate more if she was not so anxious to see to her people, who were injured in the explosion, and irritated that she was here amongst so much lavishness while she knew her own people were suffering.

Phoenix leaned on the door jamb and watched as Calista and Luxx entered the room. Luxx was wide eyed and clearly out of her element. She kept close to Calista, who wandered toward the marble table across from the bed. Set atop it was a caterer's tray with a silver domed cover concealing whatever food lay beneath. Slowly, almost reluctantly, Calista turned to face Phoenix "Thank you," she said as she caught his gaze. His smile faded as he nodded in reply.

"Don't hesitate to ask for anything else you may need."

"Who could need more than all this?" Luxx asked as she gestured to the grandeur all around her.

Phoenix dipped his chin and asked Luxx if she would like to see her room.

"I have something I would like to discuss with her; I'll show her to her room," Calista said.

"I'll leave you to it then," Phoenix replied, then shoved himself off the doorway and closed the door behind him.

As he walked down the hall, his mind spiraled with every detail of their interactions throughout the day. *During the morning meeting, she held that blade to my throat. Was she warning me? Then she broke into my palace. Was she trying to catch me off guard? How did she slip past Knoxx? Speaking of him, where the hell has Knoxx been all this time? Why didn't he tell me all this shit went down? For fuck's sake, a damn explosion! She could have been killed.*

That last thought sent a wave of chills through him. He was unsure why Calista's death would elicit such a response, but it was there, and it was hard to shake.

Other aspects of that day come to mind. She didn't appear to be wearing her Aquavass but rather a key. Phoenix was noticing a lot of things about Calista lately, and if he was being honest with himself, he might even admit that he found her attractive.

He stopped that thought dead in its tracks. Now was not the time to be having any kind of feelings, romantic or otherwise, about an opposing ruler with an attitude and a death wish.

But I still don't wish her dead.

Phoenix absently rubbed the spot on his chest where Calista hit him and wondered if his diamond-encrusted Aquavass had caused a bruise. Then Knoxx approached him, interrupting his thoughts.

"Nix, they're all set up. I'm just checking that they can't disable the lock," Knoxx said as he approached a panel in the wall between Calista and Luxx's rooms.

"Leave it, Knoxx. They're fine. they won't try anything."

"You sure about that?" Knoxx asked with an air of disbelief, further nudging Phoenix's distrustful nature.

"She's the Queen of East Marra," Phoenix said firmly. "Leave her be. When were you going to tell me about that explosion?"

Knoxx dropped his hands from the wall panel and shoved them into his pockets as he turned to face Phoenix, arranging his features into a mask of neutrality before speaking. "I'm handling it. There was no reason to involve you."

Phoenix remained quiet for several moments, questioning for the first time since Knoxx became his advisor, guard, and friend if what he said could be trusted.

"I promised to fix it. Tomorrow, I want all the details," Phoenix said finally, then turned and walked back to his private chambers.

Chapter 6
Aterna Estate
Calista

Once Calista was alone in the bedchamber, Luxx started to explore the room more earnestly. She climbed onto the bed and bounced a few times before catching a glimpse of the spectacular garden below. Luxx rushed over to the glass doors and yanked them open.

"Cali! I don't care how much we hate him, this view is stunning! I can't believe how much water there is everywhere. It's like another world."

She looked behind her to see Calista inspecting her nails and standing rather awkwardly in the middle of the room. She looked very out of place in the middle of all that opulence, standing there in her battle leathers. She was not unfamiliar with such a lifestyle, but it was not how she lived. It was not what her parents taught her to value. Calista couldn't help but smile at Luxx's childlike enthusiasm as she marvelled at the luxury that surrounded them. She joined her friend at the balcony that overlooked the garden and leaned on the carved stone railing, looking out. The fountain caught her eye again, and in a moment of calm, Calista felt the unfamiliar hum of magic. She couldn't quite figure out where it was coming from though.

"Luxx, I do need to talk to you," she said hesitantly. "I need you to be my advisor right now. I don't think Phoenix is taking us seriously. I'm not sure he will follow through with his promise to fix what happened today. I need you to make sure he follows through." Calista turned to face Luxx, who was looking at her rather strangely. "Yes, of course I'll make sure of that. That is my job, after all, and I'll protect you with my dying breath too. You know you never need to ask me that."

"I know, I know, but I can't help but feel like this whole situation is strange. The meeting this morning felt pointless, like we didn't accomplish anything, which wasn't really unusual, but there was something in the way he spoke to me when we parted ways. I almost felt like he was trying to be nicer somehow. It reminded me of when we were kids, before we became rulers. He behaved as he always did, but something in the air changed when we blessed the daggers together, like there is something else happening that I can't put my finger on."

Calista instinctively held the key that was hanging around her neck and for the first time became aware of how unusually warm it felt. She cast her observation aside, chalking it up to having had a supremely stressful day.

They stared out at the garden. Luxx pointed at the fountain that they had passed during their break in. "That fountain is glowing with magic. It looks so gorgeous. Reminds me so much of Shadow Lake. Did you notice that little bird cage at the top? It's so cute."

Calista smiled at her friend, still lost in her thoughts about Phoenix. "Yeah, it's really pretty," she replied softly.

A few silent moments passed. Finally, Luxx couldn't hold in her curiosity any longer. "Cali, what do you think of Phoenix? I mean *really* think of him?"

"He's an ass, full of himself, and has more crap than he knows what to do with."

"That's not what I mean, and you know it. You've known him since you were a child. And let's be honest, he's not hard to look at, even if he is an ass."

"What's your point?" Calista was not in the mood for girl talk.

"I saw how he looked at you, like he would stop the world from spinning if it meant he could protect you, and I saw how you—never mind. Just remember who he is and that he's not to be trusted with anything."

"I haven't forgotten," Calista replied. "And that's just the look on his face when he's met with how a true ruler behaves. Nothing more." She smiled slyly. "To answer your earlier question, yes, he's a very pretty piece of man, even if he is an ass."

On that note, Calista collected her plate off the fancy table and walked Luxx to her room next door to join her for dinner. Together the women dined on a traditional West Marraian meal of seasoned and grilled beef filet with an assortment of fresh vegetables and a bottle of red wine. It was a lovely meal, the meat a rarity for them. The raindrop cake, if one could even call it cake, was an especially ostentatious way to end their meal. They laughed over the fact that only the wealthiest of the wealthy could transform water into dessert and be pretentious enough to call it a cake.

The next morning, Calista woke with a start, squinting at the bright sunlight. *So much for leaving at first light,* she thought. She scrubbed her hands on her face to wake herself up. She had slept deeply and soundly, well past first light. She felt a pang of guilt as she climbed out of bed and walked into the bathroom. The big beautiful shower was like an oasis in the desert. She stripped down, tossing aside the silky nightgown, which was among the clothing offered to her as an overnight guest.

As she turned the ornate taps, warm water flowed from the shower like a rainfall. She stepped in and allowed herself to revel in the simple pleasure of a warm shower.

Once dressed in more of the borrowed clothing, after taking care to fold and pack her battle leathers into a borrowed bag, Calista sought out Luxx.

"Did you sleep in your leathers?" she asked, taking in Luxx's dishevelled appearance.

"Didn't you?" Luxx replied.

"Luxx, you could have taken some advantage of the amenities available to you, like a shower and maybe some fresh clothes." Calista saw the tortured look on Luxx's face and read her expression for what it was. Tortured guilt. Luxx was accustomed to living a simple life, having grown up in a rustic village at the base of the Basara Mountains in Vulnari before becoming a warrior in the Zenovia Army. She lived a frugal and sometimes difficult life, and she was more at ease in the company of others who chose to live simpler, traditional lives, as was the custom in East Marra, where the dependence on magic was still the driving force behind their lifestyle. "I know you're not used to this, but it's OK," Calista said gently. "This is how people here live."

Luxx was silent, and Calista knew why. It was hard for her to allow herself to indulge, and being there at Aterna was overwhelming. It was so unlike the Cerulean Estate back in East Marra.

After some more encouragement, and Calista taking it upon herself to turn on the water for her, Luxx reluctantly took a warm shower rather than the icy plunge in a bathhouse like she was used to.

Once she emerged from the bathroom with her long blonde hair wrapped in a fluffy towel and her body swathed in another, she looked more relaxed and younger than her thirty plus years.

Luxx dressed in typical West Marra apparel, choosing jeans and a long-sleeved knit top with sensible ankle boots. Her outfit was casual compared to Calista's choice of cream dress pants and a matching halter top vest with a pair of blush nude heels.

Together they roamed around the wing of the estate closest to their rooms, admiring the wall art and various sculptures of shapely nude women everywhere.

"What is it with this man and all these statues of naked women?" Luxx said as she gestured toward what she felt was probably the hundredth statue she had seen. "Maybe he needs these statues around to ease his *frustrations,*" she said with a laugh and a suggestive wiggle of her eyebrows. Both women dissolved into a fit of giggles that continued until they were interrupted by Knoxx, who joined in with their laughter as he approached them.

"Good morning, ladies. What has put you in such a cheerful mood?"

Calista struggled to set aside her giggling and responded with as much dignity as she could muster after being caught laughing like a child at a statue of a naked lady.

"Good morning, Knoxx," Luxx chimed in. "Hey."

Knoxx gestured down the hallway. "Ladies, breakfast is served on the main floor. Follow me." He led the snickering women downstairs.

Knoxx pushed open the doors to the dining room. Daylight poured in from yet another large set of windows overlooking the spectacular gardens. Light glinted off the flatware and silver that decorated the table. There was an abundant spread of fresh fruits, pastries, breads, rolls, coffee, tea, and juices and a wide selection of jams and preserves. Calista glanced over at Luxx, whose eyes were practically falling out of her head at the sheer volume of fresh food before her.

"Luxx, you alright?" she asked with a hint of a laugh.

"Yeah . . . fine. There's just so much food here that I don't even know where to start." Luxx wandered up and down the length of the table, inspecting the variety of fruits and pastries on offer while Calista took her seat beside Phoenix, who sat across from Knoxx.

"I thought you were leaving at first light," Phoenix said without bothering to look up from his tiny cup, filled with a thick dark liquid.

Calista rolled her eyes and reached for the tongs to serve herself some strawberries and a buttery twisted roll. "I must have overslept," she replied, "what with all the excitement yesterday and your spectacular hospitality."

Phoenix reached for a pitcher beside him and poured a mug of rich, sweet molten chocolate and then handed it to Calista. She accepted the mug, and her eyes opened wide when she realized what it was.

"Thank you," she said softly. "How did . . ."

"You always asked for it when we were on holiday on Glass Island as kids," he replied.

Calista took a long sip and savoured the sweet chocolaty flavour as she waited for the bite of spice on her palate. It was one of her favourite indulgences, even now. She gave Phoenix a quick, appreciative glance, acknowledging the kind gesture, then tried to suppress the nerves fluttering in her stomach as she turned back to her meal.

"Luxx, is there something wrong?" Phoenix asked, setting down his impossibly small cup of coffee when he noticed she had not yet taken her seat at the table.

Luxx furrowed her eyebrows. "Where's the oatmeal?"

Knoxx choked as he tried to conceal a laugh. "With all this food here, you want gruel?"

"Luxx, sit, try something new today. The fruit is amazing," Calista said, trying to protect Luxx's dignity in food choices. Reluctantly, Luxx sat beside Knoxx, shot him a dirty glance, then served herself a variety of fruits until her plate looked like a rainbow had spilled onto it.

The four sat in awkward silence for some time eating their breakfast. At one point Calista dropped her hands to adjust the napkin on her lap and accidentally brushed Phoenix's forearm. He stilled, and Calista chanced a glance at him, only to find he was looking at her with his head tilted down and smirk on his lips. The moment ended as quickly as it happened. Calista cleared her throat. "So, how are we going to settle this situation?"

The mood at the table changed instantly. Phoenix sat up straight and leaned his elbows on the table. He looked at Knoxx and then turned toward Calista. "Since our gear appeared to cause the damage, we'll cover the costs of the destroyed fishing vessels in your territory, and we'll recalibrate our systems to ensure that our gear stays in our own territory."

"OK then, now that that's sorted . . ." Calista nodded curtly, her thought cut short when Luxx jumped up and looked like she was tracking something in the garden with her eyes.

Luxx nudged Knoxx. "Was that a little Savarra?" she asked.

"Yeah, probably, little bastards." Knoxx turned to look in the same direction as Luxx. He rolled his eyes, then turned to Phoenix. "I'll call the pest company again."

"Pest company? What for?" Luxx demanded. "That was such a cute little thing."

An awkward exchange of looks around the table was followed by nervous laughter. Luxx took it as a hint to keep her comments on local wildlife to herself as she silently finished her breakfast.

"We'll leave straight away now that our business seems to be concluded," Calista said as she finished the last of her meal.

"Transport is waiting to take us to the bank of the Marra," Phoenix said. "I've arranged for my yacht to take you across the river."

"That is completely unnecessary," Calista replied. "We can secure our own passage across."

"I'm sure you can, but it is the least I can do considering the damage done to your fishing fleet. Besides, I don't like the idea of a Queen taking a floating death trap across the river where it meets the sea." On that note, Phoenix stood up and called for the food to be cleared away.

"Wait," Calista said to the staff who entered the room. "What are you planning to do with all this food?"

"We throw it away," Phoenix said. "As soon as it's been laid out, if it's not consumed it becomes trash."

Calista discreetly whispered a request to have the food sent with her to East Marra rather than be put into the trash. The server looked at Phoenix, unsure how to respond. He replied with a barely perceptible nod.

"Thank you," Calista said, unable to hide her incredulity over the thought of wasting so much perfectly edible food.

"Transport is waiting outside," Phoenix said as he passed her on his way out.

Once they had arrived at the dock, Luxx assumed her role as protection officer and boarded the yacht first to ensure it was safe for Calista.

"I would wish you a safe trip, but since it's my boat, I know it will be," Phoenix said with such arrogance that Luxx, who had just returned, looked like she had to fight the urge to slap him.

"Won't you be joining us?" Calista asked, her voice dripping with disdain. "To keep an eye on us of course."

"There is enough staff on board that I shouldn't have anything to worry about," Phoenix replied. "I have some business to discuss with Knoxx, not that it's any of your concern."

As the tensions between the four of them escalated, Calista turned on her heel and walked up the short flight of stairs without looking back. She couldn't help but feel that Phoenix's gaze lingered on her backside as she ascended.

CHAPTER 7
Kings

Phoenix

Phoenix watched his yacht sail away until it was completely out of sight. Knoxx waited patiently in the car, wanting to get on with the day. Once both men were seated comfortably in the backseat, Knoxx started in

"Glad she's out of our hair. What's wrong with those two?"

"Enough." Phoenix's irritation over how Knoxx had misinformed him about the explosion was not sitting well with him, and he was in no mood to defend Calista, especially since after their last meeting, he was starting to regard her differently. "I'm on the hook for five new fishing vessels, reparations to the families who lost their loved ones and in some cases their only source of income, plus now I need to meet with our Techs to figure out how to recalibrate *all* of our digitized fishing gear. And all you want to do is bitch and whine about Calista and Luxx?"

Knoxx turned off his handheld device before replying. "I told you yesterday that I was dealing with it. Why are you so pissed off about it anyway? You can more than afford it."

"That's not the point. I thought I could trust you, and I had no idea any of this had happened. Do you know how stupid that makes me look?" Seeing the hesitation in Knoxx's face, Phoenix sat back in his seat. "What? Just tell me."

"She's not as innocent as you think. All the nets were tampered with. Our intel showed me all the nets were stolen. Obviously, those archaic fishermen didn't know how to use them or bring them in, and they got caught. The explosion was completely their fault. Did you really have to offer to pay for everything?"

"It was the right thing to do. They wouldn't have collected the nets if they had known they were there," Phoenix admitted thoughtfully as he reflected on the humble nature of the East Marra people.

The men rode in silence until they reached the urban jungle facility on the border of the city and the forest in the industrial area of West Marra. The men went there regularly for physical conditioning. It was a space where Knoxx and Phoenix could set aside political agendas and business and behave as friends. It was also where they first met. Knoxx was hired by Phoenix's parents to assist with his physical conditioning, as it is customary for a future ruler to be trained in the art of battle, however unlikely the reality of conflict might be. Over the years of training, and given that they were similar in age, Knoxx and Phoenix grew close. Knoxx knew Phoenix's weaknesses, which was no small vulnerability for a future ruler. When Phoenix assumed the role of king, Knoxx was a natural selection to become his advisor. They had worked in tandem ever since.

After they changed into their workout clothes, they made their way into the high-tech arena, which was made to resemble an industrial wrecking yard. Knoxx nudged Phoenix. "Calista is something, eh? She has a seriously fine ass."

Phoenix nodded in agreement as he prepared to flip over a large, heavy tire. "She does have some nice assets. You and Luxx got pretty friendly in the hallway. Don't lie; you love it when a woman knows how to manhandle you."

Unadulterated disgust settled over Knoxx's face. "There is nothing appealing about Luxx. Calista on the other hand . . . I wouldn't mind taking a ride on her."

That comment stopped Phoenix dead in his tracks as he swallowed a surge of anger, feeling like a child who didn't want to share his toys. "She's a queen, man. Have some respect," he replied, his tone bordering defensiveness.

"I saw how you eye fucked her, Nix," Knoxx said bluntly. "Don't deny it."

"Please," Phoenix scoffed. "I have enough women vying for my attention. Calista is not my type. Too much knife play."

As the men wrapped up their workout and headed back to Aterna Estate to indulge in the heated infinity-edge pool overlooking the garden, Knoxx suggested they get their mind off the day's events with a night out at King's Bar.

"I'll make the arrangements," Knoxx said as he lounged with his arms spread out beside him on the edge of the pool, wisps of steam curling up around him. "You look like you could blow off some steam."

Phoenix reluctantly agreed, his mind elsewhere. The discrepancy over the fishing gear being stolen didn't sit well with him. He decided it was his turn to make an unannounced visit to East Marra—first thing tomorrow morning.

King's Bar was a favourite haunt of the less savoury members of the West Marra population. It was located on the northern bank of the West Marra river where the air was colder, and frequently obscured by fog. More than one dirty deal had gone down within those walls. It was sleazy and dark and reeked of booze and debauchery, a far cry from the pristine, open, and glass-clad Aterna Palace.

Phoenix felt like his mood matched the atmosphere. People there don't care that he was their king, and they didn't placate him. He had taken more than a few fists to the face over dumb shit in that pit of a bar. He kept going back though because within those walls he was like everyone else. He had no obligation to solve anyone's problems or worry that he was being poisoned. He chose to poison himself with endless whisky and women.

With Knoxx as his wingman, they attracted a lot of attention, both good and bad. By the way Knoxx swaggered into the bar, it wouldn't be long before he had a woman hanging off him. No one went there for anything but debauchery, including Knoxx.

The men made their way to a booth in a more private area at the back of the bar. The space was large enough to accommodate several attractive, attention-seeking women. Moments after they sat down, bartenders and wait staff began setting plates of food and drinks on the table.

A slender, scantily clad girl confidently approached the table. "How lucky am I to stumble upon a pair of kings," she said in what she probably thought was a seductive voice. She was definitely Knoxx's type. She caught that hint as she sat beside him, draping her leg over his. Knoxx slid one hand up the inside of her thigh and nudged Phoenix as if to ask him if he wanted to join. Phoenix shook his head, in no mood for a threesome.

A large, burly man approached the table. He stared down Knoxx, whose expression suggested recognition. The interaction was fleeting, a nearly imperceptible exchange. Based on his clothing and features, the man was from Vulnari. He tossed an envelope on the table. Knoxx nodded curtly and then swiped it off the table. The man sneered at the woman draped across Knox's lap before walking away. The interaction did not go unnoticed by Phoenix, but he chooses not to comment. He trusted Knoxx, who took care of lots of things that he didn't bother informing Phoenix about. The overwhelming corruption in West Marra ran deep. Phoenix knew that some deals needed to get dirty before they got done. As royalty, he couldn't be associated with anything that would suggest mistrust. Knoxx, on the other hand, had no such issue; he did what needed to be done.

"What's your problem?" Knoxx asked, sighing in exasperation.

"Nothing."

"Bullshit. Your balls are so blue they're practically glowing."

"Get fucked."

"With pleasure." On that note, Knoxx left the booth with the attractive woman on one arm. He scooped up another woman by the waist and hauled her off to the members-only section on the bar's upper level. Phoenix saluted his advisor, then settled in for a long night of drinking and people watching.

Women drifted by his table, flirting and showing an inordinate amount of skin. Usually after one bottle of whisky, he was down for any manner of depravity; he was not particular. Tonight, however, no one was hitting the mark. The food on the table remained untouched, though bottle after bottle was uncorked. He downed glass after glass until he couldn't see straight. He had a vague memory of being hauled out of the bar supported by Knoxx but nothing else.

CHAPTER 8
East Marra
Phoenix

"I'm taking my bike across. I can't handle a boat ride after last night," Phoenix said, his skin still clammy and his head pounding from the copious amount of booze he had consumed. With Knoxx having mentioned that he wrapped up the investigation into the explosion, Phoenix wanted to settle the matter with Calista sooner rather than later, unwilling to wait until next month's meeting. She obviously didn't care for the formalities of an official visit, so he figured that dropping in unannounced would be fine.

Knoxx shook his head and laughed. "Fine. We'll take separate bikes. I'm in no mood to start a bromance with you on a motorcycle." Knoxx made an exaggerated gesture as he adjusted the front of his pants. "Still a little chafed from last night," he mumbled. Phoenix rolled his eyes at the comment.

"You sure about that? Do we need to stop by Shadow Lake for some special herbs to cure whatever disease is chafing you?" Phoenix retorted with an underlying hint of annoyance in his tone.

"What the fuck is up with you?" Knoxx stepped up chest to chest with Phoenix and stared him down. Phoenix shoved him back.

"You're an asshole."

"I should have left your sorry ass at the bar for the vermin," Knoxx growled in reply.

The men were heaving heavy breaths, on the verge of an explosive argument, but Knoxx broke the tension, shouldering past Phoenix and mounting his bike. Phoenix was in no mood to fight, so he pulled rank instead. "Don't forget who the real King is here."

With those words, Phoenix mounted his bike, and they practically chased each other through the streets of West Marra to the riverbank. There, a bioluminescent water bridge conjured by the magic of the river allowed them to pass across the water. The intuitive nature of the land's magic didn't go unnoticed by Phoenix as he recalled Calista's reminder that their regions were intertwined by the intrinsic magic that was allowing them across the river. This mode of transport was only suitable for single passengers on small vehicles. The goddess of the river wouldn't allow more than one conjured water bridge at any given time. It made getting large parties across the river nearly impossible without the use of an ostentatious watercraft.

They reached the bank of East Marra by midafternoon. There was hardly any activity around them, the dock practically abandoned. The road that followed the north/south coastline was in rough shape, riddled with cracks and in need of repair. To the east was the Ash Desert, where the dead from both East and West Marra were cremated. That was a familiar enough path; however, beyond that route, Phoenix and Knoxx were basically lost. They needed to figure out how to get to the capital where Cerulean Estate was located. Apart from wanting to settle the explosion situation, he was curious to see Calista in her own territory, her own element.

"What do you mean you don't know how to get there?" Knoxx demanded.

"I've hardly ever gone there!" Phoenix shouted back. The tension between them had not dissipated on their ride over the river.

"Fucking hell, Nix!"

"Let's ride south. If we hit Shadow Lake, we've gone too far." Phoenix set off toward a small cluster of structures in the distance. Knoxx followed, racing behind him down the coastal road.

As they drove, they passed large patches of fallow land. Some people were tending the fields, but they were few and far between.

As they approached the capital, more stone buildings came into view, and the ancient structures of the former LaMarra became more plentiful. Phoenix began to recognize his surroundings. The city, if one could call it that, appeared to be stuck in ancient times. Ancient waterways now served as gutters. Old plumbing infrastructure could be seen in various states of disrepair, and everything was bone dry. Warm earth tones—soft terracotta, burnt oranges, and yellows— were the backdrop for the buildings, businesses, and residents in the capital. It was once a thriving community that had all but fallen into ruin. Cerulean Estate was at the centre of it all.

Phoenix and Knoxx looked completely out of place, drawing curious stares. Children pointed and asked the adults who were minding them about the strangers. Most people smiled, likely recognizing Phoenix's royal insignia on his bike. No one appeared to be concerned by their presence in their city.

"What a shithole," Knoxx said as he looked around, having removed his helmet to take a break.

"Really?" Phoenix looked back over his shoulder at Knoxx. If looks could kill, Knoxx would have turned to ash on the spot. It was enough of a warning to keep Knoxx silent while Phoenix asked a woman for directions to Cerulean Palace, saying they were there on official royal business.

"Hi! I'm Cara." She offered her name freely as her eyes settled on the West Marra insignia on Phoenix's motorcycle. "Keep right, and follow the main road. That will take you directly to Queen Calista's house."

"I'm not looking for her house," Phoenix replied. "I'm looking for the royal estate, Cerulean Palace."

"No one calls it that anymore, not since Calista turned it into the community hub. Just follow the road; you can't miss it." She smiled and continued on her way.

Phoenix caught the look on Knoxx's face as he mouthed the words "community hub," his eyes wide.

As the men approached Cerulean Estate, it was brimming with activity. Long tables and benches had been set up just inside the stone walls that encapsulated the palace proper. Where lush gardens used to be, tents and areas where merchants conducted business now filled the space. It was indeed a hub of activity. People were coming and going from various arches and doorways. Not a stitch of security was to be found, not a bodyguard, butler, or even a dog standing watch. People were milling about everywhere.

They parked their motorcycles and didn't bother locking them, leaving their helmets on the seats. They made their way toward what was once a grand entrance. Large stone arches led toward a courtyard with openings to several wings of the palace.

They passed a group of young children playing a game where they would lie on the ground with their eyes closed waiting for the teacher to get to the part of the song that was the signal to jump up. They were so little, all laughing and having a blast, lying in the dirt and then jumping up for no apparent reason. Even Knoxx couldn't hide his amusement at the sight. Such carefree happiness was not seen often in West Marra. Citizens there led more private and protected lives.

Calista approached them from behind, her presence given away by the group of children swarming around her knees giving her hugs, shouting, "Cali!" An apologetic teacher rushed forward and herded the children away, allowing Calista to greet Phoenix and Knoxx.

Calista picked up a child who was still clinging to her legs and balanced him on her hip, indicating to the teacher that she was going to take the child with her.

"To what do I owe the pleasure, gentlemen?" Calista asked.

"We came to further discuss the issue with the fishing vessels," Phoenix said as he watched the child paw at Calista's chest. The child inspected the key hanging from a chain on her neck, then shoved his hand back into the neckline of her top to fish out her Aquavass. The child squealed with glee as he pointed to his own Aquavass.

"If this is a bad time," Knoxx said, stopping as the child reached over toward him, wanting to be held. "I don't like touching them; they're always sticky." He took a dramatic step back, a sneer on his face.

Phoenix laughed, then took the child from Calista. The little one promptly started crying. Alarmed, Phoenix set him on the ground, and the boy ran back to his waiting teacher.

As Calista went to tuck her necklaces back into her shirt, Phoenix reached out to stop her. "Where did this key come from?" he asked, squinting as he flipped the key over in his hand to inspect it.

"It was my mom's, I think. It's been lying around for years. Luxx had it cleaned, and I've been wearing it ever since. I would say about a year at least." She looked around. "It's really busy out here. Why don't we head inside where we can speak more privately?"

She led them through a maze of arches and open-air corridors, then up several flights of stairs before pushing aside two large doors that led to a stone terrace with a view of Shadow Lake in the distance. Sails hung from nails in the walls and pillars to create some shade. Pillows, low wicker chairs, and loveseats were scattered around. They weren't the most comfortable, but they were good enough, the décor suiting the atmosphere.

Calista gestured for them to sit anywhere they liked. The terrace was empty except for them and a young girl who motioned to

Calista, pretending to hold a glass and drink. Calista nodded, and the girl disappeared to fetch beverages.

Calista pushed aside the slit in her floor-length skirt to allow her to sit with one leg crossed over the other in a wicker loveseat across from the men, who each chose individual wicker seats opposite the low table between Calista and them.

Phoenix leaned forward resting his elbows on his knees. "After further investigation, it has been brought to my attention that all the fishing gear damaged in the explosion was tampered with and likely stolen."

"Are you implying that my people brought that tragedy on themselves by tampering with and stealing your equipment?" Calista shot back, not missing a beat.

"That is exactly what I'm implying, and I'll not be replacing any equipment or paying reparations to people who committed criminal acts."

"Our fishermen pulled up their fishing nets, which had become entangled with yours and should never have been in our waters to begin with. They died trying to feed their families. Last time I checked, there's no crime in that."

Luxx crossed paths with the young lady who had gone to fetch a tray of beverages and took the tray from her. She entered the terrace carrying the tray of drinks and set them on the table for everyone. She leaned in and touched Calista's forehead before addressing the others.

"Phoenix, Knoxx."

"Thank you, Luxx," Calista said as she reached for a glass. Tensions between everyone were becoming suffocating.

"Luxx, share with them what your investigation of the incident revealed, please," Calista said as she stared at Phoenix. Feeling the air thicken further, Luxx spoke as factually and as directly as possible.

"The wreckage revealed that West Marra had planted their nets deep into our waters. This was evident by the growth of corals on the pegs that held the digitized nets in place. Our sources believe the nets were there for some time."

Calista turned to face Phoenix and Knoxx with a raised eyebrow, daring them to challenge her findings and accuse her of theft again. They remained silent.

"Our fishermen don't have the necessary equipment or skill to anchor digital nets," she said. "There's no way anyone in East Marra could have done it."

Calista stood up and walked to the balcony rail. She swung her arm out, gesturing to the land beyond. "Look around you; my people are all here within the walls of my private estate. They're hard working, generous, and humble. The only crime we experience here is minimal at best. No one here has time to do anything other than work to survive."

Calista moved to stand in front of Phoenix before continuing. "Keep your money, and your accusations," she spat. "My people will come together and help each other. I'll help them, and we'll rebuild what was destroyed. Without you."

Calista turned and started walking back into the palace. "I trust you will find your own way out of my home and back across the river," she said without looking back. Then she disappeared into the palace.

CHAPTER 9
The Fountain
Calista

Calista sat bouncing her knee and tapping her fingers on the table's surface as she waited for Phoenix in the atrium at Glass Island. Despite their last encounter at her palace and how he infuriated her with his solution of throwing money at the issue to make things right rather than owning up to his misdeeds, she had to admit that she spent far too much time thinking about him. She had invested days thinking about what to wear to this meeting and as much time considering which clothes to pack for the time she would be spending as a guest at Aterna in the coming days while the Zenovia Army Candidate banquet took place in advance of the induction ceremony, which would be hosted in East Marra. She checked the path occasionally, looking for Phoenix. In the distance she saw a dark figure approaching. As the figure drew closer, she realized by his gait and the ominous aura around him that it was Knoxx, not Phoenix. Calista stood up.

"What are you doing here?" she demanded, not bothering to conceal the annoyance in her voice.

"Always a pleasure, Calista," he replied civilly.

"Where's Phoenix? I'm in no mood for games today."

"He's attending to business elsewhere. There was a conflict that interfered with this meeting when you decided to move it up by two days."

"No one thought to tell me that he couldn't attend?" Even as she spoke the words in a controlled tone, she couldn't ignore the stab of disappointment she felt that Phoenix didn't have the decency to send his regrets. She wondered if she had read too deeply into the small kindnesses he had shown her the last time she was at Aterna.

Knoxx sat down and scanned Calista with a look that was a mixture of appreciation and lust. Calista couldn't help but feel violated by the way his gaze drifted over her, lingering on her body. Unwilling to deal with Knoxx on any level other than what was absolutely necessary, Calista made the executive decision to end their meeting.

"I'm not doing this with you, Knoxx. I have to go back with you to Aterna anyway. I'll talk to Phoenix there if I have to."

Knoxx regarded Calista for a few moments, appearing to be weighing his options. Then he nodded. "Fine. Have it your way. The yacht is waiting for us." He stood up and strode down the path. Calista struggled to keep pace and eventually gave up, resolving to walk slowly.

He can wait for me, she thought. If she was being honest, she had been looking forward to seeing Phoenix despite how she had walked out on him during their last encounter. She recalled the way he picked up and inspected her key around her neck. She wore it all the time anyway, but in anticipation of the meeting, she had it on display with a faint hope he would inspect it again. She felt silly for wanting him to be interested in her, but it was a thought that she had a hard time shaking lately.

The journey to the bank of West Marra and the ride into Aterna were awkwardly silent and uncomfortable. Knoxx, ever the gentleman, stepped out of the vehicle first and left Calista to find her own way into the palace. Calista was more than capable of finding her way to her room, which was far easier as an invited guest rather than when she was evading security while making an unannounced visit.

Once inside the luxurious room, she changed out of the carefully chosen gown of silk and organza with a plunging neckline. She admired the dress and let herself revel in the disappointment that she spent such time considering what to wear for Phoenix, who hadn't even bothered to show up. She changed into a flowing floor-length skirt with a slit to the mid-thigh and a fitted cap-sleeved crop top that just met the waistband of her skirt, showing the thinnest stripe of skin, and flat sandals. She arranged her necklaces to rest on the outside of her top. She was careful not to display her jewellery like that in East Marra, ever conscious of the ostentatious nature of the jewels. People knew who she was and that she was royalty; there was no need to beat them over the head with the finery that she still possessed as inheritance from her mother's collection and previous monarchs before her.

After admiring the garden in the bright light of day, Calista realized she had hours before she had to get dressed for the banquet reception that evening.

She took herself on a tour of the estate, quietly roaming the halls and taking note of the various art installments and silently missing Luxx, who would be giggling at the sheer volume of nudity represented in all of the artwork. Luxx had remained in East Marra, overseeing preparations for the Zenovia Army ceremony, which was to take place the following day.

Calista opened all the doors on the upper level, learning the location of the guest wing, the heated pool, and Phoenix's private chambers, which consisted of an office, a bedroom, and the study she found him in when she was last on the premises.

On the first floor, she explored the vast dining room and the butler's kitchen, which was well stocked with bar items and plenty of wine. The main kitchen's location was still a mystery. Various glass doors led to terraces and the back garden. Several rooms were connected to the main foyer and rotunda. There was also a receiving area and, to her delight and surprise, a vast, bright, well-stocked library. The sheer wealth of books in the library was staggering compared to the one she had at Cerulean Palace.

The books she possessed consisted of ancient manuscripts, some in languages long forgotten, and books to assist the budding education of the children who studied in the library. The schools around East Marra began to close as the population dwindled. Children attended school in a section of the community hub, with multiple levels of instruction happening at once. The teachers are skilled at teaching the youngest to the oldest pupils in a single albeit large room.

The vast majority of education in East Marra focused on trades, agriculture, and general-purpose skills that would support their survival. Few could afford to indulge in the arts and the history of their land. The ancient history of LaMarra had been a topic of interest for Calista since childhood. Their history was shaped by the fundamental nature of magic and all its mystery and chaos. In particular, the unexplained elements of the Goddess's magic and the strange, unknown magic surrounding Blackstone Prison had always intrigued her.

She ran her finger along the spines of the books while roaming up and down the stacks, then climbed the ladders to reach books on the higher levels. She lingered at a section of books that looked remarkably like the manuscripts she possessed in her library and wondered if they were copies. Not having read the ancient manuscripts due to the untranslated text, she decided to have a look at these ones. To her delight, the manuscripts included some translations. The wealth of information available there was as staggering as it was thrilling, allowing her to indulge her curiosity about the ancient uses of magic and how it started to fall apart.

She hauled a giant leather-bound book that measured a foot and a half long and ten inches thick down from the shelf with some difficulty, then placed the heavy book on the nearest table. The book was bound in a strange way. Rather than opening from left to right, it was encased with a binding that was latched in the centre. She unhooked the clasp and opened the leather cover to reveal a smaller, more pristine book inside that did, in fact, open from left to right. The inside of the binding's outer layer was lined with tightly wrapped scrolls. She carefully removed the interior book and set it on the table beside the cover, then opened the book to the first page.

Laid out before her was the word "LaMarra," written by hand in a script that was clearly ancient. Writing at the bottom indicated a year, but the text was so worn and written in a looping calligraphy that she couldn't make it out with any certainty. As she leafed through the tome, she saw various sections of text and pictures of what appeared to be the development of the earliest settlements of West Marra. She also found many maps, each one with pictures of keys in various places. One particularly interesting and dark hand-drawn map depicted what she recognized as Blackstone Prison in the centre of Siphon Lake. Intricate drawings of dragon heads, tails, fins, and wings peeked out of the water. The art was captivating, even if the language made no sense to her.

She put the book back into the cover and removed one of the scrolls. The paper was heavier and thicker than she expected. In fact, the scroll was so sturdy that she wondered if it was made from animal skin rather than paper.

As disturbing as that thought was, she untied the scroll and laid it on the table as flat as she could. The edges rolled up, so Calista removed the key from around her neck to anchor the edge of the scroll to the table. Drawn on the scroll was a map. At first glance it appeared to be complete, but upon closer inspection, she saw more than a few oddities. The River Marra was depicted as a thin stream, and there was a landmass that divided the north half of the river from the south half, effectively connecting the east and west landmasses that she initially recognized as the individual territories of East and West Marra.

The word scrawled across the landmass was "LaMarra." This indication that East and West Marra were once unified called up memories of the lessons she learned as a child about the war that divided LaMarra and how the two original ruling warrior Queens had turned against one another. The reason was unclear, but it had something to do with magic. Some said it was because they tried to control it. Others said that the Goddess made a grave mistake by entrusting them with the knowledge of the original source of magic. The true reason was still debated among scholars.

The map had a small decorative border that, upon closer connection, appeared to be keys connected in a chain pattern bordering the map.

Calista carefully rolled up the scroll and took out another one. Using her key to anchor the edges of the scroll once again, she realized it was another map. This one clearly depicted West Marra. However, it was drawn as if East Marra did not exist.

Her back starting to ache from poring over the maps, and feeling the need for some sunshine, Calista took two scrolls and went out to the garden. She made herself comfortable on a daybed with a full view of the spectacular fountain with shimmering neon bioluminescent water cascading out of a small birdcage and down the form of a shapely nude winged woman holding the cage high above her head.

Her perusal of the maps, which she was becoming rather engrossed in, was interrupted by Phoenix's silhouette standing in the stream of sunlight that was warming her legs.

"What are you doing here?" Phoenix asked.

"You're kidding, right?" She angled her head toward him, shielding her eyes from the sun with her hand.

"We don't meet for another two days. Why are you here now?"

Calista set the scrolls aside and stood to meet his gaze. "The Zenovia Army candidate banquet is tonight, and you obviously forgot that it was your brilliant idea to schedule our monthly meeting on the same day."

She stood back and took in the dishevelled man in front of her. *Strange. He never looks like this. He's always so polished. What has he been up to?* His hair was a tousled mess, he was wearing dirty, stained jeans and work boots with button-down denim shirt open to expose his chest and abdomen and with the sleeves rolled and pushed up his forearms. *Very nice,* Calista thought as she fought the urge to let her eyes wander down his exposed chest and fantasize about what lay beneath the waistband of his pants. His effect on her was becoming harder to ignore. She hoped the warm flutters flooding her stomach were not causing her to blush as she sensed the heat rising up her neck and face. She found herself wondering why he was covered in sawdust as well. His rugged appearance struck a chord with her, reminding her of her own people. Hard working, honest, and . . . striking.

"Something that needed my attention came up," he said in a clipped tone as he took her in. His eyes fell on the scrolls that were lying on the daybed. "What have you been doing in my absence?" he asked, nodding toward the documents.

"If you must know, I refused to discuss *our* business with Knoxx and found myself with some extra time on my hands, so I started exploring your library and found these." She gestured to the scrolls.

Phoenix flopped down on the daybed and examined the scrolls. He unrolled the one of West Marra and held it up to the sunlight. Lines appeared to reveal further details on the map, like a watermark. Calista sat beside him and peered up at the scroll.

"Where did you say you found these?" Phoenix asked as he scrutinized the map.

"I left the book out on the table in your library. They looked so interesting. I'm sorry if it's an invasion," Calista said as she watched Phoenix's face for signs of anger. To her relief, he did not appear angry. Instead, he seemed as absorbed by the map as she had been. He twisted the map to read it lengthwise. As he held it toward the light, the sunlight highlighted the distinct shape of a key rather than what Calista originally saw as indistinguishable markings.

Calista removed the key from her neck and held it up beside the map for reference. Phoenix's eyes shifted between her key and the one depicted on the scroll.

"Hmm . . . that's interesting," he mumbled.

"Yeah, I agree. They look very similar," she said as she became all too aware of their close proximity to one another. She stood up and wandered to the edge of the fountain to create some distance between them before her composure wavered.

She flicked her hand in the cool, shimmering water as she observed the ornate details carved into the wings of the statue holding up the small gilded cage. Her gaze focused on the loops and swirls that, from a distance, looked like textured feathers. Now that she was paying attention though, she noticed that the carvings were actually words written in an ancient text. She could only make out a single word here and there, suddenly wondering if a message were hidden in the wings.

"Have you ever noticed the words carved into this statue's wings?" Calista asked as she swung her legs over into the edge of the fountain and held up her skirt, so she could wade over to the statue. She moved toward the centre of the fountain and ran her fingers over the words she recognized, tilting her head as she tried to read the elegantly carved text.

"This looks like the words *Amare, Confido, Clara,* and *Lux* on this wing." She circled the statue to inspect the other wing. "*Dubium,*

Timeo, Tenebis, Nox," Calista said as she ran her fingers over the wings and saw that the same words were written over and over, forming the beautifully intricate pattern. She recognized the words to be in a language that had long since faded from common use, but the words still held meaning in that statue.

His mind elsewhere, Phoenix finally looked away from the scroll, only to realize she had waded into the fountain and was standing beside the statue, which was taller than her, running her fingertips over its wings.

"The artist who carved her told me that she represents balance," Phoenix said as he approached the edge of the fountain.

"Whoever it was, they did beautiful work. These wings are amazing. Do you know what they say?" Calista inquired as she looked at him with an arched eyebrow.

"I can't say I have the luxury of time to thoroughly inspect each one of my commissioned art pieces in such detail, so no, enlighten me," he said, his voice dripping with derision.

"I didn't realize you needed assistance reading," Calista chided as she waved him over for a closer look. She ran her fingers toward the delicate arches of the wings and the gilded cage, allowing the water to soak her completely. She squinted to focus more on the detail. "Do you at least know what's inside that little gold cage?" she asked as she strained to see for herself.

Phoenix approached the edge of the fountain and, with his considerable height advantage, peered above the spray of water and craned his neck to see what was inside the cage. "I can't tell from here. Hold on; I'm coming in."

Moments later he had removed his boots and rolled up his pants to his knees. He stepped carefully into the fountain, making a face and wincing as he waded through the cold water toward the statue. He placed one hand on the statue's wing and the other over the breast. Calista couldn't help but laugh.

"I knew it! You love to feel up all the naked lady statues!"

"Shut up!" he barked with a laugh of his own as he shinnied up the statue until he reached the small gilded cage. He carefully brought it down.

As he waded back toward the edge of the fountain, Calista became aware of a gently increasing hum emanating from the key hanging around her neck. She picked it up and found that it was warm to the touch. Phoenix sat on the edge of the fountain and set the cage in his lap while he opened its small door.

"I can see there's something shiny inside, but my hand is too big to reach it," he said. Calista reached her index and middle finger into the small opening and pinched the item inside, then pulled it out.

It was another key, slightly larger than the one she wore but similar in design.

"When the hell did you get back?" Knoxx shouted from the open doorway, drawing their attention for a moment. He directed his question to Phoenix, but his gaze swept over Calista's wet clothes, which clung to each curve of her body.

Thinking fast, Phoenix palmed the key to keep it from view. "Just now. I'm going to go up and get ready now. People will be arriving soon."

Calista rested her hand over Phoenix's hand, which concealed the key from view.

"Do you feel that?" she whispered.

"It's warm, the key . . ." He opened his hand and noticed that the keys were both shimmering faintly and emitting the faintest hum of power.

Knoxx's heavy footsteps could be heard approaching. Phoenix quickly stashed the key in his pocket and stood up.

"Here." He thrust the gilded cage at Knoxx. "It fell off. Have it fixed," he said. Then he climbed out of the fountain and stalked up the stairs toward what Calista knew was his private suite.

"Take those too and have them replaced in the library," she said with an equally clipped tone, handing him the scrolls. Calista could exercise her rank over Knoxx, as she was visiting Aterna in an official capacity. She reflected on his earlier choice of words to greet Phoenix, feeling it was very crass even if they were friends. Even in casual circumstances, a member of any royal family should never have been treated with such disrespect.

"Do it yourself," Knoxx replied with a sneer. "I don't serve you."

"Remember who you're speaking with," she warned. "I am a Queen, you know."

"I answer to no Queen," he said, then tossed the scrolls to the ground and walked away.

The interaction left her feeling enraged and frustrated. She couldn't understand what qualities Phoenix found so appealing in the man.

The scene had been witnessed by the staff idling by the doorway. A young server rushed in with a towel for Calista and then picked up the scrolls. He was about to scurry off when she called out to him. "Wait! Stop! It's fine. Thank you for the towel. I'll bring those back."

"Please, let me," he said, practically falling over himself with the opportunity to help her. "It would be my privilege to serve the Queen," he said shyly. Then he picked up the scrolls and offered a small bow before backing away. Calista mildly wondered how much of her interaction with Knoxx the server saw and if he would report it to Phoenix. The thought was cut short when she realized it was time to get dressed for the banquet.

CHAPTER 10
The Banquet
Calista

The time-honoured tradition of introducing the prospective Zenovia warrior candidates happened the night before the induction ceremony at a banquet where the King and Queen of LaMarra as well as key political figures and aristocratic families toasted the new candidates. Historically each side hosted an event related to the ceremony to remind all those involved that the army existed to protect and serve LaMarra in a divine capacity. They answer to the Goddess Marra and her divine intuition. This connection to the Goddess and the magic of the land had made the equitable division of the army between East and West impossible to accomplish.

Calista surveyed her appearance in the full-length mirror. Her dark, wavy hair was in loose curls around her shoulders with one side pinned up and away from her face using a sparkly bauble as a clip. Her dress was immaculately tailored to fit her figure. The back of the silver-threaded gown was embellished with swaths of translucent blue strips of organza and silk, forming a slight train behind her and giving her the appearance of an angel fish's tail fluttering in her wake as she walked. The front of the gown was equally stunning, bejewelled with pearls and diamonds and featuring a plunging neckline that nearly reached her navel. There was an equally revealing slit up the side of the skirt that nearly connected with the base of the plunging neckline. She was a vision of silver and blues that twinkled when the light caught the gown.

She dabbed a light floral fragrance on her wrists and behind her ears, then moved toward the door of her room and signalled to her dressing maid that she was ready to be escorted to the reception area to meet the candidates and other guests as they arrived.

Standing at the bottom of the stairwell, Phoenix watched as she descended the stairs, one hand gliding over the railing. As she approached the last few steps, he walked up to her and extended a hand, which she took. Much to Calista's surprise, he raised the back of her hand to his mouth and brushed his lips over her knuckles with a ghost of a kiss, just enough for her to feel the warmth of his lips but gone all too soon. It was a formal greeting but not an intimate one. He raised his gaze to meet Calista's eyes as she took the final few steps.

"You certainly cleaned up nicely for tonight," she said.

A sly smile crossed his face. "I've been known to turn a few heads with my appearance."

Calista sensed he was uncomfortable. People were everywhere; this was not his usual behaviour around her. She made a mental note to keep her guard up, to be aware that he was putting on a show. None of his behaviours that night would be genuine. She could see that he was not as comfortable mingling with people as she was. He was merely fulfilling his obligations.

He led her to a small gathering of people and made brief introductions before excusing himself to discuss something with Knoxx, who was brooding in a corner of the receiving area. He had taken up his role as protection officer for the evening, as was evidenced by the earpiece that connected him to his security team.

Calista felt Phoenix's gaze on her as she shook hands with the candidates. She continued to work the room with grace, completely in her element. People gravitated toward her and competed for her attention. She was captivating.

Phoenix was doing his own work, circulating and engaging in small talk and looking like he was bored to tears. Conversations with him were short and superficial. He didn't appear to be engaging in much small talk beyond benign pleasantries. Calista, on the other hand, was engaged in deep thoughtful conversations with his people, some of whom had ever met her in person before. His attention appeared to be discreetly focused on her conversations, which helped him learn that his citizens were offering condolences to her over the explosion. Some even offered to send funds and vessels to help. It didn't escape Calista's notice that this didn't sit well with Phoenix, based on his increasingly sour expression.

Ever the diplomat, Calista declined every offer of help, insisting that her people would manage and ultimately be fine. She assured them that recovery was well underway. Even when she lied, people believed her.

"Do you mean to say that what I saw last time I paid a visit to East Marra is a city that is recovering from tragedy and disaster?" Phoenix said through a smile, giving the impression that he was engaging Calista in polite conversation.

"We're fine, and we have already recovered," she replied regally. "We are a community that looks after each other."

"If that's the crap you expect people to believe, fine," he said, a touch of acid in his tone. "But I know better."

Despite the unease between them, Phoenix linked arms with Calista and led her into the lavish dining hall. They sat side by side at the head table, which was elevated above the rows of tables for the guests. Directly across from their table was where the candidates and guests of honour sat. Six women would be attending the following day's ceremony. There the candidates would confirm their commitment to life as members of the Zenovia Army and accept a blessed dagger and all the responsibility that came with it. For those who had completed their training, it was a momentous event, and having both royal families present was a rare honour to behold.

Dinner ran smoothly enough. Phoenix cast several sidelong glances toward Calista, and she did the same, ever aware of the other guests watching her and Phoenix's every move.

As dinner drew to a close, and the last of the guests left, Phoenix stormed off. Calista followed at a distance and watched as he climbed the stairs and headed toward his suite.

She followed him into the private office, aware that her scent caught on the light breeze that drifted toward him. She was sure he felt the effects of it instantly, noting how he attempted to discreetly shift his stance to conceal the evidence of his growing arousal.

"What are you trying to gain from me—from my people?" he demanded.

Calista let the silence linger for a few moments before replying. "Jealous?" she asked. A slow smile curved her full lips. She didn't know where his hostile attitude was coming from so suddenly, but she didn't want her confusion to show. Phoenix shifted his stance again. "Jealous that my people trust me and now so do yours and that they could give a Savarra's rotting tail about you?"

Calista could see that he was fighting to keep his emotions under control. Maybe it was jealousy, though not necessarily over how his people received her but perhaps that he had to share her attention with others.

Phoenix closed the gap between them with three strides. He put his hand at the base of her neck and brushed her hair away with the back of his hand. He angled her head up ever so slightly and whispered so close to her ear his warm breath sent shivers down her spine, straight through her core. "How dare you."

Calista leaned up, touching his cheek with her own. "Feeling threatened?" she asked, her voice just above a whisper.

With those words hanging in the thickening air between them, Calista stepped back, reached down to adjust the slit of her dress, then turned on her heel. When she arrived at the ornately carved marble doorway, she paused and trailed one finger down the detailed carvings. "Choose your next move carefully," she said. Then she sashayed down the hall out of sight, leaving Phoenix gaping.

"This is far from over!"

Calista smiled to herself. *I bet,* she thought, feeling satisfied that she had gotten under his skin.

Upon retiring to her bedchamber, she took a few moments to reflect on the events that had transpired throughout the day and into the evening.

What an ass! But damn if he's not a good looking one. Calista shook her head to banish the path her thoughts were taking, to no avail. *Where was he today? It's unlike him to miss a meeting, much less forget when one is rescheduled.* This train of thought returned her attention to the key that he found in the fountain earlier in the day. Calista had only worn her Aquavass that night and opted to leave her key in her room.

She was seated at the vanity in the bathroom when she heard a knock at the door.

"Coming," she called out as she ambled over to the door, still wearing her evening gown. She opened the door to find Phoenix standing there, brooding, his tie loosened and the top buttons of his tuxedo undone, his hands shoved deep into his pockets. He stepped toward Calista, each step forcing Calista to take a step back until the backs of her legs bumped into the side of the bed. Refusing to allow herself to be intimidated, she stood as straight and tall as her petite frame would allow.

"No one walks away from me," Phoenix said, his gaze flicking between her eyes and her lips. His hand moved from his pocket to the base of her neck, his thumb sliding up her chin and brushing her bottom lip.

"Are you threatening me?" Calista choked.

"I don't make threats," he replied. "I make promises." He tilted his head to the side and inched so close that she could feel the heat of his body searing all the places he touched. "And I don't make promises I don't intend to keep," he added, his voice rumbling against her lips. He angled her head up toward his and kissed her gently at first, then slowly eased his tongue past her lips, stroking her tongue and deepening the kiss. He pulled away and dropped his hand from her body. The withdrawal of heat was immediate and hit Calista with a wave of chills that caused her skin to ripple with goose flesh. Phoenix backed away, giving Calista a once-over before turning his back to her and leaving the room.

CHAPTER 11
The Initiation
Calista

The following morning, Calista joined Phoenix for breakfast. They ate in silence, an awkward tension between them. Finally, Calista was unable to contain herself any longer. "So, what did you do with that key you found?"

Phoenix looked up from the scroll he was looking at. *He must have gone back to get it after he left my room last night,* Calista thought. *Interesting.*

"I put it away somewhere safe until I know what I'm going to do with it." Nothing about his behaviour gave away the intimate interaction they had shared the previous night. Calista had been unable to sleep, her mind reeling with thoughts of other promises he could keep. She hadn't been prepared for the effect his close proximity and touch would have on her.

Phoenix stood up abruptly, and Calista joined him. "We should get going," he said. "The ceremony will start soon."

Calista headed out of the dining room. As he followed her, she got the sense he did so on purpose, as if to conceal an embarrassing albeit natural reaction he might be experiencing as he also reflected on the previous night's events. *This is going to be a damn long ride to East Marra*, she thought with amusement.

Calista stood before her vanity dressed in her full royal military regalia. She knew Phoenix would be dressed the same.

What made you offer him space here to get dressed when he has that entire yacht? Calista thought, chastising herself for her weak attempt at hospitality.

Luxx let herself into Calista's dressing room and stood beside her, taking in their reflection in the mirror. She was dressed in her finest military regalia with her blessed blade prominently strapped in her side holster, tucked up tight against her ribs. The hilt was polished to a gleam. She handed Calista her own freshly polished blade and gave her a critical once-over before the two women leaned in to touch foreheads. They were as ready as ever. It was time to make their way to the East Marra Amphitheatre north of the capital, which would serve as the location for the induction ceremony.

The significance of having new candidates take their oath and receive their blessed blades in the ancient amphitheatre was no coincidence. The ancient ruin had been used for the ceremony since its inception to remind those present of the commitment the Zenovia warriors had to serve the people of LaMarra, regardless of their affiliation to the ruling family of the East or the West. The stage sat in the valley, the lowest level, while the rows of seats that formed a semicircle around the stage rose up and backwards, away from the stage, giving the audience an elevated view of the action in front of them. Every angle of the stage was visible; there was complete transparency. The northern Basara mountains served as the backdrop for the theatre. To the west was the bank of the Marra, and to the east was the Ash Desert.

As Calista approached the dais, not surprisingly, Phoenix was already there. As expected, he was dressed in his royal military regalia as well. It was the male version of her own attire, designed to show that there was no distinction to be made between East or West Marra when it came to the Zenovia Army.

Calista and Luxx approached the dais and formally greeted the guests, first Phoenix with a bow of the head and then a handshake for Knoxx, who was standing to Phoenix's right. Calista took up her position on Phoenix's left side with Luxx beside her. The four of them stood facing the candidates, whose backs were to the spectators. Then a trumpet played the anthem that signified the ancient calling of the Goddess to bless the land. With that the ceremony began.

Luxx and Knoxx took their seats on the far sides of the stage, giving Calista the crowd's full attention. She gestured for everyone to sit. Phoenix stood several paces behind her as she delivered the opening remarks.

"Welcome, everyone," she began, the confidence and conviction of her words ringing out across the amphitheatre. "Today, only days before the celestial solstice is upon us, we find ourselves honoured to induct six new candidates into the divine Zenovia Army." She paused to make a visual connection with each candidate.

"Being a woman is a traditional part of being a Zenovian warrior, for women who are inducted as warriors in the divine army are given a blessed blade that allows them to take the lives of their adversaries or to take someone's life in an act of mercy without the recourse of being sent directly to Blackstone Prison."

Anyone who committed murder was instantly whisked away into Blackstone. Once trapped within the prison's walls, release could be negotiated with the counsel of water dragons, who were the keepers of the prison. The only way to be released was to replace the life that had been taken by whatever means was available. Men and women had been known to sacrifice their own offspring to secure their freedom.

Calista paused for a moment to allow the weight of her words to sink in.

"Wars are a time when protecting people against a threat results in lives lost. However, lives can only be ended justly by the hand of a Zenovian warrior who wields a blessed blade. Our men fight valiantly and defend us all with strength and valour, paving the way for our warriors to take the lives of those who threaten our people and to send those who are hurt beyond repair into the peace that only death can offer. Our warriors are vicious defenders as much as they are gods of mercy."

The crowd was deathly quiet, absorbing the impact of her words. She stepped back, and Phoenix stepped forward to begin the induction portion of the ceremony.

"For the defenders of LaMarra, today we sanctify you with our favour and provide you with a dagger that has been blessed in the waters of the Goddess Temple by the hands of Queen Calista and myself. These blades are blessed and imbued with the Goddess's strength."

Phoenix glanced at Calista. Then they moved toward the side table where the tray of daggers sat waiting to be distributed. Phoenix picked up the tray, and Calista plucked a blade from it and approached the first candidate. Holding the sheathed blade across the palms of her hands, she asked the first of three affirmation questions.

"Do you accept the bonds of commanding a blessed blade of the Goddess Marra?"

"Yes." The response was clear, and the young candidate's gaze never left Calista's eyes.

"Do you swear allegiance to the Goddess Marra, protector of LaMarra and her people?"

"Yes."

"Do you choose this path freely?"

"Yes. Absolutely." A large smile appeared on the candidate's face as she said the last word. Her gaze flicked between Calista and Phoenix, who mirrored her happiness.

Smiling widely, Calista leaned forward and touched her forehead to the young candidates for a moment, indicating that they are intimately connected by their status as Zenovian warriors and shared a connection unique to members of the divine army.

"This blade is yours," Calista said, speaking the final words of the induction.

"Use it wisely. May you always carry the favour of the Goddess with you."

Gripping the hilt firmly, the newly inducted Zenovian warrior picked up the blade and admired it with reverence before sheathing the blade in its holster on her breastplate. She mouthed the words "Thank you." to Calista and Phoenix before she resumed her formal demeanour and stepped back, allowing the next candidate to be inducted.

Phoenix stepped forward and asked the same series of questions of the next candidate and was met with the same level of enthusiasm. Finally, Calista approached the final candidate. She had had a brief conversation with her at the banquet the night before and was pleased that the young woman had ultimately decided that this was the right path for her. Something seemed off though. The young candidate was sweating, and her hands were fisted at her sides, her eyebrows drawn together. She met Calista's gaze with a sharp nod.

When Calista asked the first question of affirmation, the young candidate agreed. Calista shot Phoenix a glance as she continued with the second question. Again, the candidate answered in the affirmative. Calista proceeded with the final question.

"Do you choose this path freely?" A long silence stretched between them. The candidate held her eyes shut so tightly, she almost looked like she was willing the tears to stay at bay. Finally, she opened her eyes and looked at the blade that was resting across Calista's hands. From the crowd, an older woman's voice could be heard.

"Go on, say, 'yes,'" The candidate flinched, recognizing her mother's voice. Calista and Phoenix exchanged glances. Then the candidate finally spoke

"Yes. Wait, no, I—" She took a steadying breath and then looked directly into Calista's worried eyes. "I'm so sorry. No, I do not choose this path freely." With those words barely out of her mouth, she hurried off stage, batting away her parents, who ran after her, uttering apologies toward the stage where Calista, Phoenix, and the other candidates remained.

Calista moved to follow the girl and her family when she felt Phoenix's hand on her shoulder. The subtle shake of his head was enough to prompt Calista to conclude the ceremony. She and Phoenix stood back and allowed the candidates to turn and face the crowd.

"Aria, Maeve, Daria, Eloise and Val," Phoenix announced proudly. "The newly inducted Zenovian warriors of the divine Army."

The five women turned and unsheathed their blades, holding them high as the crowd cheered for them.

After a lengthy period of cheering and accolades, the trumpeter led the crowd in the traditional procession toward Cerulean Palace, where they would have a reception feast to celebrate the new warriors. The warriors led the crowd, with Calista and Phoenix bringing up the rear. It was a scenic walk along the bank of the River Marra, one of Calista's favourite parts of the ceremony.

"I want to find Daisy," Calista said, her eyes searching the crowd as they filed past. "I'm worried about her."

"I see her," Phoenix said, much to Calista's relief. "She's behind that wall. Give it a minute until all the people pass. She's probably mortified."

As the final members of the congregation filed past, Daisy approached Calista and Phoenix. Her face streaked with tears, she reached out to touch Calista's forearm. Calista pulled her into a tight hug. The young lady began sobbing as she muttered the word "Sorry." over and over again. Once she had calmed down, she pulled away from the security of Calista's embrace.

"I've disappointed everyone," she said. "I know how important being a Zenovian warrior is to my family, but I just couldn't do it."

"You made the right choice, Daisy," Phoenix replied, placing a hand on her shoulder. "Knowing yourself and what you're capable of is what being a warrior is about."

Calista echoed the sentiment. "You didn't disappoint anyone. Accepting the responsibilities of being a warrior with a blessed dagger are so profound, you need to choose that life freely."

Daisy nodded, having calmed significantly by then that she had begun walking alongside Calista and Phoenix.

"Now that you have all this time freed up since you don't have to attend basic training, what do you want to do?" Phoenix asked.

Daisy hesitated for a moment before speaking. "I've always been interested in healing. I'll become a centenary healer, if I get to live that long that is," she added with a laugh. "But I really want to learn about it now. I want to help people now. Being a Zenovian was one way I could help the dying. I love the part about being a god of mercy, but I don't want to put people out of their misery. I want to help people now."

Calista's eyes lit up as Daisy spoke, realizing that this young woman held potential beyond what a member of the Zenovia Army could do. She smiled. "I know somewhere you can go to get started."

The elation on Daisy's face was enough to drag a laugh out of Phoenix and Calista.

"Come find me after the celebration," Calista said. "I'll introduce you to Jade. But for now, go and talk to your parents. They'll be relieved that you have bigger plans than being a soldier." Daisy thanked Calista and Phoenix, then gathered them both into a tight hug.

As Daisy caught up with her parents, Phoenix and Calista continued walking behind the procession. Calista could feel Phoenix looking down at her, noting the slight movement in her peripheral vision.

Was that his hand brushing mine again? Why is he looking at me like that? Engrossed in her thoughts, Calista was annoyed with herself for being so hyper aware of his presence beside her.

Phoenix appeared lost in his own thoughts as well. He had maintained a professional distance during the ceremony, but it seemed like his mind was elsewhere. Calista wondered if he was thinking about their kiss the night before, then tried to banish the thought before it could take hold of her, but her hopes of another kiss got the better of her.

"Something on your mind?" she asked, hoping she did not sound desperate. Phoenix gave her a sideways glance, then smiled crookedly before responding. "You were great today at the ceremony and with Daisy."

"Thank you," she replied as she fussed with the detailing on her outfit, aware that nervousness was out of character for her, but somehow he brought that out in her. As they continued walking, they fell farther and farther behind the crowd, discreetly seeking a little more privacy.

"Have I mentioned that you look very nice today?" he asked casually, almost shyly, making Calista silently swoon. "I have to admit that I prefer those long slitted skirts though. They leave just enough to the imagination." With that admission Calista couldn't keep herself from smiling.

"Oh, I bet," she replied as she nudged his shoulder, relishing the brief contact they had and hoping he wouldn't ridicule her poor attempt at flirting.

The festivities lasted all night, continuing until sunlight sliced through the darkness and announced a new day. As the celebrations died down and the families started going home, Calista and Phoenix found themselves alone on the open-air terrace. As they leaned against the balcony's stone railing, Calista felt his hand on her lower back. She looked up at him but didn't move away. He angled his head toward hers and slid his hand up her spine until it was under her chin. She took a breath to speak, but he silenced her and dropped his head down to meet her lips again. He kissed her gently and sweetly. The feeling consuming her, Calista allowed herself to indulge in the intimacy of the moment. She rose up on her toes and pressed into the kiss, deepening it a little more. She felt his response to her touch against her abdomen. He sucked in a sharp breath and broke their kiss, speaking with his lips against hers.

"We should stop."

"Hmm . . . yes we should," she replied.

They stayed locked in that awkwardly intimate moment, neither one able to pull away. Calista's hand wandered from the firm muscles in his back to the solid wall of his chest. She pushed gently but couldn't bring herself to use much force. With his hand still on her back, he pulled her against his body. There was no hiding his arousal. Calista leaned her forehead against his chest

"We can't do this; we both need cold showers," she muttered with a breathy laugh. Letting the weight of the moment settle in on her, she felt conflicted by her feelings about him. Their core values were so different, but she found herself questioning if that was still true. Her feelings for him were changing. She recalled how she never really felt hostile toward him until she became Queen, and the role seemed to demand it of her.

Phoenix reluctantly relaxed his grip on her and they slowly separated. "OK, you're right," he said.

"Bye, Nix."

"Goodnight, Cali," he said with a wink, then turned to show himself out. His reluctance to leave had her wondering if maybe his feelings were changing as well.

As Phoenix rounded the corner, he bumped into Luxx. Calista heard him say goodnight. Then she saw the look on Luxx's face. Calista's heart sank a little at her friend's disapproving expression.

"I'm going to shower before turning in for the night," was all Calista offered as an explanation for being found alone with Phoenix. On that tight note she slipped into her private bedchamber, leaving Luxx in her wake.

Once she was alone, Calista's thoughts were like a hurricane whipping around in her head. She let herself wander down a rabbit hole of thoughts about Phoenix, unable to get his face, his touch, or his scent out of her mind.

CHAPTER 12
Vulnari
Calista

In the aftermath of the induction ceremony and with the celestial solstice approaching, Calista turned her attention to the other regions of LaMarra, going on a short overnight visit to the Vulnari district.

"I've already made the necessary arrangements for us to get to Vulnari by horseback," Luxx informed Calista rather curtly as they walked through the estate toward the hardly used motor court at the front of the palace. "The inn we're staying at will be sending horses to the base of the cliff for us to take back up." Although Calista's parents had a fleet of vehicles, they felt it was wasteful to keep all of the vehicles maintained. That left Calista with a single all-terrain vehicle that was in decent working order but was known to break down on occasion.

"Did you make introductions between Daisy and Jade?" Calista asked in an attempt to soften the tension between them.

"Yes. Is this everything we need? Are you good to go?" Luxx pinned Calista with a no-nonsense stare, waiting for confirmation.

When Calista nodded, Luxx circled the vehicle and climbed into the driver's seat.

They pulled away from the palace just as daylight made its full presence known. Calista stifled a yawn while Luxx drove, not missing her friend's epic eye roll.

"We could have delayed this trip for a day, so you could rest up," Luxx said. Calista shook her head and sat up straighter.

"No need. I'll be fine. Just tired after all the excitement of the reception last night."

"Among other things," Luxx spat.

Not wanting to engage in a full-on argument, Calista took a different approach, wondering if perhaps Luxx had seen her and Phoenix together or if Luxx's attitude was tied to something else entirely. "Say it, Luxx. Just get it off your chest. I don't want you to be upset with me the entire time we're up north."

Inhaling deeply, Luxx glanced at Calista then turned back to the road before replying, letting the silence stretch out between them. "Cali, I am saying this now not as your advisor or your protector but as your friend and sister." The mention of the word "sister." caught Calista's attention. Luxx only used that term if she was worried or feeling protective.

"Go on."

"You're letting him get too close to you. I saw you at the ceremony and again afterwards. You looked very cozy. I don't like it. I'm worried not only that he'll hurt you, break your heart, but the consequences of him getting too close to you could hurt the people who depend on you as their Queen."

Calista was quiet for some time as she absorbed Luxx's words, realizing that Luxx must have seen her and Phoenix after the ceremony. *Consequences, consequences, consequences.* She let the word roll around in her head as she reflected on the conflicting emotions she already had about Phoenix.

"You're right to be worried, Luxx. I'm worried too. I find myself getting a little confused when it comes to him. I want so much to trust him, but I don't know. Something is holding me back."

"Holding you back? From what?"

Shit! I've said too much. Does she suspect we kissed? It's Luxx. I can tell her, can't I? Should I? Calista let those thoughts settle before she spoke up.

"Nothing. It's nothing. I just don't want to get caught up in his bullshit."

Luxx scoffed. "Yeah, I'll bet."

They rode the rest of the way in relative silence, Luxx allowing Calista to catch up on sleep before they reached the foot of the cliff that would lead them on a winding path up to the Vulnari district.

At the base of the cliff face, two horses were waiting to take the women up the winding path into the Vulnari district.

"West Marra has a rest stop just across the river at the base of the cliff. I'm not going to lie; it looks pretty convenient," Luxx griped as she attached her and Calista's bags to horses' saddles.

"I thought you liked camping and roughing it," Calista said as she mounted her horse. While on their journey north, travelling through the Zenovia training grounds, Calista was reminded of how she and Luxx met.

"Being up around here always reminds me of my training days," Calista offered as an olive branch to encourage Luxx into more pleasant conversation.

"How could I forget?" Luxx replied as she recalled how she and Sapphire the centenary healer camped out for the night near the training grounds. Luxx didn't sleep because she became enraptured with the strength and skill that other women her age had. It was the first time she saw Calista, then merely a princess, who was training among them.

"When I saw the Zenovia warriors training for the first time, I remember thinking that not one of these women would ever have been taken advantage of."

Calista smiled at Luxx's recollection and thought fondly of how she took Luxx under her wing, and they became inseparable. They fought together as equals, friends, and warriors of the army, like sisters.

Despite their fond recollections, Calista couldn't help but notice that Luxx still seemed lost in thought. Then or now, Luxx had never shared the details of her life prior to when they met, She still held out hope that one day, that might change.

Once securely in the saddle, Calista ran her hand along her horse's neck and brushed a spot that looked like an injury. She inspected it more closely and saw that it was a slash mark. Feeling sorry for the animal, she clucked her tongue and made soothing noises before spurring the beast toward the path. The drive had taken them the better part of the daylight hours, and night was falling. The trek up the cliff would take a few hours at least, and they hoped they would make it before nightfall.

While they rode, their conversation continued on a darker subject.

"Luxx what do you know about the renegades?"

"Well, that's a little random. Why do you want to know?"

"I noticed my horse has a scar. Looks like a knife mark, and it made me think about the ex-cons who wear the offences they commit on others on their own bodies as if they inflicted them on themselves. Do you think we'll run into anyone around here?"

"Well, you know as well as I do that the risk is always there. I have received some intelligence that there have been some riots over in West Marra, but that's hardly any of our concern. Prince Charming and his henchmen can deal with that."

Luxx's mention of Phoenix sent Calista's thoughts drifting back to him and their last encounter. She shook herself and pulled her mind out of the rabbit hole that was swirling with promises of lust before she gave herself away.

"Hmm . . . OK. Well, if you think there's nothing for me to worry about, then that's fine. I trust you. What did they say the riots were about? It seems they're happening more often."

Luxx appeared to hesitate before sharing what she did know. "The riots have been little more than vandalism. No one has been hurt yet. It's like they're making their presence known, perhaps looking for something, but I don't know what. They display allegiance to someone in West Marra based on their chants about the true king, but whoever is claiming that title, I have no idea. It's interesting how they have left East Marra alone—so far anyway."

Calista spent a moment considering this information. Since her region was not affected yet, she had no business interfering, especially since her people and lands didn't seem to be the target. She resolved to keep this information in the back of her mind just in case things did escalate. Needing a change of pace in their discussion, she steered the conversation in another direction.

"So, what's the first order of business when we get the Vulnari district?" Calista asked, as much to keep herself alert as to find out what she needed to do. The journey north has been tiring, and it was on the heels of a rather charged evening, leaving her sleep deprived and emotionally unsettled.

"After we check in, I'm going to my Mom's for dinner. You should come with me. She would be thrilled to have you."

"I would hate to impose Luxx—"

"Let me stop you right there. You're coming to dinner. I need you there," Luxx said with an arched eyebrow.

Unsure what kind of turmoil existed between Luxx and her Mother, Calista decided she would tread carefully that night.

The Baraf Pahar Inn was a cozy chalet-style building with a rustic kitchen that served as a local restaurant. On the second level, it also had several rooms available for travellers passing through the district. It is a large establishment and well known to those passing through the village of Vulnari. Several times per year, travellers from the Basara Mountain villages came down to Vulnari to restock on essential items and to get their hunting knives sharpened and tended to. The trek was anything but convenient, and they usually sought shelter for a night or two before returning to their villages. Sage, the innkeeper, had been the proprietor of the establishment for nearly eighty years. He was practically a centenary and was well known for his hospitality and spectacular mushroom-and-ale stew.

"Your Highness of Godliness and most beautiful Queen Cali! Hello, and welcome to my humble abode!" his voice thundered as he burst through the doors of the restaurant's kitchen the moment he saw Calista and Luxx approaching.

Smiling broadly and blushing at the ridiculous level of fanfare he exuded with his introduction, Calista dismounted and approached him with her hand outstretched. Sage ignored the polite gesture and wrapped her into a bear hug that warmed her heart and her sore bones.

"It's so wonderful to see you again, how have you all been?" Calista asked as she disentangled herself from his warm, fatherly embrace.

"I'm glad you asked. Things are OK, but with the celestial solstice coming we have been busy . . ." His voice trailed off as though his thoughts were becoming clouded, and he was hesitant to continue.

"What is it?" Calista prompted as Luxx moved behind Sage and caught her eye. She shook her head, indicating that Calista should not pursue the conversation any further. Catching the hint, Calista quickly linked arms with Sage and feigned feeling a cold breeze. "Sage, let's go inside. It's freezing out here, and I can't wait to have a mug of your delicious spiced cocoa."

Together they walked inside while a young man took the horses to be tended to.

Once inside the warm, cozy inn, Calista could see that things had changed. The building looked like it was falling into disrepair but only in one area. The booth toward a hidden corner looked shabby and unkempt, very unlike the rest of the tidy but rustic space.

Sage's eyes flicked toward the booth before they turned to Calista "You will be safe here tonight. The renegades won't be back for a while, I hope."

"The renegades? Have they been here giving you a hard time?" she inquired.

"No, not really, but they do have a presence, and they tend to run off my friendlier patrons. They keep to themselves usually. Ever since that fellow Knoxx has been coming here more regularly without the King, the other renegades have been coming around more. Makes people feel uneasy."

Calista shot Luxx a look that spoke volumes. It seemed her weariness and general dislike for Knoxx was not unique to her. She turned back to Sage. "I know we are safe here with you. Thank you for having us."

After some stern negotiations with Sage, Calista lost her battle against having two rooms. She and Luxx were assigned the two largest and coziest rooms atop the inn. After freshening up and changing into significantly warmer clothing, they set out to see Luxx's mother.

"I always forget how chilly it gets up here," Calista said. Luxx appeared to be lost in her thoughts, and it took her a while to respond. Even when she did it was offhanded and distant, as if her thoughts were consuming her.

"Luxx? Luxx?" Calista prompted to no avail until she placed a hand on her friend's shoulder and plucked her out of the depths of her thoughts. "Luxx, is everything alright? You're not yourself."

"Of course I'm not myself, Cali!" she practically shouted, the sharpness in her voice highly unusual. "Did you really need to give Sage such a hard time about the rooms? So what if he wants to make a big deal about having royalty at his inn? And did it ever occur to you that maybe I would want some privacy for once?"

Calista was taken aback by her outburst. She would need to tread very carefully tonight. Luxx was clearly working though some issues that had nothing to do with Calista. It made Calista wonder what Luxx had been keeping from her. Guilt washed over her as she wondered if she had been so wrapped up in her recent infatuation with Phoenix that she had missed something major happening in Luxx's life.

Luxx stopped walking and stepped in front of Calista, effectively stopping her in her tracks. Facing Calista, Luxx glanced around to make sure no one could overhear her next words. "Forgive me for being so nasty with you, but being here is bringing up a lot of old memories, not all of which are good. You don't know much about my history; I've never shared it with you because I'm ashamed of a lot of it. When we met it was like starting over for me. I didn't have a good life, Cali, not until I learned what it meant to have self-respect and confidence. I have you to thank for that. I'm grateful you never pried into my past, but here in this place, it's unavoidable." Luxx's brows knit together, and her eyes were glassy as if she were fighting to keep a flood of tears at bay. It was so out of character for her.

Calista rubbed her shoulder. "You can tell me anything anytime. It will never change how I see you. Let me be here for you."

Luxx brushed away a stray tear. "I'm coming home for the first time in a long while. Last time I was here, we had a disagreement, my mother and I. I don't know what's going to happen at dinner tonight. That's why I need you there. But there's more. I never told you because I was too embarrassed, but I would rather you hear it from me than anyone else, and it may come up at dinner anyway."

Calista used her gloved hand to wipe away Luxx's tears and listened earnestly as Luxx continued. "My mother, Maia, was a prisoner at Blackstone for murder. She killed the person in self-defence, but it didn't matter; it was still murder. It was a long time ago. She was released when I was born, but time is different in prison. It's slower, and the magic in the prison is strange. No one really knows how it works." Luxx hesitated before continuing. "I . . . she's different, my mom, her views, her way of speaking. I just want you to know she's a good person."

"Luxx, I would never judge you or your mother for your past; you know that," Calista said gently. This vote of confidence earned her a small, relieved smile from Luxx.

Luxx nervously played with her Aquavass and advised Calista to keep hers tucked inside her shirt to avoid any lengthy or uncomfortable questions about her mom's favourite topic, the excessive wealth of the south districts. Many of the inhabitants of the Vulnari district did not distinguish much between East or West Marra. To them it was all the same; they were the southerners, rich, and entitled, and it was where the royals lived.

Luxx's childhood home was not far from the inn. The two-bedroom structure was just on the outskirts of the village. Night had fallen, and the stars were the only light. Luxx pinned Calista with a stern look, her eyes becoming glassy. Calista was unsure if it was from the cold bite in the air or from emotion.

Luxx knocked on the door and was met first by the large, furry dog that leapt up with his giant paws on her chest, nearly knocking her back. Luxx laughed and batted away the beast as she fought her way past the open door, leaving Calista to figure out how to keep the excitable beast from licking her face into oblivion. While Calista calmed the large but friendly dog, Luxx walked toward her mother, whose back was facing her as she stood at the stove fussing over a large pot.

"Ma," she said quietly. "Ma, it's me, Luxx."

Maia turned around and saw Luxx standing there. It took a moment for her to react. She closed the distance between them and wrapped her frail arms around Luxx in a tight hug. Tears sprang to Luxx's eyes as she returned the affection.

Calista watched quietly from the doorway as she absently petted the dog. After an extended silence, Luxx gestured to Calista.

"Ma, this is Que—Calista, my very good friend."

As Luxx was about to say the word "Queen," Calista silenced her with a look. It was not the time or place for pomp and circumstance. Her mom knew who Calista was, and this was a social visit.

Maia fixed Calista with a penetrating glare that felt so familiar. Luxx had the same hair colour and build as her mother, but something else was oddly familiar about her, the way she looked down her nose at Calista. She had a hardness about her that was so different from Luxx but also familiar. Calista couldn't quite put her finger on it.

"Calista, welcome to my humble home," Maia said as she made an awkward attempt to bow.

Calista stooped to lift the older woman upright, smiling gently at her. "Thank you for having me to your beautiful home. Please allow me," Calista said as she pulled out a wooden chair from the kitchen table. Maia sank heavily into the chair and coughed as she inhaled a few strangled breaths. Calista looked at Luxx, whose face was the picture of worry and concern. Calista went to get the mug of tea beside the pot on the stove and offered it to Maia. She took a few sips and caught her breath.

"Ma, why didn't you tell me you were sick?" Luxx asked. "You could have sent someone to get me."

"Girl, I'm not sick. I'm old, broken, and tired, but I'm not sick! I overdid it at the shop. Solstice is coming up, and we're busy!" Maia huffed, then stood to make her way back to the stove. "Go make yourselves useful and set the table. You too, Queen. A little hard work never killed anyone."

Calista smiled and began setting out the plates on the table while Luxx put out the flatware and glasses. Once they were all settled around the table, Maia served each of them a heaping bowl of stew. It was warm, thick, and rich, smelling of hearty meat and vegetables.

"It's Savarra Stew," Maia said with a sneaky smile and a wink at Luxx.

"It's what she calls it when she doesn't want to say what's in it," Luxx explained. In her youth when times were lean, and they had to make do with whatever limited resources were available, it became a running joke to call whatever Maia made for dinner Savarra Stew. Luxx assured Calista it was likely not Savarra meat and probably wild boar.

"This tastes wonderful," Calista said around a mouthful of stew.

She was truly warmed to be with Luxx and her mother. She felt the familial love envelope her as the meal carried on. Conversation was a bit strained at the beginning, but as second and third helpings were served, Calista found herself laughing and sharing in the easy banter that sprang up between Luxx and Maia. Maia also started to shed the elderly appearance she had when the women arrived. She was dressed like a centenary, and she was clearly run down, but her features were young. She had a youthful glint in her eyes that was so striking. She resembled Luxx a lot, especially when she smiled.

"So, Luxx, what made you feel like you needed to bring a Queen home with you unannounced?" Maia asked pointedly as she folded her arms in front of her on the table.

"Ma, she's not like the old Queens you remember. She's also my friend, and I thought you would like to meet one of my friends."

Maia cast an uncomfortable look at Calista, choosing her words carefully. "Your Highness, I'm not sure if you have already been informed, but the hospitality you have been provided tonight comes from a former inmate of Blackstone." She cast her eyes downward as the silence in the room thickened. Calista glanced at Luxx, unsure of what to say. She had no intention of making anyone feel uncomfortable.

"Maia, please call me Cali. There's no need for any formalities. Luxx is a friend, a sister to me. I'm grateful for all your hospitality this evening." Calista hesitated before continuing, not wanting her next words to offend Maia. "Your past deeds are just that, in the past and nothing to be judged by today, certainly not by me. I consider you a friend, as you are Luxx's mother, and I'm grateful to you for raising such a wonderful person who I am proud to have as my advisor, protector, friend, and sister."

Maia finally lifted her gaze to meet Calista's. "Thank you."

Calista felt Luxx's hand squeeze her knee under the table as Maia smiled, the brightness returning to her eyes as she mouthed the words "Thank you." to Calista. With the tension broken, the evening gave way to drinking local wine and comfortable conversation.

After Calista and Luxx said their goodbyes and exchanged warm hugs all around, they set out into the cold night air on their way back to the inn.

"There's more to the story about how my mom got out of Blackstone," Luxx said.

"Well, I'm sure it wasn't easy," Calista replied. "She looks like she's lived several lifetimes worth of distress, and leaving Blackstone is only one chapter among them."

"That's not what I meant," Luxx replied hesitantly.

"What is it?"

"Well, you know that she was imprisoned for murder, and her release was negotiated based on her giving back a life to replace the one she took. I don't know how she made it out, but I do know from the stories she told me that I was born in the prison and a water dragon showed her mercy and brought us both across Siphon Lake."

Calista's eyebrows knit together in confusion. Something did not make sense. If Maia was pregnant, she would have had to give up her child in the negotiation for an early release from Blackstone. Who replaced the life of the one she took? Calista kept this thought to herself as Luxx continued her explanation.

"I don't know how my mom managed to keep me safe after having me in prison. Maybe one day I'll get it out of her," Luxx said, seemingly lost in thought.

Upon arriving at the inn, the women pushed open the doors and saw Sage's beaming smile from behind the front desk.

"Message for you!" Sage waved an envelope and handed it to Calista.

"Thank you," she said as she tore open the envelope and unfolded the parchment inside.

Luxx, I heard you were in Vulnari. I sent this message when you didn't respond to my bond message. Come see me. - L

Calista handed Luxx the note. She snatched it from Calista's hand and fixed her with a look that could incinerate her.

"It's nothing, Cali."

"Who is contacting you through your bond?" Calista demanded. "Are you in trouble?"

"No! Just leave it, Cali."

Luxx started up the stairs toward their rooms, Calista close on her heels. "Luxx!" Calista hissed. "Don't cause a scene. What the hell is this about?"

"Nothing, Cali. I'll meet you tomorrow morning downstairs. Just leave me alone."

Calista's nose was nearly caught in the door as Luxx slammed it. She placed a hand on the door, ready to knock, then thought better of it and decided to give Luxx her space for the moment.

Calista retreated to her own room, her mind swirling with a myriad of intrusive thoughts.

What the hell has gotten into Luxx? What is it about Vulnari that has her so edgy? First her mother, and now she's bonded with someone?

This new information baffled Calista. For as long as Luxx had been her advisor, Calista couldn't remember a time when they kept things from one another. As that thought crossed her mind, she was flooded with guilt, realizing she was keeping her true feelings about Phoenix to herself, however confusing they were.

Feeling the full impact of the day's physical and emotional tensions take over, Calista climbed into the warm bed and, without even undressing, fell asleep, her mind racing with thoughts and images of Luxx, the mystery person, and Phoenix.

CHAPTER 13
Maps
Calista

The following morning, Calista went downstairs to see if Luxx had emerged from her room. As she approached the table that was reserved for her, Sage sauntered up in his overly exaggerated way, beaming with pride that he had the honour of serving a royal.

"Will you be having the same thing as Luxx this morning, Your Highness?" he asked

Calista's eyebrows drew together as she realized she must have missed Luxx.

Where on earth could she have gone in such a hurry? she wondered as she arranged her features into a smile before replying. "Yes, thank you, Sage. I'll have whatever Luxx had and some of your spiced cocoa, if you have any." Calista was not about to let on that there was something amiss between her and her advisor. Perhaps knowing what Luxx had for breakfast would give her a clue.

As she waited for her meal to arrive, Calista was consumed with worry. She discreetly dipped her little finger into the glass of water on the table and traced the symbol that she and Luxx shared when they created their bond—a question mark. Hoping that she could at least figure out if she was OK through their water bond, Calista waited patiently for Luxx's response. Finally, after what was actually seconds but which felt like hours, a heart symbol shimmered to life on Calista's forearm, indicating Luxx was OK. Although this settled her mind momentarily, Calista knew she would have to conduct a further investigation later. But for now she needed to carry on with the business at hand.

"Breakfast is served!" Sage presented Calista with a platter large enough to feed several people.

"Luxx ate all of this for breakfast?" Calista asked, her eyes popping at the sheer volume of food in front of her. It was a far cry from the oatmeal that Luxx favoured at home. Laid out on Calista's plate was an assortment of meats, eggs, potatoes, and vegetables and nearly an entire loaf of toasted bread, each slice coated in butter. "Thank you, Sage. Had I known this is what she ordered, I would have asked for less."

"Eat up, Your Highness. It's cold out, and you will need your energy."

Calista smiled. "At least join me, Sage. There's more than enough for both of us here." Sage's cheeks turned rosy as he smiled.

"I would be honoured to join you."

He sat down, and they tucked into their breakfast. His mouth full of the delicious food, Sage drew his eyebrows together and looked at Calista. "I imagine your advisor has gone ahead of you to secure the area before your arrival?"

Calista marshalled her features into as natural an expression as she could muster. It seemed she would be learning a bit about Luxx's whereabouts sooner rather than later.

"Yes," she replied.

Ever the innocent, Sage continued to spew information. "Yes, I imagine you have some serious business. Going up to Siphon Lake, Blackstone Prison, perhaps?"

Calista swallowed her mouthful whole before she looked directly at Sage, not wanting to give away that she had no idea what he was talking about. "Is that where Luxx told you she was headed this morning?"

Sage put down his fork and wiped his mouth with the back of his hand. He looked directly at Calista, all pretense of pleasantries gone, his pleasant expression replaced by concern. "Your Highness, I am a jovial man, but I am also very perceptive. Have I said something to cause offence?" He leaned back and waited for Calista to respond. Still not wanting to reveal her ignorance, Calista hesitated before replying.

"What makes you think she went to Blackstone?" Calista asked, settling on the tactic of responding to a question with a question.

"She didn't say specifically that she was going to the Blackstone. But she did ask for a sturdy horse and a riding cloak. She seemed pained, and if I'm being honest, she gave me the impression that she did not want you to know where she went."

"Why have you told me then?" Calista asked, her eyebrows drawn together in worry and panic beginning to mount even though Luxx had confirmed she was OK.

"We all have a past. No matter how hard we try to forget it, sometimes it can follow us. While I don't know for sure that she's going to Blackstone, I do know that she's headed for Siphon Lake. She didn't want to worry you, but I feel like you should know. You're clearly more than a ruler to her. You're her friend, and you deserve to know. Luxx also asked me to keep an eye out for you to protect you in her absence."

Calista searched the depths of Sage's eyes as she formulated a response. She decided it was best not to ask any further questions for the moment. If there was anything about Luxx that she needed to know, Calista wanted to hear it directly from her. It was true that everyone had a past, but what was it about Luxx's past that needed to be kept so secret?

"Thank you for this meal and sharing the information with me. I'll leave this matter with Luxx until later. You're right that we're friends, and when she feels she can come to me, she will." As Calista reflected on what Luxx had told her the night before, she knew that if Luxx needed to tell her anything, she would, but she wouldn't allow it to be coerced out of her.

Calista and Sage finished their meal in comfortable silence. Then Calista set out on her day's errands, meeting with the citizens of Vulnari. She had planned to shop for some solstice gifts as well as visit the various caves and mines that the Vulnari region was known for. The caves and mines were where the material for the weapons for East and West Marra is mined.

Sage offered her the use of a horse to get around the village. Calista accepted the offer as well as a heavy riding cloak. The practical clothing she had brought from home was warm enough, but in the mountains the wind slashed through the fabric of her coat.

As she rode toward the base of the mountain range to explore the caves and mines, she was grateful for the heavy cloak and wrapped it tightly around herself to ward off the bitter cold.

Calista tied her horse to the nearest post and smiled as she greeted miners, who were going back and forth into the mouth of the cave, hauling the materials used to make various weapons, blades, and other defensive tools.

"Hello, Your Highness!" A man covered in dirt from head to toe but smiling broadly approached Calista with an outstretched hand. "Sage sent word you would be visiting," he said as Calista approached him.

"He did, did he?" Calista replied, smiling. "Whom do I have the pleasure of speaking with?" she asked as she shook his outstretched hand.

"I'm Blake. I run this operation. It's a busy time right now, especially with the request from the other Highness."

"The other Highness?" Calista asked.

"Yeah. He sent his advisor, the big burly bald guy, Knoxx. He asked for a ton of ardement. He met with the weapons master too, designing a new kind of blade or something. I'm not too sure, but he wants the most heat-resistant material available and a lot of it."

"Ah, I see. That's interesting," Calista said as more questions spiralled around in her head. What was meant to be a relaxing visit was becoming so informative. Between visiting the Vulnari Mountains, learning about Luxx's childhood, meeting Luxx's mother, and now discovering Phoenix's increased demand for ardement, the trip had led to so many questions.

Shaking off her mounting anxiety over all the new bits of information, she asked for a tour of the caves.

Blake broke into a giant grin that showcased his crooked teeth. He was charming in his own way, and Calista couldn't help but take his hand as he led her toward the mouth of the cave. As he approached other workers coming and going, Calista noticed he was trying to keep his composure as he explained that Calista was here on important business and that the men should keep working.

The entrance of the cave was decorated with carvings depicting various scenes from Vulnari's history. Blake talked non-stop as he described the various tools and procedures used to collect the materials to make weapons. He was blissfully unaware of Calista's minimal interest in what he was explaining. Her occasional responses kept him chattering away, allowing her to marvel at the images on the cave walls.

As they reached a dead end in one tunnel, Blake announced that the tour was finished and offered to take her back to the entrance. Calista took a moment to look around, placing her hand over one of the carvings.

"Oh yeah, those drawings, they're pretty cool. They're as old as the hills too," Blake said.

"Do you know what they're meant to depict?" Calista asked.

"Uh, no, not really. There are some pictures of ancient animals, stuff that doesn't exist anymore. Some pictures of swords and stuff too."

"Hmm . . . I see," she said absently as she traced her finger over an image. Dust fell away from the wall, revealing more of the image. Calista wiped away more dirt and dust, struck by the image's familiarity. It was the same map that she had been studying in West Marra.

This looks so similar, but it can't be. It's much bigger, Calista thought as she studied the map, noticing that it appeared to be divided. To the far east, the Ash Desert was clearly marked. That area must have been known to serve as a place for the dead even in ancient times. In the far west, on the other side of the line that divided the map in two, was a clear marking that showed a small body of water. Slowly, it dawned on her that the body of water was Siphon Lake, and the line dividing the map was the River Marra. The primitive map depicted the whole of LaMarra before the war, possibly even before it was known as LaMarra. It seemed to predate everything she had ever learned about LaMarra.

Calista thought back to her time as a student when she was learning about the history of her people and her land. The teaching was specific to East Marra and only briefly touched on West Marra. The information never seemed to be complete, but the scholars said that was all that she needed to know. However, her curiosity regarding the land's ancient history never left her. From time to time her education alluded to legends and stories of ancient goddesses and a myriad of water- and sky-dwelling beasts, all of which she thought was nonsense, but this map was a physical piece of the story, causing her to wonder if such stories were reality rather than fiction.

This realization settled into Calista's mind, mingling with all the other questions she had about Luxx and Blackstone Prison. Spurred on by the need to find out more, and wanting to reach out to Phoenix

A World Divided

to share this news about the map, she wondered if his education had fewer gaps than hers and if he perhaps knew something more about ancient LaMarra than she did. Calista returned her attention to Blake.

"Do you happen to have any parchment with you?" she asked. Not wanting to disappoint her, Blake hurried out of the cave.

"I'll find something. Anything for you, Your Highness."

While Blake went off in search of parchment, Calista uncovered more of the map, revealing a tiny indent in the far south that she thought could represent Glass Island. Right beside it was the insignia of the Goddess Marra. *How interesting,* she thought. *All this information, all this history, and I knew none of it. What else don't I know?* Calista's mind spiralled deeper and deeper into a rabbit hole that she was sure would lead to more questions than answers. The war that had divided LaMarra was common knowledge, but it seemed that the division was more impactful than she learned about as a child. She had always known that the chaos of magic was why West Marra and East Marra stood divided, but now she wondered if that was the whole story. What exactly happened in the war?

Blake returned with a large swath of parchment and proudly presented Calista with a lump of coal as well. "I brought this in case you want to draw something on the wall." Blake smiled broadly, clearly very pleased with himself for thinking ahead. Calista graciously accepted the parchment and spread it against the wall covering the map, then began rubbing the coal over the parchment, effectively etching the map onto the parchment.

When she was done, she rolled up the parchment and tucked it into the deep interior pockets of her cloak. Blake marvelled at her intelligence. "That's why they made you a Queen. So smart."

"Thank you, Blake. It's been a pleasure, but I should meet with the others in the area."

Not wanting to be a hindrance, Blake led her to the cave opening and made sure she was securely mounted on her horse. He thanked her profusely for her visit and wished her well.

Calista spent the rest of the day visiting the other mines. Later in the afternoon, she meandered through the shops, purchasing an item in each shop she entered. She acquired gifts for Luxx, Maia, and Sage. She even picked up an item for Phoenix. As she reflected on their most recent interactions, she couldn't ignore the warm flutters that flitted through her core whenever she thought of him. His effect on her was growing.

By the time she returned to the inn, she was exhausted. Dinner was brought to her room. After she ate, she had a warm bath. As she undressed and slipped into the warm water, scented with mint and lavender, she let her mind drift. So much new information had come her way that day that she couldn't help but wonder if she really knew Luxx at all. What secrets was she keeping? And what was Knoxx up to? Did Phoenix even know? And that map . . . So many questions.

CHAPTER 14
The Gatekeeper
Luxx

Luxx slowed her horse as the cottage came into view. She dismounted and tied the steed to a nearby tree with a long enough lead that he could graze and drink freely from the nearby stream. She set aside her feelings of guilt over how she left Calista in the dark about her intentions for the day, though she took some comfort in letting her know she was safe. Eventually, she would explain everything, but not until she had figured things out for herself first.

Pulling the hood of her cloak down over her face, she slowly approached the cottage. The mist coming off of Siphon Lake was thick at this time in the morning, and the forest was quiet except for the crunching of the snow with each of her steps. The early morning sun began to burn through the mist that was rising off the snow, making everything shimmer. It was quiet there and peaceful, a direct contrast to the storm raging in Luxx's mind. Her heart thundered in her chest as she approached the cottage. She thought more than once about turning back, but she couldn't put it off any longer. Anxiousness churned in her stomach, threatening to make her throw up the excessive breakfast she had consumed a short time ago. She had sought the comfort of food, hoping it would drown out the emotions that threatened to consume her.

She approached the wooden door and knocked. She stood on her toes and peeked through the small window in the door when she was startled by the sound of footsteps approaching behind her. The deep timbre of a familiar man's voice caused her to whip her head around. The hood of her cloak fell back, revealing her bright blonde hair.

"You never were the patient type," the man said as he looked Luxx up and down. He dropped the large bundle of wood at his side and pushed his long hair off his face, revealing a scar that went from his left eyebrow down through his eye and ended at the top of his cheekbone. Upon seeing his scar again, Luxx couldn't help but recall the story of how she was responsible for disfiguring the water dragon who stood before her. He had been sentenced to assume a half-human existence, known as a falso-humanis, because of what he had done to protect Luxx.

Luxx pulled herself out of the depths of the memory and became aware of the light snow that had begun to fall and was collecting on her hair. The man reached forward to brush the snow from her shoulder.

"My ray of light. I'm glad you came."

Luxx stood frozen on the spot, as if time had stopped. She reached for his hand and looked up at him. "Lev . . . I . . . It's snowing," was all she could say. Her mind was fracturing from the wave of thoughts that prevented her from speaking coherently.

"Let's get you inside, Ray," he said as he pushed the door open and held it for her. He ushered her inside with a broad hand on her lower back.

Luxx removed her cloak and shook out the snow that had accumulated on it as Lev smoothed back his hair and removed his thick outerwear. An awkward silence filled the space. Then they both attempted to break the silence at the same time.

"I felt you were close—" Lev started

"Lev, I—" Luxx watched him walk over to the butcher block in the kitchen, putting space between them.

"Are you OK?" he asked. "When you didn't respond, I, well, you know what I was thinking. I knew from our bond that you were alive, but that was about it."

Luxx swallowed hard before answering. "Yes, well I'm obviously alive." Her response sounded more sarcastic than she intended as anxiousness swirled around in her chest, making her feel lightheaded. Lev was at her side in an instant, catching her when she swayed to prevent her from falling.

With his large hands supporting her, he guided her toward the armchair by the fireplace in the living room. Luxx shrugged away from his touch, trying to preserve her independence and the façade of strength, but that only ignited the temper that was lying just below the surface of Lev's calm exterior. He dropped his hands and slammed his fist and forearm into the doorframe.

"Damn it, Luxx, you're my mate. I can feel you!"

Luxx squeezed her eyes shut, his words like a slap across her face, and tried to grab her cloak from the hook by the door, but Lev intercepted her, wrapping her small body in his warm embrace. He cradled her head against his chest and shushed her until she calmed down. Lev didn't loosen his grip until her anxiety faded, and her heartbeat resumed a normal rhythm.

Luxx pulled away from Lev and inhaled deeply before speaking. "I know you can feel everything I'm feeling. As soon as I set foot back in Vulnari, I was overwhelmed with you, through our bond, in my head, everywhere. That's why I came to you. I knew you needed me. I wasn't sure you wanted me though, not after how we left things."

This confession from Luxx was heartbreaking for him to hear. As he released her from his embrace, he directed her back toward the living room. She went willingly this time and sat down, curling her legs under her. Lev sat on the sofa across from her, leaning his elbows on his knees as he looked at her. The intensity of his stare made her fidget.

"Ray, it's time, and we need to decide," he said, his voice low and deep.

Luxx stared at him as she contemplated her response. There was so much to say and so many feelings to sort through.

"Don't call me Ray. I hate that nickname. It's not me, not for a long time."

"You will always be my ray of light," he replied. "I don't care what you say. You're and always have been the light in my life, and you always will be."

"Stop it, Lev. I can't . . . I don't deserve the things you say or what you did for me, not then and certainly not after I left you."

"Ray, we're mates. We're connected now and, well, our mating bond is not like any other bond. Our connection runs deeper than a simple water bond. We feel each other here." He put his closed fist to his chest over his heart. "That makes our bond stronger. I can feel when you are hurt, sad, happy, everything. Every. Single. Thing." His voice was desperate, almost pleading.

Luxx felt the swell of emotion in Lev, and it threatened to suffocate her. She stood up and began pacing in front of the fireplace.

"You were young," he said. "There was so much we didn't know. We were in love, and that was all it took. Then you left." His voice cracked on the last word. He cleared his throat before continuing. "That night I found you all bloody, half dead on my doorstep. I suffered right there with you, but I couldn't die. At that moment I wanted to give my life over to you, but I couldn't. Then you were gone."

Luxx clamped her hand over her mouth to hold back the sobs that were threatening to gush out. There was so much more to the story than she had told him. Things that caused her great pain, pain she desperately wanted to protect him from. The only way she knew how to shield him from her pain was to leave Vulnari. The greater the distance between them, the weaker the bond became.

"I just can't," Luxx choked out. She made a dash for the door, but Lev was faster. As she reached for the doorhandle, his large hand slammed the door shut above her head.

Luxx leaned her forehead against the door and let her tears fall freely. Lev stood behind her for a few moments, waiting for the tension to diffuse before he scooped her up and brought her to the sofa, where she let the emotions that wracked her body consume her. When there were no tears left to shed, Lev held her close to his warm body.

"It's time."

Luxx sat a little straighter, taking in Lev's appearance. His strong jaw was covered in stubble, and his left eye only added to his brooding presence. The deep scar was a constant reminder of how they had entered each other's lives.

Luxx reflected on the story that Lev had told her when they first began living together. When Luxx was an infant, her mother had to transport her across Siphon Lake. Maia had collected sharp stones from the shore at the base of the prison and tied them around Luxx's arms and body like protective armour. Lev, full name Leviathan, was the water dragon that shot out of the depths to demand the blood token for payment to cross the lake. Her mom hesitated but ultimately chose to prick one of Luxx's fingers to draw blood. Only centimeters away from Luxx and all the sharp stones tied to her, Leviathan turned his large head. In that instant, Luxx's arms began to flail about, slashing across his eye. Wracked with pain, he sprang out of the water, roaring and slashing his talons in fury. Despite the injury inflicted by the infant, Leviathan refused the blood token and agreed to carry Luxx across the lake to the bank of Vulnari. Knowing the frail infant could not care for herself Leviathan reluctantly brought Maia along as well. The journey across the lake established the bond between Luxx and Leviathan. The moment of pain they shared joined them on the deepest level of emotional consciousness, allowing them to feel each other's emotional state wherever water was present. Leviathan made a silent vow to protect Luxx forever.

As Luxx reflected on his appearance, thoughts surrounding his origins crept into her mind. Lev was a water dragon who had refused to accept a blood token from an infant to secure safe passage across Siphon Lake from Blackstone Prison. For denying the blood token, he was sentenced to live as a human but not a mortal on the shore of Siphon Lake as their gatekeeper.

Anyone who straddled existence between the realms of beast and human was known as falso-humanis. Such individuals were few and far between, their existence an enigma. Time was a relative term when considering the unexplainable magic that existed in and around Blackstone Prison. The time, however, had come, and he was being summoned back to Siphon Lake's inky waters. The infant he had chosen to protect from the bloodletting to secure passage across the lake was now his mate. He had made a vow to protect her, and nothing had changed. His feelings for her intensified as she became older, and they realized the strength of their bond as mates. The intrinsic bond between them was forged by the magic of the lake and the vow of protection made by Lev. Their destinies were intertwined from the beginning; Luxx was still coming to terms with the unconditional and all-consuming love that the bond brought with it.

"I've been summoned back to the lake," Lev said.

"What happens if you don't go back?" Luxx asked

"I don't know, but I know I won't be here for you any longer."

"They'll kill you?"

"Maybe."

"What if you go back and then do something wrong. They will just sentence you to be a falso-humanis again."

Lev chuckled at the childlike naiveté of her reasoning. He smoothed her hair back from her face and kissed her forehead. "That's not how it works, Ray."

"Then how does it work?" Luxx shot back with mounting frustration. "Explain it to me!"

Lev sucked in a deep, steadying breath. "When summoned, I can return to become a water dragon again and the vision in my destroyed eye will be restored. If I commit another crime, there is no telling what punishment I'll suffer. They may even kill me. But they will not send me back to live as a human."

"But how do you know?"

"Because they know I love you, and being here with you is no longer a punishment, no matter how much pain you put me through."

Luxx sighed heavily, searching his eyes with her own, praying the answer to their problem would come to her. "What happens if you tell them you want to stay here?" she asked. "What happens then?" The hopefulness in her voice was Lev's undoing. He let his frustration show in his response.

"If I deny the counsel of water dragons and choose to leave them, I'll become mortal."

"Why would that be so bad?"

"Because it would mean I'd age, become weak, and die, leaving you forever! I can't leave you. I won't. You're mine." Lev tightened his arm around Luxx, bringing her close to his chest in a crushing embrace, as if letting her go would end him on the spot. "I would be given a one-hundred-year lifetime as a mortal, then I'd die. You would most certainly outlive me. I'd have no choice but to leave you. I don't know if I can live with that."

Luxx stayed silent for a long time, letting the weight of this choice settle over her. There was no denying that they shared a unique bond. How could she ask him to die for her? She couldn't, not after the pain she had put them both through.

"Go. Go back to being a water dragon," Luxx said, her voice quivering. She locked eyes with Lev before continuing. "I can't give you the life you want—children, a happy home. I don't deserve you."

"What are you talking about? Children? A happy home? What shit is this?" Lev's features contorted into a grimace that displayed his confusion and incredulity. "Where's all this coming from? I never asked that of you. You're more than enough. You're everything to me."

Luxx moved out of his embrace, feeling the hostility her words created roll off him in waves. She backed away, putting distance between them. "There are things you don't know, things I'm sure you felt me suffer through, but I never explained. Things that make me a truly awful person."

Lev drew his eyebrows together quizzically. "Yes you did go through a rough phase when you were young. Thank the gods you survived."

"No, there's more to it than that, so much more. I was—I am too ashamed to tell you."

"Tell me." The command in his voice grabbed her attention. As she locked eyes with him, the pain, the need to know, was written all over his face. She knew she owed him an explanation for the heartache he had felt all those years ago. He never questioned her, not once; he was just there to pick her up time and time again. He watched her destroy herself over and over again, and all he ever did was try to protect her. There was no way he could help her though. Luxx needed protection from herself and no one else. Luxx finally broke her silence and explained everything.

For months Luxx had sought out the company of men in bars. She would drink to calm her racing mind, and she never said no to anyone. Her slender, womanly figure and bright blonde hair made her a favourite among the patrons of several seedy haunts. As she became more brazen about the company she kept, she fell into violent encounters. In her absence, Lev felt everything. Occasionally, she would turn up on his doorstep a shell of a person, strung out and barely conscious. Lev brought her back from the brink of death over and over again.

One night, the most disturbing of all, Luxx reminded Lev of a time when she was tortured. She recalled how the pain she had suffered dragged him from the depths of deep sleep, pulling on the bond so sharply that Lev told her he was sure she had met her end. Frantic with worry, he fought to get to her, but to no avail as the magically enforced borders of his land prevented him from leaving the area around siphon lake. Then, in the early morning hours on the border of his land, he saw her. She was lying prone on the ground, half naked, bleeding, and beaten, left for dead. The vision of her, his ray of light, nearly destroyed, was almost his undoing.

He brought her to the cottage and nursed her back to some semblance of life. When she was finally consistently conscious and appearing to heal, Lev slept for the first time in days. When he awoke, she was gone yet again.

After sleeping her way through half of the Vulnari male population and nearly succumbing to the brutal rape and beating, Luxx needed to drown her emotions and bury them deep. Sapphire, a wandering centenary healer, found her huddled in an abandoned cave, sheltering from the onslaught of rain and snow that was cascading off the mountain range. Sapphire urged Luxx to fight and not give up. The Queen and King of East Marra were recruiting warriors for the army. After everything that Luxx had survived in the recent months, she reluctantly succumbed to Sapphire's request to at least consider a future as a Zenovian warrior. That decision to go with Sapphire put her on the path to her future as Calista's advisor. It was a decision that she had never regretted.

CHAPTER 15
Decisions

Luxx

"Lev, I never told you what happened and why I spiraled downward and then left. I never wanted to hurt you," Luxx said, emotion choking her words. She forced herself to continue. "When I got pregnant and learned that it could kill me, I couldn't tell you. I had no business causing you any more pain than I had already, so I took care of it. But you felt it anyway."

Lev's gaze bore into her before he turned his head away from her, unable to conceal the wave of anger that was consuming him. He stood up suddenly. Luxx felt the absence of his body heat so acutely that she shivered.

"Yeah, I did feel it. Damn fucking right I felt it!" he spat. Luxx watched him pace the small living room, anger rolling off him in waves. Tears streaked her cheeks as she watched Lev process the confirmation of what he had always suspected.

"Why did you leave? Ray, why did you leave?" he shouted.

There was nothing she could say, so she let the silence speak for her. Then Luxx decided there was nothing about her past worth hiding, so she explained the circumstances that had led her to leave.

From time to time she would venture into the village to acquire supplies and food. On one such trip, she discreetly met with Sapphire to remedy what she thought was a new ailment, only to discover she was with child. Being that she had possibly been impregnated by a falso-humanis, there was no way she could bear the child. Carrying such a beast to term could kill her. If it didn't, giving birth to it certainly would.

Recognizing the abundance of affection that she and Lev shared and not wanting to cause him any heartache, she chose to end the pregnancy. She also vowed never to tell Lev what she had done to spare him the pain of her decision.

Soon after the procedure, Luxx returned home to Lev, but her mood had darkened, and she refused to accept his affections. Within a short time, she spiralled into the dark depths of her mind. Pursuing any means to numb her emotional state, she sought out drink, drugs, and emotionally empty carnal activities, one of which resulted in Luxx suffering a brutal sexual assault that nearly ended her life.

Lev turned to face her, the deep emotional turmoil he was feeling was bubbling right under the surface. His eyes were glassy as he spoke in a dangerously calm tone. "You degraded yourself with how many sick fucks after that. Then I found you left for dead and thought for sure you were gone. I had failed to protect you. I would have given anything for me to take your place. The second you could move you left, and I never saw you again."

Luxx was silent, tears flowing down her face, paralyzed by the truth that was being held up right in front of her. She could see with crystal clarity the pain she had caused, the one thing she never wanted to do.

"I had to find out from a convict going to Blackstone that you had become a member of the Zenovia Army and that you had risen to the rank of royal advisor when the King and Queen in the east disappeared." Lev scrubbed his face with the palm of his hand, then pushed his hair off his face before turning to face Luxx. Long moments passed between them.

Luxx stood up and went to Lev. She rested her head on his chest and wrapped her arms around him, hugging him tightly. Lev did not respond at first. Then he wrapped his arms around her and kissed the top of her head. He angled her chin upwards to face him.

"I love you," he whispered. "You're my mate." He gently kissed her lips. Luxx surrendered to the intimacy for a moment before breaking away.

"Become mortal," she said, not facing Lev.

"Excuse me?" Lev asked.

"Fuck the water dragons. I need you here with me for however long you have. You're no good to me here locked up by magical barricades. If you're my mate, then *be* my mate."

The finality of those words was enough to shock Lev into action. He swept Luxx into his arms and walked her over to the sofa. He plopped her down and knelt in front of her, so they were both at eye level. "Do you know what you're asking of me?" he said, his face deathly serious.

"Yes, Lev. After I became a Zenovian warrior, I learned how to face my demons. You're my mate. You're part of me, and the strength I now possess is because you vowed to protect me. If being by my side means you need to be mortal, then be mortal with me. Let me protect you."

Lev let out a laugh. "I would be honoured to have you protect me," he said.

"What happens now?" Luxx asked. "Do you shout, 'Hey Dragon!', and hope that one of them pops out, so you can tell them you're out of the water dragon game for good?"

Lev's eyes widened as he let out a deep chuckle and pulled Luxx into a crushing hug. Their bond was alight with emotion driven by Luxx's elation at not only accepting the mating bond but also vowing to protect Lev in return.

"It's a little more complicated than that," he said, "and I'm sure there will be some bloodshed. They will demand a blood token from me and perhaps more, but no price is too high if it means you and I will live out the rest of our days together."

Luxx threw her arms around his neck. Lev picked her up, and she wrapped her legs around his waist. Lev crashed his lips into hers in a kiss that spoke of years of unrequited need. He cradled her head with one hand and tilted it to the side to expose her neck, planting kisses along her jawline and down her throat. With her head tilted back, a moan of pure desire escaped her. The sound ignited Lev's arousal, and Luxx felt his length press against her abdomen.

A low groan that came from deep in Lev's chest vibrated against Luxx, fuelling her need to be with him. Her legs still wrapped around his waist, he walked over and laid her on the bed in the corner of the cottage. In one smooth motion, he reached back and grabbed the collar of his shirt, pulling it over his head and tossed it aside. Luxx's cheeks flushed at the sight of his broad, muscular shoulders, which bore the markings of an ancient warrior. Unlike traditional tattoos that stained the skin, Lev's skin appeared to have been embossed with the telltale signs of battle. His left shoulder depicted a pattern of swirls and scales that resembled the scales of a water dragon's skin just below the shape of a clawed foot with sharp talons. Close inspection of the markings revealed his name embossed across his chest: *Leviathan*.

Heat rushed through Luxx's body in waves. Lust clouded her vision as she took in the sight of her mate, her protector. Lev wasted no time removing his pants, his cock hard and ready. He dropped to his knees and reached under the oversized sweater that Luxx was wearing, only to discover that she was naked beneath it. With a devilish glint in his eye, he slid his large hands up the sides of her abdomen to cup her breasts. Then he pulled the sweater over her head and tossed it on the floor. Without wasting a second, he pulled the waistband of her pants over the swell of her hips and pushed them down, revealing her lack of underclothing for a second time. He let out a throaty chuckle as he positioned his head between her thighs.

Luxx's breath hitched as she felt the first touch of his tongue along the tight bundle of nerves at her apex. She was drenched in seconds, a detail that did not go unnoticed by Lev. He teased her with his tongue as he slowly penetrated her entrance with his finger, pushing into her wet flesh and stroking her as his tongue brought her closer and closer to release with each delicate flick.

Within moments Luxx was on the brink of ecstasy, unable to control her guttural moans as she shattered beneath his expert touch. While she was still heaving from the intensity of her release, Lev positioned himself over her. He lined up the crown of his large throbbing cock with her entrance and slowly began to push himself into her welcoming warmth.

Luxx winced and gasped slightly as he moved inside her

"Did I hurt you?" Lev asked, pausing his movement as he waited for her answer.

"You're bigger than I remember," Luxx admitted as she adjusted herself beneath him, angling her hips to accommodate his size. She tightened her grip on his hips with her legs and urged him to go deeper. Lev complied and thrust into her until he was fully seated in her tight warmth. He started to move, thrusting at a relentless pace that drove them both closer and closer to release. Lev used his thumb to massage the bundle of nerves as her body began to constrict around him. Lev groaned loudly as he picked up the pace, signalling he was close to his own release. His guttural, primal noises set Luxx off into her own release, and they rode through the seemingly endless waves of pleasure together until they were completely spent.

Lev and Luxx spent the remainder of the day catching up, basking in the afterglow of reconnecting their minds, bodies, and souls. Finally, Luxx reluctantly gathered her things, explaining that she needed to return to her duties as Calista's advisor.

"I thought she was your friend," Lev prompted.

"She is, but she's also my Queen. I want you to meet her."

"I would love to, but only after this is all sorted."

"Of course."

Luxx planted a deep kiss on Lev, then she made her way to the tree where her horse was tied.

The last time she left that place, she was an emotional wreck. This time she felt a lightness, an assurance that everything would be OK.

Before leaving she told Lev about Calista's recent interest in a series of ancient maps. She promised to share more information with him soon.

Lev watched her ride off toward the village, secure in the knowledge that they would be together for as long as their lifetime would allow. Now all he had to do was deal with the counsel of water dragons.

CHAPTER 16
Savarra
Calista

"Thank you," Calista said over her shoulder after Sage packed her and all her belongings on the horse. She was going to ride down the cliff face accompanied by a stable hand, who would tend to the horses and bring them back up to the inn.

The pair rode in relative silence, with Calista following the stable hand. She remained lost in her thoughts, dwelling on the map etching she had made in the cave. Her mind circled the layout of the land and the distinctive marking at the base of the waterfall. She had seen the same marking on one of the maps in Phoenix's library. This detail piqued her interest, and she made a mental note to ask Phoenix about it, hoping he could fill the gap. She let that thought roll around in her mind as she considered what was so important about that destination on the map. Another feature was the rough shape of a key. *Keys, they keep showing up,* she mused. *Maybe the key unlocks a secret door to a land full of little people who live blissfully unencumbered by the realities of LaMarra.* The thought brought a brief smile to her face.

"You're all set now, Miss—I mean Your Highness—I mean Calista." The young man fumbled over his words, clearly nervous.

"Calista is fine. Thank you for guiding me down the cliff safely," she replied with a warm smile. She gave him a hug before she climbed into her vehicle, saying a silent prayer that it would start.

Much to her relief, the engine roared to life, and she set off on her way. She had a long drive ahead of her, but she expected it to be a relatively peaceful one. Her mind was still buzzing with a myriad of things. The maps, the keys, the celestial solstice, and of course, Luxx.

As she drove along the coastal road that passed through the training ground for the Zenovia Army, Calista was reminded of how she and Luxx met and the instant friendship they formed. In the years since then, their friendship had grown, and the scars of Luxx's past seemed to fade away. Rumours persisted surrounding Luxx's virtue, but Calista never pushed to know more, figuring Luxx would talk to her about it eventually. That conversation never happened though, and Calista maintained her conviction that the past was just that and should remain there. Becoming a member of the Zenovia Army was a new beginning for Luxx, and Calista didn't want to spoil that for her. However noble those thoughts were, Calista couldn't help but feel like she had failed her closest friend by not asking more questions or trying to understand her more. Maybe that time was now.

As night fell, Calista's thoughts kept her alert enough to continue driving. She was on a stretch of road near the capital flanked by an open field and the bank of the River Marra when, seemingly out of nowhere, a small figure darted out ahead of her car and bounced off her windshield. She slammed on her brakes and then leaped out.

Calista couldn't see anything outside the glow of her headlights. She felt around on the ground, touching the tires and praying that nothing had gotten caught in them. Then her hand brushed over a small form. It was shimmering ever so slightly with bioluminescence, right under the passenger side of the vehicle beside the tire.

"There you are, little thing. Are you hurt?" Calista crooned as she reached for the creature, silently thanking the gods that she hadn't run over the poor creature. She gathered up the small Savarra into her hands and cradled it close to her body, wrapping it in the folds of her jacket.

Once she was back in the driver's seat, she unwrapped the creature and realized it was only stunned and not too badly hurt. She bundled the purple Savarra in some clothes and then secured it next to her in the passenger seat. Then she continued toward home.

"It's OK, little one. We'll be home soon, I'll look after you."

As Calista kept watch over the small animal, listening to its whimpers, she recalled how much Luxx loved the little creatures.

"I'll hold off naming you. I'll let Luxx do that," Calista said as she pulled up to the motor court. She carried the Savarra and the small bag she had packed up to her private chambers, leaving the vehicle to be tended to later.

CHAPTER 17
celestial solstice
Phoenix

"Really, Kings? That's where you plan on spending the celestial solstice?" Phoenix asked Knoxx as they flipped massive tires in the training complex.

"Yeah. Why the hell not?" Knoxx responded through a grunt as the tire landed with a thud.

"Because we usually host something at Aterna, and I'm going to need my protection officer present, especially if those rumours about renegade riots are true."

"Relax. The renegades are under control. You don't need me there. The security specs are up to par. Besides, I thought you might be spending it with that piece of ass across the river."

Phoenix let his tire fall with a loud thud and levelled a nasty look at Knoxx. "First off, what the hell are the renegades rioting over anyway? From what I've seen, it's little more than vandalism, petty crimes, and making their presence known. And what is your fucking problem with the Queen of East Marra?"

Without skipping a beat, Knoxx flipped his tire. Then he looked back at Phoenix with a sinister and disturbing smirk. "She's under your skin, and you don't even see it. She's manipulating you. And I already told you, I've got the renegades under control, or don't you trust me to do my job?"

"How is she manipulating me? She's been nothing but kind, honest, and . . ." His voice trailed off as he watched Knoxx's eyes widen, as if to prove his point.

"She made an ass of you at the banquet, letting everyone fall all over her while they looked at you like a fucking sucker."

"So, she's charming and knows how to work a room. She's royalty. What else do you expect?"

"She knows how to work more than a room. And you damn well know it. I know what you've been up to."

Phoenix narrowed his gaze at Knoxx as if to remind him who he was talking to. "Need I remind you that it's your *job* to keep me informed? Something I can't help but notice has been exceptionally lax on your part lately. I shouldn't have to ask you what's going on, and yet that's all I seem to be doing lately."

The silence stretched out between them for a few tense moments. Knoxx cleared his throat, then stood up straight and looked down his nose at Phoenix. "When were you going to tell me about that key?"

"It's a key. So what?" Phoenix replied with indifference.

"That's what you think. I've been picking up strange readings from that thing ever since you liberated it from the statue with your precious little piece of ass plaything."

"Just spit it out! What's your problem? I shouldn't have to decipher anything you tell me. You work for me."

"Yeah that's right; I work for you, Your Highness," Knoxx replied as he dropped his tire with more force than necessary, then turned to walk away.

"Where are you going?" Phoenix asked.

"To take a piss. Why, you want to hold my dick? Make sure I'm not lying?" Knoxx said without turning to face him. The deflated tone underlying the comment was enough to push Phoenix into a guilt-riddled sigh. He stooped down to pick up their towels, then caught up to Knoxx and nudged his shoulder.

"Meet me in the sauna."

An unspoken truce ended their tense conversation.

What the hell is going on with Knoxx? Phoenix wondered. *How can I trust my advisor when he makes me drag information out of him? If I can't trust Knoxx, who can I trust? Is he right? Am I letting Calista get too deep under my skin? Then again, something about her makes me feel like there's more to her than meets the eye. I feel like I can trust her. But should I?*

Phoenix let those thoughts marinate in his brain as he and Knoxx resumed an easy conversation about their latest fitness goals. No matter the direction of the conversation, Phoenix reminded himself to use caution, to listen and observe. Trust was never freely given. Knoxx would need to work to regain the level of trust they once shared. Not enough water had passed under the bridge between them to drown Phoenix's uncertainties.

CHAPTER 18
Shadow Lake

Calista

Calista dressed in her usual style, choosing something slightly more festive. She opted for a long deep-red silk dress with an open back and deep V-neckline and light lace shoulder straps that draped down her upper arm. The slit exposed her tanned leg, and the waistband was a delicate lace that allowed her skin to show through.

"This is appropriate for the celestial solstice, right?" she asked the young woman who was tidying her chamber.

"You look great, Calista! You always do," the young woman replied as she picked up the basket of linens and left the room. The Savarra leapt out of the basket and scurried off toward the terrace in search of the sun-warmed stone it liked to rest on.

Luxx would tell me everything wrong with this outfit, Calista thought as she inspected her reflection in the mirror. She missed Luxx, but Calista knew her advisor would be back from Vulnari soon enough. The thought of spending solstice alone was weighing heavily on Calista though. It occurred to her that Phoenix would also be alone. She allowed the thought to flourish, musing about how beautiful the celestial solstice night sky was, especially when viewed from

Shadow Lake. *After all the events he has hosted in West Marra the least I could do is invite him to join me at Shadow Lake for the longest night of the year. It's the least I can do* . . . Calista smiled at the thought, romanticizing it perhaps a little too much. However, she felt it was important to invite him soon, before she lost her nerve.

She scribbled a note and put it into a small piece of leather, then rolled it into a tight scroll. She had to move quickly to get the note to one of the messengers who was going across the river to deliver some medical supplies that Jade had collected in anticipation of the solstice. She had thought to collect all the delicate herbs before the entire population of East Marra descended on Shadow Lake and potentially ruined the supplies that she had so carefully curated.

Calista raced down to the edge of the estate where the supplies were being checked and bundled for safe passage across the river.

"Wait! Hold on!" she shouted, catching the attention of a young sailor who was the last to climb onto the back of the truck.

"Here." She placed the scroll in his hand. "Take this please. Make sure it gets to Pho—the King of West Marra and only him. It's important."

The young sailor nodded and smiled. "Of course." Calista could tell he was pleased to be entrusted with a task set specifically by her. She had faith that the message would reach him. She was less confident that Phoenix would actually attend, but she would know soon enough. The celestial solstice was that night.

Calista and members of the East Marra community made their way south toward Shadow Lake on foot. The solstice was a time to connect with people, nature, gods, and herself. It signalled a time of renewal and change. On the day of the celestial solstice, thanks and praise were shared in celebration of the longest night of the year and the bounty it brought. The night sky was alight with stars so bright it was as if a sea of diamonds had been scattered across the sky's dark inky depths. It had been described as many things over the years, but the overwhelming reality was that it was a humbling experience that reminded everyone that they were all connected. The night also caused precious deep-water plants to surface where they could bloom and share their bounty with the healers who recognized their healing powers. It was viewed as much as an entertainment event as a divine moment. Many believed it was a way for Goddess Marra to share her blessings with all those present to witness the magic of the moment.

Calista walked alone, waving occasionally and offering smiles as people passed and offered her polite greetings. She nervously played with her Aquavass, more to keep her hands occupied than anything else. The twilight sky was breathtaking as darkness descended. She was nervous and extremely bad at hiding it.

As she tried to distract herself with the changing colours drifting across the sky, she absently scanned the crowd for him. *Stop looking for him, and focus on your people,* she chastised herself.

"Calista? Something on your mind?"

Calista turned quickly, startled out of her own thoughts by the question, which was posed by Daisy.

"Ha! Hi. You scared the life out of me," she replied, laughing. "I'm OK. I'm just thinking. How are you enjoying the celebrations so far?"

"Thinking about what—or should I say whom?" Daisy replied with a smirk.

Calista laughed. "Is it that obvious?"

"That you're searching for someone? Yes. You're an open book, Calista, and you look like you could use some company. Where's Luxx?"

"Oh, she's spending the solstice in Vulnari. I'll be fine."

"OK. I should find a good place to watch the deep-water plants bloom. Would you like to join me?"

"It's OK. Go on. I'll check up on a few things and join you later," Calista said, then sent Daisy off.

Darkness had fully enveloped Shadow Lake by then. Calista found a tree on the edge of the mangroves that clustered around the shallows. She enjoyed watching the community come together and mingle. Some families had spread a blanket on the sand, so they could lie back and stargaze. Others were perched on various rock formations and fallen trees that were scattered around. Jade was poised on the water's edge, ready to wade into the lake the moment the underwater plants surfaced and bloomed and collect some samples. Daisy took up a position close to Jade but kept a distance so as not to interfere. Some young children were playing with the bioluminescent waters that were gently lapping at the shore. Lost in her observations, Calista did not hear his approach.

Phoenix picked up a flat stone and tossed it past Calista and into the water, skipping it across the surface. Calista turned quickly and saw him standing in the shadows of the trees. The darkness was punctuated with starlight, which was bright but not bright enough to fully reveal his form. He stepped out of the shadows and slipped his hands into the pockets of his dark trousers as he pushed aside his suit jacket. His white shirt picked up the neon light cast from the lake, causing it to glow slightly. His Aquavass glinted in the starlight, catching her attention.

"Hi. Thank you for coming," she said as she turned to face him.

"Hi? That's how you greet me?"

"What else you expecting? Me to launch myself into your waiting arms?" she replied sarcastically, perhaps a bit nervously. "I see you got my note."

Phoenix pulled the rolled-up note from his pocket and waved it at her. "Oh, I most certainly did." He paused for dramatic effect as he unrolled it and then cleared his throat and read aloud. "Phoenix, join me tonight at Shadow Lake. C." His eyebrow arched as he looked up.

Calista smiled and blushed, praying it was dark enough to conceal her glowing cheeks. "Sounds a bit direct."

"Direct!" he barked, followed by a laugh. "Yeah, that's one way to put it. More like a summons."

"Sorry. I should have thought it out better and asked you formally," she said.

Phoenix stepped forward to close the distance between them. Standing close enough that she could clearly see his chest rise and fall with each breath, he raised Calista's chin, so she was looking at his face. His proximity was enough to turn her nervous insides into a flurry of confused butterflies. Words failed her as she let the silence drag out.

Phoenix raised his hand to touch her elbow, a motion that Calista was all too aware of, when the tension was broken by the sounds of violent splashing and the crowds cooing and chattering in awe as the deep-water plants broke the surface and began to bloom into large, stunningly beautiful blossoms. Their fragrance filled the air with floral sweetness while droplets of neon water beaded up on the thick foliage. As each bloom surfaced, it would start off a deep purple colour, then would slowly transition to fuchsia, then light pink before finally fading to white. The white petals would break off and drift toward shore, where people would roll them up to take home. This went on for several hours, marking the middle of the longest night of the year. With Daisy's help, Jade made quick work of wading out to each bloom to collect the contents at the center of each one as well as a few of the white petals.

Once the water plants had finished blooming, the crowd's attention turned back to the skies, where the stars continued to twinkle brightly. As Calista watched, she was reminded of how truly connected they were by the magic of the land. It might be a little chaotic and unpredictable, but it was beautiful and life giving as well.

She chanced a glance at Phoenix and wondered if the magic of the moment was on his mind as well. His features gave nothing away, but he was watching the sky as intently as she was. By that time many of the families had started to make their way home.

Neither Calista nor Phoenix spoke as they watched the display, transfixed by the magic in the air. Calista waved as people passed her on their way home, bidding them goodnight. She noticed that they looked toward her, even from a distance, their eyes flicked to the man standing beside her. Everyone knew who he was, and yet they maintained a respectful distance and allowed Calista the peace of not questioning her.

When only a few stragglers were left on the shore, Phoenix and Calista made their way to a larger open section of the beach and sat on the flat, smooth rocks that protruded from the shallow water and onto the sand. Once they were alone, Phoenix finally broke the awkward tension between them.

"Is it like this all the time for you?"

"Like what?"

"Calm, no one fussing over you, your people just waving and not badgering you with questions or stupid reasons to talk to you."

"Is that what it's like for you?" Calista asked, her eyebrows drawn together in concern.

"West Marra is different, so formal, I—" He stopped short, not wanting to reveal too much.

"Go on," she urged as she rested her hand on his knee. He looked down at her hand, recognizing the act of comfort for what it is before continuing.

"I have to be careful about everything. I almost didn't come tonight because Knoxx had other plans. But something made me jump on my motorcycle and come down here moments after I saw your note."

A slow, gentle smile curved Calista's lips. "I'm glad you came. With Luxx away I didn't want to spend the solstice completely alone. Besides, I got you a little something while I was up in Vulnari."

"You didn't have to do that."

"I know, but I noticed that you never eat or drink anything that isn't brought to you by your own staff, so when I came across this . . ." She reached into one of the pockets concealed in her dress and produced a slim box approximately the length of her hand.

Reluctantly, Phoenix accepted the box and opened it. Inside was a slim pen knife made of sleek black stone and monogrammed in gold with the West Marra insignia. It was discreet enough to be tucked into his suit jacket or the pocket of anything he wore.

"This is nice. Thank you. But what made you think of this for me?"

Calista took the pen knife from his hands. The brush of her fingers across his palm sent a shock through her core, heating her insides to the point that she needed to fight to conceal her feelings.

"When you deploy the tip of the blade by clicking here, like this," she said, demonstrating, "the knife will change colours if it detects poison in the surrounding area, including your food or drink. It's an ancient form of natural technology."

Phoenix took the knife back and inspected it again, clicking it open and closed a few times. He arched an eyebrow and looked at Calista with a bemused smile. "I see you've been paying attention. This is very thoughtful."

"I am a Queen of the people, after all," she replied shyly as she looked out at the reflection of the stars on the water's surface.

Phoenix reached into his jacket pocket and pulled out a small green velvet sachet held shut by a drawstring, then got on one knee in the sand.

"Give me your leg."

"Excuse me?"

"Give me your leg, please," he repeated as he reached for her exposed ankle.

Calista adjusted herself to face him as he put his large hand around her ankle and slipped her sandal off her foot. The slit of her dress fell away to reveal her entire leg nearly up to her hip. Phoenix placed her foot on a smaller rock, so her leg was slightly bent, and he had full access to her upper thigh.

"What are you doing?" Calista asked, intending to sound authoritative, although it came out sounding very breathy.

"Shhh, hold still."

Phoenix opened the sachet and pulled out several lengths of gold chains with a delicate leather strap that had a snap-style closure. Letting the chains fall, he slipped her foot through the leather strap. Then he slid the chains up her leg until he reached the thickest part, he snapped the closure shut and arranged the tiers of chains into a decorative pattern of diamonds down her thigh, coming to a point a few inches above her knee.

"Stand up for me," he said.

Calista found herself obeying his order immediately, unsure why she was so compliant. Nevertheless, she couldn't help but admire the new piece of jewellery.

"You aren't the only one who has been paying attention," Phoenix said as he admired Calista's newly decorated leg.

"This is beautiful. Thank you."

"You're welcome."

"What made you choose this as a solstice gift? If you don't mind my asking." Calista gently moved the delicate chains around on her leg, admiring how they glinted in the starlight.

"Unless you're storming my estate in battle leathers, I noticed you like to show some skin in your regular attire. I thought it might benefit from some . . . decoration," he said, revealing a shy, crooked smile.

Calista grinned at Phoenix "Knoxx wouldn't approve."

"HA! No he would not! But he's right about one thing."

"What's that?"

"You're stunning, distractingly so."

Calista's expression changed from bemusement to shock. She was at a complete loss for words. Phoenix cleared his throat as he took a few paces back.

"This has been nice."

Calista blinked a few times as she tried to bring her reeling mind back from the shock of the blunt compliment Phoenix had just paid her.

"Of course. Yes, um, thank you for coming—and for this." She gestured to her leg. "It's beautiful. You're beautiful." She stumbled over her words, a veritable fountain of verbal diarrhea. "Uh, you know what I mean," she said, laughing nervously.

Phoenix approached her and placed his hand under her chin, tilting her face up to meet his. He kissed her, then spoke with his lips against hers. "I do know what you mean."

As he moved away, Calista felt her heart pound in her chest, threatening to escape with the force. She calmed her nerves as best as she could and organized her thoughts. After taking a few steadying breaths Calista remembered there was something important she wanted to share with him.

"Before you go, I did want to share something else with you."

"What is it?" The question was laced with what Calista now recognized as concern whereas before she would have assumed it was suspicion.

"While I was in Vulnari, I found another map. It's unlike anything I've ever seen before. I wanted to show you."

Phoenix was quiet for a moment before replying. "How is it possible you've never seen a completed map before now? We suffered through the same teachings about the ancients."

Calista dropped her head, reflecting that her education was more focused on survival and leading her people. "I was always interested in ancient history, but I wasn't able to indulge that interest as much as I would have liked. It was always considered secondary to the skills required of a future ruler."

Phoenix nodded, perhaps realizing for the first time that even though they were both of royal descent, they had not learned how to rule in the same way. Calista realized that their animosity toward each other was driven by circumstance and not their true feelings. Maybe that moment could be the beginning of a new era. As she ruminated on such thoughts, Phoenix's voice brought her back to the present.

"Come to Aterna tomorrow. We can look at the maps then."

Calista nodded. "OK, tomorrow."

CHAPTER 19
The Library
Calista

The following morning, Calista was mildly surprised to find that Phoenix had made arrangements to have her brought to his estate. She made her way down to the court at the entrance of her estate and found Knoxx there, greeting her with a scowl.

"Get in. I'm taking you to Aterna," he said in a clipped tone.

"Good morning to you too," Calista responded with as much respect as she could muster for the thug that Phoenix kept as his advisor.

"Where is the other one?" he asked as he swivelled his head around.

"If you're talking about Luxx, she's due back later today."

"Figures. That's why he sent me to pick you up." Knoxx barely glanced in Calista's direction as he shoved the luxury vehicle into gear and sped off toward the bank of the River Marra where, no doubt, Phoenix's yacht would be waiting to speed them across to Aterna.

Much to Calista's relief, Knoxx was able to drive the vehicle directly onto the boat, allowing them to part company for a short time before continuing to drive to Aterna Estate. It made their journey relatively quick, if uncomfortably silent.

"We're here. Get out," Knoxx said as he pulled up to the same gates that Calista had attempted to break into several months earlier.

"This is the gate," she said as she glared at his bald-headed, stoned-faced profile.

"Yeah, and the last time I checked, you had two working legs." His response left Calista only too willing to get as far away from him as possible.

She stepped out of the vehicle and touched the keypad on the intercom at the side of the road to indicate her arrival. To her surprise, Phoenix himself answered. "Cali, where's Knoxx and the car?"

"Never mind, I'm here. Can you please let me in?"

Not even a second later, the large gates began to swing open. Calista took her time wandering up the long tree-lined driveway that ended at the grand front entrance of Aterna Estate. As she approached the front doors, the waterfall security feature parted for her, and she walked right through like an expected guest.

Phoenix greeted her on the opposite side of the door. Calista couldn't help but notice how relaxed he seemed compared to the last time they were standing in that same spot. He was dressed casually in a pair of soft gray slacks, athletic shoes, and a white T-shirt. It was unusual to see him dressed in such a way but not unwelcome. Calista chose comfort for herself as well. Believing when she chose her attire for the day that she would have to find her own passage across the river, she had opted for a pair of casual training leathers that were lightly equipped with only her blessed blade. Besides, leather looked good on her.

The Aterna library held an extensive collection of works. Calista's previous explorations had also revealed something interesting. The maps were specific to the area and did not expand beyond to include East Marra, including only a few details of the northern Basara Mountain range. The map etching that Calista made while in the

A World Divided

caves of Vulnari showed a primitive but complete map that spanned the entire landmass.

She unrolled the parchment on a large table, using several tchotchkes to pin down the corners. Beside the etched map was the oldest detailed map found in all of West Marra. The dates on the maps indicated they were 200 years old. That was relatively recent in terms of the LaMarra's history, but it still made them the oldest maps in recorded history.

"Some of the older maps I've seen of East Marra include the northern regions and Blackstone in the middle of Siphon Lake but nothing else," Calista said. "On the southwestern side of the river there's usually nothing but an empty landmass. The waterfall is there, but it's not marked as a site of importance."

Calista shifted her attention to the detailed map of West Marra. She pointed to the edge of the map at what was identified as Gold Leaf Forest and traced her finger up toward the base of the waterfall coming from Siphon Lake and the Blackstone Prison. "No East Marra map shows this area in any detail," she said.

Phoenix leaned over to inspect that area of the map, contemplating the geography. "Hmm, yeah, this is a fairly recent map of the west, but see there?" He pointed to the same area on the map etched from the cave that indicated the waterfall. "There are keys on every single map as well. There must be a connection between those keys we have and these maps." Phoenix turned his attention to Calista. "Speaking of keys, I've noticed you've stopped wearing yours."

She nodded. "I misplaced it somewhere. I'm sure it will turn up. You're right though; those keys are featured on each map. I don't know the area well enough to be sure of the connection."

"I can't be sure either until I see it for myself," he replied. "I've spent some time in Gold Leaf Forest, but there is a lot of area I've yet to explore."

"What is it about that area and those keys?" Calista asked.

"If memory serves me, LaMarra was built up around the river that is fed by Siphon Lake. Siphon Lake is older than anything else around here. Those keys are as much of an enigma to me as they are to you."

Calista thought for a moment before replying. "Have you ever been to the waterfall?"

"I can't say that I have," Phoenix said, shaking his head as he studied the maps further. "How about if we go there now?" He straightened up and looked at Calista expectantly.

"What do you mean?" she asked. "Like go on a hike to find this waterfall?"

"Yes!"

Calista took a moment to consider what she might be getting herself into. Ultimately, she decided she had nothing to lose.

"Let's go find us a waterfall then," she said. "There may be something there to help us figure out what made our ancestors decide that magic was so chaotic that it was worth trying to extinguish it."

Phoenix smiled, pleased with Calista's decision.

"It must be a significant place," he said. "It shows up on all the maps in some way even if not in great detail. I'll have the car brought around; we can go right now."

CHAPTER 20
The Cabin
Calista

As Calista and Phoenix walked through Gold Leaf Forest, rain began to pour down in torrents.

"Follow me! I know where we can go!" he shouted over the rain. He grabbed Cali's hand and led her toward a cabin.

They rushed inside, closing the heavy wooden door behind them, both of them looking like they had just swam across the River Marra.

"We can wait out the worst of it here before we continue on toward the waterfall," he said. Calista nodded in agreement, thankful to be out of the pouring rain for the moment.

Phoenix laughed as he shook out his short hair and raked his fingers through it, pushing the rich dark-brown strands away from his face. He made his way toward the bathroom as Calista wrung her hair out in the sink in the small kitchen. Moments later, Phoenix emerged from the bathroom and approached Calista with a towel.

"You can get out of those wet clothes if you want," he said, pointing to the bathroom.

Phoenix seemed to hesitate for a moment. Then he began to strip off his shirt, which was fused to his chest, and unbuckle his belt so he could peel his pants off. He mumbled and cursed that he hadn't thought to leave any clothes at the cabin. As he hung his soaked clothes on the back of one of the kitchen chairs to dry, Calista watched him discreetly while toweling off her hair. Then she scooted toward the bathroom, clutching the towel to her chest.

While she removed her clothes, she took advantage of the moment of privacy to process the flood of conflicting thoughts that was invading her mind. Judging from the few glances he had sent her way, she suspected he had caught her looking at him. She felt heat rise to her cheeks and the flutter of those damned butterflies in her stomach again. How could one stolen glance produce such a reaction in her? Calista became acutely aware of her state of undress. She was wearing nothing but a cold, wet towel. *There's no way I'm going to parade around here naked,* she thought. *I don't care how uncomfortable I am. This towel is staying on.* She tightened the towel more securely around her chest, careful to keep the edges from slipping open and revealing too much. She couldn't let her guard down, especially now, no matter how much she craved his touch. As quickly as the thought came, she banished it, realizing how inappropriate it would be but wanting to feel him physically close to her all the more.

By the time she emerged from the bathroom and hung her clothes on the other kitchen chair, her hair had mostly dried into soft waves, though it lacked the fresh fragrance it usually had after bathing. She was very aware of the damp, earthy scent that seemed to cling to her skin. It was not entirely offensive, but it was not in line with her usual orange blossom scent of choice.

Calista caught Phoenix stealing a glance at her as she moved around the small kitchen, rising up on her tiptoes to see what was stashed in the far reaches of the cupboards. Feeling the back of the towel rise up over her thighs as she reached up, she quickly smoothed her hand down her backside, trying to preserve a modicum of modesty.

"This is a cute little place. How did you know it was here?" she asked as Phoenix began lighting a fire in the fireplace.

"I put it here," he replied dryly.

"What does that mean?" Calista asked.

"It means I built this cabin, so I, in fact, put it here."

Calista thought back to that day at the fountain, the odd way he was dressed and all the sawdust. She realized he must have come from building this very cabin. She abandoned her exploration of the cupboards and leaned against the counter, watching while he lit the logs in the hearth.

"Oh, I didn't realize you built this," she said in a more civil tone. "I had no idea . . ." She trailed off, not knowing how to finish the sentence. She sensed it was not the moment for a snarky retort. "You did a great job. It's sturdy." She rolled her eyes as soon as the words left her mouth, silently scolding herself for not having anything better to say. "Is there anything to eat here?"

"I don't know. It's been a while since I've taken inventory. There may be something in the cupboards," Phoenix answered as he finished with the fireplace. Calista returned her attention to the few cupboards that she had not explored.

"Aha! Found something!" Calista said gleefully as she pulled a jar of almond butter and a jar of blackberry jam out of the cupboard. She opened another cupboard and smiled. "Crackers! And wine."

Phoenix had been observing her from the living room. He rose to his full height and secured his towel around his waist before joining Calista in the kitchen. He smiled as he reached above her and pulled out two empty glass jars from a higher shelf.

"These will have to do for the wine, I'm afraid," he said as he placed the jars on the table beside a plate that Calista had found.

She surveyed the odd assortment of foods in front of her and then sighed. "Well, let's see if I can make something palatable out of this."

Phoenix poured them each a generous serving of wine. Calista set to work spreading almond butter on each cracker, topping each one with a dollop of blackberry jam. She brought the plate to the coffee table in front of the fireplace and sat on a cushion on the floor, leaning her back against the sofa. Phoenix handed her a jar of wine, then continued toward the floor-to-ceiling window that overlooked the rain-soaked trees. The torrential rain had tapered off and was now falling steadily, accompanied by low rumbles of thunder in the distance. It didn't look like it was going to let up anytime soon.

"Dinner is served," Calista said as cheerfully as she could, although her voice was a little strained. She watched him carefully as her voice seemed to break him out of a trance.

Phoenix made his way to the sofa and sat down as far from her as he could. He reached over and took a cracker off the plate. They ate quietly, immersed in their thoughts as they savoured the wine. Calista sensed the tension between them, amplified by her awareness of her state of undress. She couldn't help but be affected by his closeness. As the wine warmed her from the inside out, she found her thoughts drifting toward him. So close yet so far. He was within arm's reach. All she needed to do to feel his warmth was reach out. She could touch his knee, even lean against his legs, but she kept her distance, knowing the whole situation was so wrong.

"This is excellent wine," she said as casually as she could, hoping her voice didn't betray how conflicted she felt. Phoenix went to the kitchen to retrieve another bottle and uncorked it. He topped up her jar.

"I have to admit this is one of my most guilty pleasures." He smiled shyly and drank deeply from his own jar. Then he took up a new position on the sofa, closer to where Calista was sitting. She felt a flutter in the pit of her stomach and took a sip of wine, hoping to quell the feeling.

"So, is this your little love den?" she asked, leaning into the liquid courage that the wine had afforded her.

She stood up to further explore the small space, adjusting the edges of the towel to pull them more tightly together. Under normal circumstances, she had no issue showing her legs. All of her skirts sported deep slits, after all, but she felt so much more exposed in the towel with no undergarments on and the possibility it could fall off if she didn't clutch it tightly. The way his gaze followed her nudged at her insecurity. The last thing she wanted was to appear desperate.

Phoenix didn't answer right away. He seemed to be contemplating his response as he casually followed her movements around the cabin. Calista walked around looking out various windows, poking her head into the small closet beside the front door, then opening the door next to the bathroom.

"Ah, the bedroom," she said, closing the door with a soft click of the latch. She walked back to the sofa and sat beside Phoenix, close enough to touch but keeping her hands to herself. She observed him for a moment while he stared into the fire and sipped his wine.

"Actually, if you must know," he said, hesitating before continuing, "I've never brought anyone here before. Not another living soul."

The pit of Calista's stomach tightened when he said that, and she felt bad for mocking him before. "Oh, really," she said softly. "I didn't realize this was such a private place."

Phoenix turned toward her, his face a mask of neutrality. His guard was up again. Calista felt his mood shift as he closed himself off. "We have a long hike tomorrow," he said. "You should get some rest." He nodded toward the bedroom.

"No, you sleep in the bedroom," Calista protested, rising to her feet. "I'll stay out here. It's the least I can do."

"You made me dinner, or what passes for a snack anyway," Phoenix replied, levelling his gaze at her. "You've done enough. Now, you can either walk into the bedroom yourself, or I'll pick you up and put you there."

Calista's eyes widened at his words. Then she sat down on the sofa in a huff. "Nothing good ever come from mixing almond butter, jam, and wine. It seems my cooking has gotten you all riled up," she said, attempting to diffuse the tension over who got the bedroom with a little humor at her own expense.

Phoenix didn't waste any time. Before she knew what was happening, he stood up and threw Calista over his shoulder, then carried her into the bedroom. As she felt the warmth of his hands on the back of her naked thighs, any words of protest died in her throat. When he dumped her unceremoniously on the bed, she bounced up and quickly adjusted the edges of her towel to cover the tops of her legs. Phoenix strode toward the door, then turned back to face her.

"Leave the door open, so the heat from the living room can warm the bedroom," he said, his voice sending a strange shiver down her spine. She couldn't help but think—or, rather, hope—that he wanted the door to stay open for another reason.

Calista nodded, then slipped between the sheets, ever aware of Phoenix in the next room. She considered removing the damp towel but decided against it, not wanting to be caught in the nude. No one in her adult life had seen her naked. She wasn't sure how Phoenix would react. He might mock her for being like a child, as he had during their meetings, and it was not a chance she was willing to take.

Sleep evaded her. She was freezing, and she couldn't find a comfortable position that would allow her to settle. After some time, Phoenix appeared in the doorway.

"Everything OK in here?" he asked, his voice low and gruff.

Calista sat up, clutching the covers to her chest. "No. I'm freezing."

Without bothering to reply Phoenix walked around to the empty side of the bed, removed his towel, and, without hesitation, slipped between the sheets beside Calista. He put his hands behind his head, lying back and stretching out.

"What are you doing?" Calista asked, a note of incredulity in her voice. In a slight panic, she leaned over to look out the open bedroom door and saw that the embers of the fireplace had dwindled and mostly gone out. "I thought you wanted to sleep in the living room," she said.

Phoenix lazily turned to face Calista. "Take off that damp towel, and you'll warm up."

Her eyes nearly popped out of her head at his request. "And sleep beside you, naked?" She clutched the blankets tighter to her chest. "Absolutely not, get out!" The conviction in her voice was genuine, but part of her was thrilled by the opportunity to be in bed with him.

Phoenix, chuckled. "I'm not going anywhere, naked or otherwise," he drawled with a smirk.

She huffed and dropped her head onto her pillow, facing away from him, then moved as far away as she could. She was still freezing, her damp towel not helping. She lay there quietly, listening for the even sounds of his breathing. When she was sure he was asleep, as discreetly as she could, she removed the towel and snuggled into the sheets avoiding the damp patch left by the towel making her very aware of her proximity to him. Immediately, she felt the soft sheets warm her chilled flesh. She convinced herself she would wake up early and get dressed before he woke up, and he would be none the wiser. On that note she snuggled under the sheets and within moments fell into a deep sleep.

A slice of bright sunlight peeked through a slit in the bedroom curtains. It cast a streak of light across the spattering of short dark hairs that covered Phoenix's defined chest and landed across Calista's eyes, rousing her from a deep sleep.

As she woke up, she found that over the course of the night, she had gravitated toward Phoenix's warmth and was shamelessly draped across his large body. His heavy arm was draped across her midsection with his thumb brushing the underside of her breast. Calista tried to disentangle her body from his, praying desperately he would not wake up before she could slip out of bed and get dressed. Just as she lifted her leg off his body and attempted to turn her back to him, she felt him stir and tighten his grip on her midsection, his thumb lazily stroking the underside of her breast. Thick with sleep, Phoenix leaned his face down toward the top of Calista's head. "What's your rush?" he asked sleepily.

A wave of embarrassment threatened to consume her as she felt the warmth of his touch. *Well, he certainly knows I'm naked,* Calista thought as she wriggled to free herself from his grasp. If she was being honest, his touch was not unwelcome but she knew it was inappropriate. She wriggled a bit more until they were in a spooning position. Phoenix pulled Calista's back tight against his chest and nestled his face into the crook of her neck and shoulder.

The heat of his lips close to her neck sent shivers through Calista in the best possible way. She snuggled closer and felt the length of him press into her backside.

Phoenix accepted that nudge against his manhood as consent to start exploring more of Calista's body. His hand drifted lazily around her belly, stroking the soft skin and slowly drifting up and down her abdomen, creeping lower and lower with each gentle stroke until he had his palm lightly stroking her inner thigh. Then, with achingly slow movements, he curled his fingers into the space between her legs cupping her most intimate parts between his fingers. Calista wriggled again and pressed herself closer still against his hard length, then raised her arm up and around the back of his head, threading her fingers through the soft hair at the base of his neck. He placed a gentle string of kisses along her neck and up along her jawline, slowly making his way to her lips, his kisses intensifying until they began to devour each other.

He slipped his tongue past her parted lips and stroked her tongue with his. As he deepened the kiss, he allowed her to explore the heat of his mouth with her own tongue and nibble on his plump fleshy lips.

Calista reveled in the sensations that were shooting through her with such intensity that she could barely keep up with the torrent of emotions. She was becoming completely enveloped in the intimacy of the moment, her insecurities fading as Phoenix's hand drifted upwards again and cupped her breast, pinching her nipple between his thumb and forefinger, then cupping her breast feeling the full weight of it while he massaged her. Calista let out a muffled moan that was echoed by a low primal groan coming from deep in Phoenix's chest.

Behind her, Calista felt his cock twitch as it grew more rigid, and she ground her backside against its firm, velvety length. Surprised by her own boldness, she decided to let go and surrender to his touch, though her emotions warred within her as she wondered how someone so forbidden could make her feel so good.

Phoenix's hand drifted back down to the apex of her thighs where he spread her folds and felt her slick flesh. Calista rolled her hips slightly, pressing into his hand as he stroked her entrance. He teased her with one finger at her opening and the base of his hand pressed tightly against her sensitive flesh. He slid his finger around the apex of nerves, drawing a throaty moan from her. Calista ground herself against his hand, desperate for more friction.

"I'll give you what you need," Phoenix whispered against the side of her neck.

She didn't need any more encouragement than that. Her heart was slamming into her chest. With her sexual experiences limited to what she could accomplish on her own, she was overcome by how something as gentle as his touch could affect her so much. Her senses heightened to his touch. She knew what she liked enough to get herself to climax, but having him explore her in that way was next-level stimulating. Their rivalry be damned; this felt too right.

Phoenix stroked her until she began to tingle. She felt her body contracting tightly as his fingers stroked her until her release claimed her and sent her over the edge. She rode it out, breathing hard as she came down, and her heart rate returned to normal. She was riding high on feelings of ecstasy driven by her first taste of shared intimacy. She was as conflicted as ever, knowing she had surrendered to her temptations and that it could negatively impact her reputation should anyone find out. Despite the consequences she might face, she knew deep down that this was just the beginning.

Phoenix's hand stilled and then withdrew slowly from the heat between her legs, settling on her stomach as he pulled her toward him. Calista turned to face him as he sat up, resting against the backboard. Without saying a word, Calista straddled Phoenix's hips and tucked herself up close to his shaft as she gripped him at the base.

"Hey, slow down, there's no need to rush," he rasped.

Calista cocked an eyebrow at him. Through her lust-filled gaze, she tightened her grip slightly. "Like this?" she asked.

"Mmmm, yeah," he groaned, shifting beneath her touch.

Phoenix tilted his head back, sucking in a breath as she stroked him from base to tip.

"Easy," he said in a low voice, wincing as she gripped him harder. "I'm going to need you to do what I tell you . . . before one of us gets hurt." At that moment Calista realized he had noticed her inexperience. She paused, not wanting to reveal the depth of her innocence but not wanting to hurt him either.

"OK then. Tell me."

She rocked her hips against him as she stroked him with increasing pressure and intensity. His breathing picked up pace.

"Slow down, or this will end too soon," he said through clenched teeth. "I want this to last." he added as he relaxed into her grip. "Now move up and down." Calista followed his instructions, "A bit harder now...that's it" he urged her on "move a little faster" her gaze never leaving his. She moved in tune with the cues of his body and when she noticed the bead of moisture collecting on the tip of his shaft she used her thumb to rub it around his sensitive flesh. "Like this?" her shy question earned her a deep groan of approval that sent chills of pleasure through her. Leaning into the intimacy, feeling her inhibitions melt away, she became increasingly confident in her ministrations.

Calista smiled and raised an eyebrow as she watched his cock throb under her touch. She picked up the pace slightly, and within seconds Phoenix let out a guttural moan, his release spilling all over his stomach and down the length of his shaft. He leaned his forehead against Calista's, his eyes closed. Having never witnessed a man's release before, Calista was slightly surprised but inexplicably satisfied with herself.

She cupped his face and held him for several moments. "So, is this what we get up to when we're together now?" she murmured. Phoenix smiled shyly as he pulled back to appreciate the view of the naked woman in front of him.

"Well, this," he said, gesturing to their tangled limbs, "is definitely better when we're together." His words sent Calista's stomach fluttering, and she was sure she was blushing furiously.

A loud pounding on the door caused them to jump, pulling them out of their afterglow bubble. As the pounding intensified, Phoenix moved Calista off his lap and threw the bedcovers over her naked form as he scooped up his towel and tied it around his waist.

He strode to the door and yanked it open, ready to tear a strip off whoever dared to interrupt them. He came face to face with Knoxx.

"You need to come now," he said in a rush, his voice charged with urgency. "They've stormed the palace."

CHAPTER 21
Riot
Phoenix

"Hurry up and get dressed. Your armour is in the car," Knoxx said as he flung a set of leather garments at Phoenix from the doorway.

Phoenix looked at his battle gear and then looked over his shoulder toward the bedroom. Calista was gone. He scanned the room and saw that she was already getting dressed in the clothes she had worn the day before, which, thankfully, were her battle leathers, including by some stroke of luck a blessed dagger.

At least her clothes are dry, he thought. As he buckled the various straps and adjusted the fit of his own leathers, he noticed Knoxx was already geared up and armed to the nines.

What the hell happened since yesterday to cause all of this shit? Phoenix wondered as he shot out the door with Calista on his heels.

"She's going to have to find her own way back across the river, Nix. We don't have time to play chauffeur today," Knoxx said, sneering at Calista. She appeared to take no notice of Knoxx's hostility.

"Like hell I'm going back. I'll fight with you," she said as Phoenix helped her into the vehicle.

"Why would you want to fight?" Phoenix inquired as he strapped every manner of blunt object to his front breastplate. "It's dangerous." Every item could deliver a fatal blow but at great cost to the person who did it. Only Calista had a blessed blade to truly and justly kill an attacker.

Asserting her position as a ruler, she replied as diplomatically as ever. "A threat in West Marra could easily make its way over to East Marra. I'm a trained Zenovia warrior. I should at the very least offer a neighbouring region my support. Divided or not, a threat bold enough to take on the most fortified estate in the capital of West Marra is a threat worth keeping an eye on. These riots, although seemingly without purpose, seem to be getting worse. I'll fight alongside you."

Phoenix got the sense he was working with an equal. She was no longer a child; she was a true Queen, a warrior. Though not entirely new to him, that side of her felt different now that she was willing to work with him and not against him. He wondered when that had started to change.

"Take this," Phoenix said, tossing a short baton into her lap.

"I'm good, Nix." She patted the sheathed blade on the side of her leathers and offered a weak smile, followed by a nasty sneer at Knoxx, who dutifully ignored her. The tension in the back of the car was thick and uncomfortable. Phoenix was trapped between his most trusted friend and advisor and Calista, his opposing ruler who had offered her help in a fight and . . . his lover? He had no idea how to define what he and Calista had become over the last few hours, but it was not the time to be mulling it over. There were more important issues at hand.

"Knoxx, get me up to speed what the fuck happened since yesterday."

"I spent the day tracking and trying to find a way to infiltrate the renegades. They have a strong leader, a stealthy son of a bitch. They snuck right through the front gates, and then the riots started. They burned their way southward and had just breached palace security when I left to get you."

"Why didn't you use the bond?"

"Your cabin blocks magic, you idiot." Knoxx levelled Phoenix with an incredulous stare before continuing. "I would ask what the fuck you've been up to, but it's damn obvious."

Calista seized the moment to interject, her voice filled with venom. "And what exactly is wrong with what you suspect we were up to, Knoxx?"

Knoxx ignored Calista, speaking to Phoenix as if she was not there. "Nix, of all the bitches out there, you picked this one to fuck? What the hell kind of stupidity is that?"

Phoenix was having none of it. His eyes widened, filled with enough rage and contempt that it could have levelled mountains. His chest heaved with the harsh breaths he drew as he launched himself at Knoxx, wrapping his hands around his throat and squeezing. His knuckles turned white with the amount of force he was exerting.

"Don't fuck with me, Knoxx. She's royalty, and you will treat her as such."

Knoxx's eyes began to bulge, his face turning red as he struggled for breath. After a few moments, Calista placed a hand over Phoenix's hand. "Let go; you'll kill him." Moments later, Phoenix loosened his grip. Knoxx gasped for air and massaged his bruised throat while he nodded to Phoenix, indicating that he understood.

As they made their way toward the capital, evidence of the destruction left by the renegades was visible but not severe. Mostly broken shop windows and some vandalized parks and green spaces. No one appeared to be hurt until they arrived at Aterna. The gate was mangled, and the gardens looked like they had been torched. Several people were engaged in hand-to-hand combat, mostly men.

Calista leapt out of the car and jumped right in, striking the first person who came at her. A renegade with a bat swung wide. Calista ducked and took him out with a blow to his midsection. His head bounced off the stone ground, and he lay prone, bleeding from his nose and ear.

She stepped over him and spun around, looking for Phoenix. He was engaged in hand-to-hand combat with two men. He was holding one off while he savagely kicked the other one in the chest, sending him crashing into another group of men who were torching the furniture on the terrace.

Phoenix shouted for Calista to see if the secondary security was engaged.

Calista dashed inside to look for the control panel that would engage the protective shields on the remaining unbroken windows to limit further access to the palace. Renegades were scaling the building and smashing every window. Thankfully, the windows were reinforced enough that it took considerable force to break through. That bought her some time.

Phoenix was close on her trail, shouting directions as he ran. "The entrance to the control room is concealed behind the woman upstairs!"

Calista shot up the stairs and found the statue. It was the same one that she and Luxx had giggled about several months earlier. She pushed the statue aside and saw that the baseboard was broken into several sections. She kicked the middle section, and the wall swung open to reveal a small closet-size room with several electrical panels lining the walls. Overwhelmed by the sheer number of buttons and switches, she had no idea what to do. Knoxx, who seemed to appear out of thin air, pushed past her and started slamming his large hands over sections of switches, setting into motion the secondary security system.

He shoved her out of the small room, and she backed into a renegade who was tearing his way through the upstairs chambers. The man reacted fast, slamming Calista to the floor. Phoenix leaped on him while Calista struggled to her feet, clutching her ribs and breathing hard. The rogue had Phoenix pinned to the floor, his knee on his back between his shoulder blades. Calista launched herself at the man, blade drawn and ready to slice him to ribbons. She grabbed him by the back of his scalp and yanked his head back, the tip of the blade positioned in the tender hollow at the base of his skull. One thrust and he would be dead. The rogue loosened his grip on Phoenix, put his hands up in surrender, then took off running down the stairs the moment she released the handful of greasy hair she was clutching. As the shields slammed down on every window with a deafening crash, the last of the renegades who had infiltrated the palace fled like Savarras from a sinking ship.

Calista and Phoenix helped each other to their feet. "Where's Knoxx?" Calista asked, looking around.

"We'll find him later," Phoenix rasped as he grabbed Calista's hand and dragged her behind him. His mind was racing with what he just experienced. He had been trained in the art of hand-to-hand combat, but he had never fought anyone outside of controlled training sessions. He was blown away by Calista and her fighting skill. She displayed no hesitation. She was so focused and deadly if she chose to be. Before that day he never would have thought a woman warrior could be so sexy, but her strength, her poise, and her willingness and ability to protect him had his blood running hot in his veins.

He took large, purposeful steps directly to his bedchamber. Thankfully, it did not appear to have been breached. Phoenix scanned his retina to gain access to his room and then pulled Calista inside after him.

He slammed the door and shoved Calista up against it. Both of them riding high on the adrenaline of the fight, they consumed each other. Phoenix's mouth landed on Calista's, crushing her. Her passion matched his as she tore at the buckles and fasteners that held their battle leathers together. A lock of hair fell over Phoenix's forehead as he tore his lips away from hers, biting her lower lip and breathing hard. His eyes were hooded and filled with lust. Calista made quick work of undoing the bindings of her battle leathers, expertly pulling apart the buckles at the waist that held her pants and breastplate together. She tore them off and stepped out of them. Standing in nothing but skimpy undergarments, she went to work on the many buckles that held Phoenix's pants up.

She shoved them down his muscular backside as he tore off his own breastplate and then stepped out of his pants. He kicked the heap of clothing out of the way and descended upon Calista, more ravenous than before. He picked her up and held her against the door, one large hand around her throat—tight but not enough to choke— keeping her head in place as she wrapped her legs around his waist. She rolled her hips against his raging erection, signalling her consent. He was so hard; a deep primal groan escaped his lips as he held her close and thrust his tongue into her mouth, stroking her tongue and tasting her. Phoenix pulled his cock free of his undergarments and gripped the thin, soaking wet fabric that covered Calista's sensitive flesh, tearing it clean off her body. She gasped as the sudden movement, perhaps as a reaction to cool air touching her scorching-hot skin.

Her sudden intake of air and the breathy sound she made, made it nearly impossible for him to contain his need for her. He glanced down at her breasts as they rose and fell with her ragged breaths. He felt torn between burying his face in her soft flesh and using his tongue to tease her peaked nipples. He could hardly formulate a coherent thought as he attempted to speak through his laboured breaths. "I need you to want this as much as I do."

Upon hearing his words, Calista rolled her hips again, squirming restlessly. She managed to find the words to express what Phoenix could only assume was her own mounting need for release. "I need you, Nix." The sound of his nickname or her full lips was his undoing.

Phoenix gripped the base of his cock and angled the head of his throbbing shaft at her slick entrance. Then, with one smooth motion, he drove into her right up to the hilt. He paused for a moment, his breathing ragged, and leaned his forehead against Calista's, his eyelids hooded.

"Are you OK?"

Calista looked like she could barely breathe as she shifted slightly to accommodate his size within her. She nodded and looked down to where they were joined. "I'll be fine, I just need a moment to—" She cut the thought short as she moved her hips to adapt to his length and considerable girth.

"Hmm . . . you like to watch me fuck you?" Phoenix said with a groan as he too looked down and withdrew almost the full length of his cock. With his hands supporting her backside and thighs, Phoenix couldn't deny how hot she looked in that position, legs spread wide apart, willing for him to thrust deeply into her slick flesh.

He paused as he noticed a bright streak of red along his shaft. Alarmed, he looked into Cali's face. "I've hurt you."

Calista rolled her hips, desperate to gain more friction as she shook her head. "No, I'm not hurt. Isn't that supposed to happen the first time?" she asked as she continued to squirm, eager to bring them closer together. "I've waited far too long. More. Give me more."

Phoenix looked at her in wonderment, hardly able to believe this was her first sexual interlude. The shock made the experience all the more enthralling for him for reasons he did not have the brain capacity to explore at that moment.

He slid himself back inside her, his eyes never leaving her face, watching for cues that he should stop. She winced as she braved the briefest pinch of pain and then moaned. The smile on her lips and her eyes half closing and clouded with lust was all the encouragement he needed that she was enjoying their carnal act. He set a steady pace, moving within her. To help her along, he reached a hand between where they were joined to massage and tease her slick and overly sensitized bundle of nerves, driving them both over the edge of ecstasy, panting and moaning as their release gripped them. Together they rode out the pleasure until they sank to the floor, a tangled heap of sweaty, bloody limbs.

Once they finally caught their breath, they stood up. Calista winced as she stood to her full height and cupped her breast as she examined a tender spot on her ribcage that was starting to turn purple. She touched it gingerly, then flinched when Phoenix's warm fingertips gently made contact with the tender flesh.

"Oh, that looks painful," he said, his eyebrows drawn together as he examined her.

"You look like hell yourself," Calista said, her voice soft and concerned. She reached up to touch the cut on his cheek that ran along his chiselled jaw. He jerked his head away from her touch, hissing in pain.

"Sorry," she muttered as she pulled away from his face.

He led her into the bathroom where he ran a heavy stream of water into an enormous soaker tub. Phoenix directed Calista to sit on the edge of the tub while he searched through an array of vials and fancy bottles of potions and lotions that littered his vanity. He dumped some shimmery blue scented liquid into the running water, and immediately the room filled with the scent of Phoenix—Citrus, and fresh pine. The shimmering blue water began to foam up with the most luscious and fragrant bubbles. Calista reached her hand into a cloud of bubbles and blew them away gently.

"I have something to help with those bruises," Phoenix said as he knelt in front of Calista with a small pot of thick translucent salve scented faintly like sea salt and sage.

He dipped his finger into the salve and applied a small amount to the various cuts and scrapes on her body, taking extra care around the tender bruise on her ribs. He placed the palms of his hands on her knees and pushed them apart. Then he dipped his head and placed a soft kiss at the apex of her thighs. He looked up at her and noticed her blushing furiously, but she didn't resist his touch.

"After what we just did, now you're shy?" he said, smiling while he brushed the inside of her thigh with the stubble of his cheek. It sent chills through her core.

"I don't usually let anyone *this* close to me," Calista replied.

"Yeah, I know that . . . now," he said quietly. The heat of his breath as he spoke against her sensitive skin sent a tingle into her belly and heat surging through her veins. Calista couldn't resist the urge to run her fingers through his thick hair as he lingered around her most intimate areas.

Phoenix pulled back from her and inspected her folds. With his eyebrows drawn together, he dipped his thumb into the pot of salve and ever so gently applied it to her sensitive flesh. He chanced a devilish glance at her as he circled the tight bundle of nerves at the top, sending chills through her core once again.

Slowly, Phoenix stood to his full height. As he stood between Calista's legs, she was eye level with his member. He was already hardening. Without a coherent thought in her mind, Calista reached up and held him at the base of his cock, stroking the velvety length of him to the tip and back down again. He groaned and let his head fall back before he gripped the back of her head and looked down at her. She slowly licked him from base to tip, closing her eyes and planting a gentle kiss on the tip of his cock before taking the tip into her mouth and pushing him as far back as her throat would allow without engaging her gag reflex. She had her fist around the base as she withdrew and felt him shudder while she gently dragged her teeth along his shaft. Growing harder still, Phoenix withdrew from her warm, soft, and dangerously sensuous mouth.

"Not like this," he said as he stooped to pick her up under her knees and stepped into the tub cradling her against his chest. As they sank down into the warm, bubbly water, the heat of his body and the water soothed her aching bruises.

He settled her between his legs as he leaned against the tub and cradled Calista's back against his hard body. He lazily stroked her breasts and stomach, drifting occasionally between her legs and causing her to squirm against him. Each time she wriggled her backside against him, his cock twitched until he grew painfully hard again. They did not speak as Calista turned around and straddled Phoenix's hips. He eased himself into her, and she rode him slowly at first. The water around them shimmering and swirling around the motion of her body. As she ground herself into him and drove herself closer to release, Phoenix began to match her thrust for thrust.

Calista cried out as she reached her climax, clenching tightly around Phoenix as he found his release. He drained himself inside her, and she fell against his chest, her breasts pressed up against him. Together they caught their breath. Then Phoenix gently withdrew from Calista. She winced slightly as she moved to rest her back against the opposite side of the tub. Phoenix was the picture of contentment as he rested against the other side, basking in the afterglow of great sex.

Bubbles swirled between them in the shimmering water.

"How do you feel?" Phoenix asked

"How do you think I feel?" she responded, smiling.

Phoenix laughed. "I mean your ribs and cuts. They should be healing."

Calista took a quick inventory of the areas where he had applied the salve and appeared surprised to find that the bruises didn't hurt anymore, and the cuts had already begun to heal.

"I feel good, actually," she said as she looked into Phoenix's face with mild astonishment.

"Good." He smiled earnestly and raked his fingers through his hair, pushing it back off his forehead.

"How many have there been?" Calista asked, biting her lower lip. With a rush of air escaping his lungs, Phoenix tried to formulate a response. It was his turn to blush now.

"Are you taking anything right now?" he asked.

"That's not what I asked you, Nix."

"I know. But I don't know what to say. How is it possible that I'm your first?"

"I . . . I didn't intend it to be that way. It just happened. I've had interests and other experiences, but with everyone so close all the time, privacy to be this intimate with someone is not a luxury I was ever afforded." Calista busied herself by playing with the bubbles, unable to look directly at Phoenix. "I have been anticipating—rather, hoping for it since I was eighteen. I've been taking the potion since then, but . . . obviously, I've not needed it."

Phoenix nodded. "I'm on the potion too, but, well, it saved me more than once, since we're being honest."

The awkwardness of the intimate conversation gave way to laughter as Phoenix caught Calista's foot and began massaging it.

"It was an honour and a privilege to be your first. I hope I didn't disappoint," he said, arching an eyebrow as his eyes locked with hers.

"I must admit I did enjoy watching you fuck me." It was Calista's turn to laugh out loud and give him an exaggerated wink.

There's no turning back now, Phoenix thought in the aftermath of their conversation and lovemaking as he admired her lounging in the tub across from him.

How am I supposed to let her leave my sight now? What the hell am I supposed to do? No one can know about this. Damn it, Knoxx is going to drop my balls in a damn vice if he finds out. He already suspects. Shit, I can't let her go. She's mine—I need her. Why were we ever meant to hate each other?

Phoenix watched her climb out of the tub and wrap her toned body in a large bath towel.

She's fucking stunning. Stop staring at her like a creepy asshole. She won't hesitate to drop-kick your ass. More lust filled thoughts clouded his mind as he followed suit and towelled off.

Shit, she caught me staring, and now I look like I'm playing with my balls. Get it together, Nix!

Calista's quizzical expression brought him back to reality.

"Are you OK?" she asked, watching his expression for signs of illness.

"I'm fine. You must be starving. I'll call down and see if they can bring us something to eat."

Calista fidgeted a bit before replying. "That sounds amazing, but things seem to have died down around here, and I really need to go back across the river. Luxx is probably wondering what's happened and, well, I need to go back. I'm so sorry."

"Once you leave, how am I going to know that you are safe?"

I need to know you're safe.

"I'll be fine. I'm always fine. We've been apart before. It's not like you can come back with me and stay in East Marra anyway."

CHAPTER 22
Afterglow

Calista

Alarm bells were sounding within Calista's mind. *Luxx can't know about this! How am I ever going to explain this to her? Will she know? Will she be able to tell I was with him?* Such thoughts raced through her mind as she dried off, twisting her insides until the gravity of the situation settled on her like a ton of stones.

I feel different, but I don't look different. Can people see how I feel? Gods! How am I going to face Luxx? She'll know for sure. I don't want to leave him. I want to stay here naked with him on the floor, in the garden, and up against every surface he'll take me on!

Calista's emotional surges threatened to consume her. Her desire to stay and indulge in endless carnal activities with Phoenix threatened to overwhelm her better judgment. She had to stay focused though. She was the Queen of East Marra, not Phoenix's plaything. But damn if it didn't feel good to be his plaything.

Over the last thirty-six hours, Calista had become privy to a whole other side of Phoenix. His vulnerabilities had been laid bare before her, and she had been just as exposed. They had been raised to be wary of one another, to keep their distance, coached from childhood to be friendly around each other but not too friendly. From their respective sides of the river, they viewed each other as enemies. When forced into close proximity, they were instructed to put on a show of good faith but to never let their guard down. Never say too much, don't give anything away, protect their families' interests and secrets. Now all those years of careful coaching and guarded behaviour lay between them in a proverbial pile of ashes.

Calista felt a connection to people in general. That was how she ruled, by connecting with people. The connection she felt with Phoenix was different, more intense, cosmically destined to be. Forces well beyond her comprehension were hard at work. The connection she felt filled spaces in her mind, body, and soul with a sense of peace, driving her toward new heights. She wondered if Phoenix felt the same. Time would tell. For now, the matter at hand was getting back to Cerulean Estate unnoticed and then facing Luxx.

CHAPTER 23
The Water Bond

Phoenix

Phoenix went into his vast closet and came out shirtless, wearing only a soft pair of cotton pants held up by a drawstring at the waist. The pants hung low on his hips, exposing his perfectly sculpted torso and a trail of dark hair that disappeared beneath the waistband. He approached Calista, holding out a large white dress shirt.

"Your battle leathers need cleaning, put this on. It will fit you like a dress; you're so tiny," he said as he held the shirt open for Calista to thread her arms through the sleeves. She stood before him in the shirt, the first few buttons undone, and spun around for his inspection. She looked like a child playing dress-up. Phoenix smiled in spite of himself, then went back to the closet to fetch a tie for her to cinch at her waist like a belt.

"This will have to do," he said as he stood behind her, planting soft kisses along her temple and down her neck while his hands slipped under the hem of the shirt to cup her behind and stroke her between her thighs.

"Stop that," she said with a hint of a giggle. "I don't have any underwear on!"

"I know—you dirty birdie," Phoenix replied, continuing his exploration of her most intimate region. With great reluctance and sheer force of will, Calista stepped out of his intoxicating embrace and put some distance between them.

"It's time to go."

"It's late," he replied. "Spend the night here with me . . . please."

His plea yanked hard on her heartstrings, and Calista wanted nothing more than to stay, but her responsibilities as Queen were ever present and calling out to her. It was pure torture.

"Nix, please don't do this. I want nothing more than to stay here in our fortified little bubble, but I can't. Neither of us can," she said, the reality of having to leave that bubble of contentment causing emotion to creep into her voice.

Phoenix raked his hand through his hair and stalked off to his closet again. A moment later he came out wearing a leather jacket and boots and holding two helmets.

"I'll take you back then," he said with an air of finality.

Calista slipped on her hiking boots, the only footwear she had since arriving in West Marra and leaving on their hike through Gold Leaf Forrest the day before.

"How exactly are you planning on getting me back across the river?" she asked as she accepted the helmet he extended to her.

"Trust me," he replied.

He took her by the hand and walked her through a hidden door in the corner of his bedchamber. It led to a narrow hallway that followed the shape of the building along the inside walls, another security feature.

"I had them add this hidden hallway, so I could slip out undetected. Knoxx doesn't even know about it," Phoenix said as he guided her through the maze of halls and narrow stairwells that exited into a garage several levels below ground that housed multiple vehicles. For the second time he had felt compelled to share private information with her, first about the cabin and now his secret escape route. *I can trust her,* he thought. The realization stunned him as much as it comforted him, knowing he had found his other half.

Calista's eyes widened in astonishment at the sheer number of armoured cars and other vehicles parked in the garage. Tucked away in a corner was a selection of motorcycles.

Phoenix mounted the one in the middle and reached out to secure Calista's helmet before putting on his own. She closed the visor and mounted the bike behind him. She pressed herself as close to him as she could, her legs squeezing hard on either side of his thighs.

"Don't tell me this scares you," Phoenix said, unable to conceal the amusement in his voice.

"Terrified," was the only response she offered before clutching his waist with a vice-like grip.

Phoenix laughed as they took off into the night, speeding toward the bank of the Marra. When they arrived, Calista started to dismount.

"Hold on," Phoenix said, resting a hand on her leg.

"We're at the edge of the water, and there's nowhere left to go," she replied,

"I told you to trust me," he said in a low voice as he squeezed her leg.

Calista closed her eyes in anticipation of another wickedly fast ride. Instead, she was surprised to see a bioluminescent swell of water form a bridge across the river. The water collected a few feet ahead of the motorcycle's front wheel, allowing Phoenix to drive them across the river on a stream of water fuelled by magic.

As they made contact on solid ground at the entrance to Shadow Lake, Calista hopped off the back of the bike and cupped herself between her legs. Phoenix watched her for a moment in confusion before realization dawned on him

"Sorry. I guess that's not the rough ride you were expecting to have without panties." He laughed at his own joke while Calista massaged herself for a moment. Then she punched him good-naturedly in the arm.

"I wouldn't object to you kissing it better."

"With pleasure," he replied, gathering her up in the protective cage of his arms.

"Come with me," Calista said as she led him toward the shore of Shadow Lake. A centenary healer could be seen lurking around in the darkness, tending to the wild flora and fauna.

"Who is that?" Phoenix asked with a start, squinting into the darkness. Calista turned to see what had captured his attention. "I thought you said no one would be here."

"That's Jade. She's been here for at least twenty-five years, ever since she became a healer. She's harmless, and she won't say anything. She doesn't leave Shadow Lake unless it's absolutely necessary." Calista waved at Jade and was granted a soft smile before Jade turned away and disappeared into the thick, leafy canopy.

Calista started to take off her boots and gestured for Phoenix to do the same as she scanned the shore looking for something. With his shoes off, Phoenix looked at Calista in confusion.

"What are you looking for?"

"Here we go," she said, smiling as she held up a scalloped seashell. "Come stand in the water with me. Take off your jacket,"

He looked at her with eyebrows drawn together in confusion. "What for? What are you doing?" He watched as she waded into the shallows, in the same general area where they had exchanged solstice gifts. Deciding that there was no reason to keep his guard up around her, especially after recent events, he followed her lead. He was tired of fighting his impulse to keep her at a distance. It never felt right when he was around her, and yet he fought to keep her and everyone else at arm's length. To appease whom? He had no idea, and now it didn't really matter.

They stood together ankle deep in the shimmering, healing waters of Shadow Lake. The stars were plentiful and shining brightly, the air cool but comfortable. One of the few luxuries afforded to that section of East Marra, the temperature was eternally on the cusp of late spring and early summer.

Calista reached into the shirt and took out her Aquavass. "I want to link a water bond with you," she said, looking up into Phoenix's face.

Water bonds were a rite of passage, made using the water in the Aquavass given to everyone in the LaMarra region. The water contained and protected by an Aquavass was gifted at birth. It was drawn from the reflection pool at the temple of the Goddess Marra, and it was gifted to each newborn soul as a connection to the Goddess and her divine energy. Mixing the water from an individual's Aquavass connected families and friends. The bond was an intimate communication link between partners, sometimes included during a marriage ceremony if a bond had not already been established. Some bonds were deeper than others, depending on where the people involved in the creation of a bond were when they created their connection. Ancient scripts suggested that an especially divine and precious water bond existed that has the ability to connect one to their chosen partner with an emotional link so profound that each person could sense the emotional state of the other as if it was their own emotional experience. In the rarest cases, and only when the Goddess made her presence known during the bond, the bond could produce visions that were shared in the mind's eye. How bonds deeper than communication alone were formed was a mysterious and largely unexplainable form of magic. Some believed it depended on the amount of magic present when the bond was created; however, no one in living memory had reported experiencing an emotional link in their bond or one that produced visions.

Fully aware of the magnitude of what creating a bond entailed, Phoenix picked up his own Aquavass, pinching and spinning it between his fingers as the weight of creating a bond with Calista settled over him.

"You're sure you want to do this?" he asked softly. Making his indecision known was a risk he had to take. Phoenix was sure his feelings for Calista were far greater than he had ever let himself realize before. Creating a bond with her was akin to marriage, albeit in their current state of affairs a highly secretive marriage and one not validated by witnesses.

Without hesitation Calista opened her Aquavass and emptied it into the shell. As she watched the small amount of shimmering liquid pour out, she smiled. "I've never been more sure of anything in my entire life." Her bold statement and her assurance that she was ready and willing to bond with him settled his nerves and gave him the clarity of mind he needed to abandon the last of his reservations about what people would think of him for literally and figuratively getting into bed with a woman and ruler whose reputation was that of an adversary to the King of West Marra. They had decided five years earlier to rule differently than their parents, although Phoenix was fairly sure this was not what he intended. However, now he was ready to accept the challenges that would come his way when his relationship with Calista was eventually revealed.

Phoenix unlatched his own Aquavass and tipped its contents into the shell. The water swirled around, sparkling and producing small effervescent bubbles, effectively sealing them together in a bond that defied time and space as long as there was even a single drop of water available to engage a connection.

The breeze picked up, and the waves gently lapping at the shore became larger swells that reached past Calista's knees. The turbulent water settled as quickly as it started, and the tide pulled back, almost calling Phoenix and Calista to wade deeper into the lake.

Calista poured the water back into each of the vials in their Aquavasses and then leaned in to kiss Phoenix. He returned the affection and grasped her hand as he led her deeper into the water. When they were chest deep in the lake, Phoenix took it upon himself to undress Calista, who, in turn, removed his soaked clothing. They floated on the surface of the lightly shimmering water and soaked in the serene atmosphere. The water was calm, and the sounds of the night insects and birds were soothing, yet somehow the air felt charged with power. Phoenix felt his skin ripple with the energy that imbued the water and the air around him. He reached out and felt goose flesh covering Calista's arms and body.

"You feel it too?" he asked as he brought her close. Her warmth sent new waves of lust coursing through him.

"Mmm . . . yes, among other things," she replied as she arched an eyebrow and reached between them to stroke his growing arousal. He groaned, and suddenly a large swell of water lifted both of them and washed them ashore, almost as if the lake itself was telling them to get a room. Laughing and gathering up and wringing out their clothing, they got dressed and then sat on a jetty of stones on the beach.

The bond being forged that night was just the tip of what could be. Recent history did not speak to what happened when two royals created a bond. That fact alone made their bond unique. With this bond, Phoenix and Calista could reach out to each other with a message that appeared on their forearms in the presence of water.

Calista opened her Aquavass and dabbed her index finger into the water, then traced a small letter "b" on her forearm, followed by a horizontal line across the top of the letter to make a capital "T." She instructed Phoenix to do the same. This symbol when traced on either of their forearms with as little as a drop of water would immediately activate their bond, allowing them to communicate privately. The symbol glowed brightly on their skin. The stars also seemed to glow brighter, and ripples in the lake caused shallow waves to lap against their legs.

Lost in the moment, Phoenix slid his hand up Calista's arm and rested his hand under her chin, angling her face up toward his. He kissed her gently, lovingly. Then he ran his thumb over the shimmering symbol on Calista's arm. As the symbol faded, he locked gazes with Calista. "Better together?" he asked.

Calista nodded. "Yeah, better together."

The air around them changed again. The slight breeze became stronger as the sky began to brighten, and the sun started to rise. The threat of discovery was far greater in the light of day.

"You need to go now," Calista urged. "No one can see you here."

Hesitation slowed his movements. He knew full well that they couldn't afford to be caught. With great reluctance he mounted his bike and then shot away over another magically conjured bioluminescent water bridge, back to West Marra.

Calista set out on foot toward Cerulean Palace. Anxiety gnawed at her insides as she anticipated what would happen upon her return.

CHAPTER 24
Revelations
Calista

The walk to Cerulean Palace was as therapeutic as it was tiring. As she walked, her mind churned over the events of the past few days, particularly the last few hours. The waterfall they never found, the maps, Phoenix, oh so much Phoenix. As Calista absently reached up to hold her Aquavass, it occurred to her that she needed to find the key she had been wearing. Not for the first time, it dawned on her that there was a magical hum whenever she had the key and was around Phoenix. The connection continued to nag at her, and she needed to find out what it was. She resolved to ask Luxx to help her find it. But later. Sleep first then Luxx.

Upon entering the open court of her estate, the community was buzzing as people set up produce stands, and the nursery children ran around gleefully. Calista's appearance did not escape those who saw her walking her first and very obvious walk of shame.

Why should it be a walk of shame? I'm not ashamed of what I've done. I'm a Queen, after all, and a woman. A woman in love maybe. Yes, for sure. Maybe. Well, I'll sort that out later. There's nothing shameful about walking through my palace wearing an oversized men's shirt and no panties.

Calista tried to reason with herself, as if what she was doing was perfectly natural. Deep in her heart, however, she knew she was being judged. The judgment came from a very kind community of people, but it was a judgment nonetheless.

After stopping by the kitchen for a quick snack, Calista couldn't fight her exhaustion any longer and made her way toward her suite. She collapsed onto the daybed on the balcony and fell asleep, not bothering to change her clothes or even put on panties, for that matter. The events of the last few days had drained her.

An indeterminable amount of time later, Calista was momentarily disoriented as her sleep-clouded brain was nudged awake by Luxx. "Hey, wake up." She nudged Calista's upper arm as she coaxed her into consciousness. Luxx was sitting on the edge of the daybed looking very concerned.

"You're back. How was the trip down the cliff?" Calista asked, her voice thick with sleep. She started to sit up, only to realize she was still dressed in Phoenix's shirt.

"Fine, thanks. Uh . . ." Luxx cocked an eyebrow as she gave Calista a very clear once-over. "What happened to you? Are you OK?"

Looking down at her partially unbuttoned shirt and realizing it had bunched up around her waist, she was grateful someone had had the kindness to drape a blanket over her legs, which was all that was protecting her modesty at that moment.

"Yes, I'm fine, thanks. Why do you ask?"

"Because you're naked from the waist down, wearing a man's shirt, it's nearly seven in the evening, and you appear to have slept the day away on your terrace. Shall I go on?" Luxx's list of observations was enough to bring Calista crashing back into the reality of her current circumstances.

"Luxx, I really missed you, but we need to talk." Calista sucked in a deep breath and then exhaled.

"That sounds serious."

"Don't mock me. I am serious. I've never seen you behave like you did in Vulnari, and . . ." Hesitation threatened to choke her final words, but she pressed on. "There are other things I want you to know." She gestured to her attire and raised an eyebrow, indicating the conversation was going to be a big one.

"I have some questions of my own, but first . . ." Luxx bent her forehead to touch Calista's. She stayed there for a moment before pulling back. "I missed you. Let's eat something and then go from there."

Calista went to stand up and almost stepped on the little purple Savarra that had been sleeping close by, then jumped up as the little creature crawled up her leg and settled on her shoulder.

"Who is this cute little thing?" Luxx squealed with delight as she reached out a finger to pet it between the eyes.

Calista coaxed it into the palm of her hand and offered it to Luxx. "We, uh, we met on my way back from Vulnari. The little stinker bounced off my windshield. I actually wanted to give it to you for solstice."

Luxx smiled broadly and widened her eyes as she whispered a heartfelt thank-you to Calista. "Go shower. You kind of smell bad. Plus, I want to bond with Amari."

Calista laughed and shook her head, then made her way to the shower in her private chambers, mumbling to herself.

"Wow, that was quick," Luxx said a short time later. Freshly showered and dressed in clothing more suited to her regular style, Calista sat with Luxx as they ate from a spread of fresh fruits, cured meats, and cheeses, along with copious amounts of wine.

Calista crossed her legs, allowing the slit of her skirt to fall to the side, revealing her leg and its newest decoration.

"Where did that come from?" Luxx asked as she ran a finger over the delicate chains.

"Just a solstice gift. Nothing special."

"Except that thigh bands usually suggest ownership of some kind. Who gave it to you?"

Calista pulled her leg back and covered her thigh band, smiling. "It's not important. What I would like to know is what got you so worked up that you thought it was a good idea to snatch a note from me, slam a door in my face, then ditch me for the last night I was in Vulnari without so much as clue as to what you were up to."

Luxx drained her glass of wine and refilled it before resigning herself to deal with the moment she had been dreading for so many years.

"Calista, I love you like a sister, and I respect that you never pressured me to reveal my past in any great detail, but being in Vulnari brought up elements of my life before I met you that there is no escaping from."

"You're a sister to me, and I never pressured you because when we met on the training ground, it was an opportunity to start a new life, and I didn't want to be part of the past that drove you away from your home by making you remember it or relive it."

"I know that, and you do know some of it, but there's more. Before we met I was involved with someone."

"The person who left you that note?"

"Yes." Luxx paused and drained her glass, then refilled it again.

"Did he try to hurt you?" Calista asked, her tone shifting into one of fierce protectiveness. Luxx shook her head.

"He's my mate."

CHAPTER 25
Return to Glass Island
Phoenix

"What more is there to discuss?" Phoenix asked as he closed his folio and leaned back in his chair. He and Calista had not had any in-person interactions since they parted ways after becoming bonded. They shared the odd message using their bond, but they were both kept fairly busy with their usual day-to-day tasks leading up to their monthly meeting. He missed her and was anticipating seeing her that day. However, she seemed distracted. Something was on her mind. Her body language gave it away, and even though she seemed calm as ever, something was there. He wondered for a moment if perhaps she was regretting bonding with him.

A young server approached with a tray of beverages for Phoenix and Calista and set it on the table before nodding respectfully at both of them and backing away through the curtain of the atrium.

"They always seem so nervous," Phoenix said, raising an eyebrow as he reached into the interior breast pocket of his jacket and pulled out the knife that Calista had given him for solstice. "Actually, you seem a little . . . I don't know, distracted. Is there something you want to tell me?" He decided to just put it out there. His feelings for her were continuing to deepen, and if she was having regrets, he wanted to know before it was too late, if it wasn't already.

"Who's nervous now?" Calista said through a laugh as she watched him stir the drink with the open blade, revealing that the beverage was not poisonous. Her light laugh was slightly strained, He knew she was teasing, but there was something else about the way she spoke that made him push a little more.

"Cheers." He raised his glass and winked as Calista did the same.

"This really does taste like when we were kids," he said as he drained the bubbly blue drink. "I haven't had one of these in ages."

"That's because you're paranoid. Wait, scratch that. A neurotically suspicious man who barely trusts himself," Calista said with a lightness that was tinged with truth. "You're right though," she continued. "There's nothing left to discuss. We'll start recruiting or at least advertising for more candidates for the Zenovia Army and see what happens," Calista said, concluding the official business of their meeting.

Phoenix reached across the table and laid his hand over hers as she fussed with the glass in front of her "There's something bothering you," he said. "What is it? I can't help but notice you've been distracted this whole meeting."

Calista sighed heavily and then lifted her gaze to meet his. "It's nothing, or maybe it's not. I'm not sure. Luxx shared something with me, and I'm not sure what to do with the information."

Her confession instantly set him on edge. "What did she say to you? How much does she know about us?" he asked, his instinct to protect Calista overriding every other thought and emotion.

Calista raised her hand and rubbed her forearm in the same spot where bonded messages appeared. "Relax. There's nothing to be angry about. It has nothing to do with us. She just has a life that I didn't know anything about."

Phoenix nodded as he measured her words and. "What makes you think I'm angry?"

Calista brushed away his comment with a shrug. "You just seem agitated, and I'm not sure, but I thought I felt my arm tingle like when I'm about to get a message from you. It's obviously nothing. I'm just thinking about everything and nothing."

Phoenix hesitated but then accepted her reasoning, resolving to talk to her about it later. At the moment, other matters demanded their attention.

"There is something else though," she said hesitantly. "Remember those keys?"

Phoenix nodded. "Yeah. I noticed you stopped wearing yours a while ago."

"That's because I can't find it. I took it off on the night of the banquet, and I thought I brought it back home with me, but I can't seem to find it anywhere. I wanted to compare the key to the maps we were using to locate the waterfall."

"That's strange."

"Where did you put the key we found in the cage?"

"I locked it in my safe. But now that you mention it, I need to check on that. That safe hasn't been working right since I put the key in there. The damn finger pad keeps heating up, and I'm almost positive I've heard things crashing in there."

"Crashing? What could you possibly have in there that could make a crashing noise? It's not like there are people in there," Calista scoffed, but the laugh died in her throat as she saw the expression on Phoenix's face. "Don't tell me your safe is big enough to hold people!" she exclaimed.

"Let's just say I use the term 'safe.' loosely. It's more of a secret chamber that has multiple purposes, and only I have access to it."

"What about Knoxx?"

"Nope."

"Hmm . . ." Calista said as she stood up, ready to leave. Phoenix followed her and pushed the curtain of the atrium aside, allowing Calista to pass through first. As she passed him, Phoenix placed the palm of his hand on the small of her back. He felt Calista lean into the heat of his hand as he made contact with her skin, and the light touch of his fingertips caused her to shiver and blush. He leaned in close, his lips brushing the shell of her ear.

"Come back with me," he whispered in an intoxicatingly low voice.

Calista turned her face toward him, her lips barely brushing his. He could see he was having an effect on her. She could feel the heat of his breath on her skin, and it was causing her to squirm and her breath to hitch in a way she couldn't seem to control.

"No one knows about us. What if we're seen?" Calista whispered as Phoenix ran his hand up the length of her back and toward the base of her head, where he gently tugged her hair, causing her to tilt her face upwards. He kissed her with a fierceness that defied her will to pull away. Calista melted into his embrace and allowed his tongue to caress hers in a slow, seductive way that caused her breath to catch in her throat. Finally, she forced herself to break away. "Nix, we shouldn't do this here."

"Why so shy?"

"I'm not shy, I just—no one knows about us."

"And what are we exactly?" He pulled away, clearly agitated

"I don't know, but I need time to find out—without an audience!" Calista fired back. "This time you come with *me* back to Cerulean."

"There's less than no privacy there."

"Privacy is not a luxury I can offer, but at least we won't be judged, and gods help me, I want you more than I can stand right now." The honesty in her words caught Phoenix off guard.

"If you want me so much, does it matter where we go?"

"I want you, all of you, but we need to do this carefully. Knoxx already suspects, and that man hates me. I don't want him to see us. I want to get Luxx on board with us. So come back with me."

"Lead the way, Queen." He planted another deep kiss on her and nodded.

They boarded a rickety fishing vessel back to East Marra. As helpful as ever, Calista assisted with the rigging while Phoenix lent his strength to shoving away from the dock. The fishermen on board regarded him politely if not a little reservedly.

"Why do they keep bowing and nodding to me?" Phoenix whispered once they were on route.

"They don't know how to act around you, so they're being formal. You being here with me helping is probably very strange to them, especially considering the pomp and circumstance that goes into setting up for one of your visits and making sure the dock is sturdy enough to hold your yacht." As if to prove her point, Calista approached one of the men, who was busy reeling in a fishing net, and started hauling alongside him. He smiled and accepted her help but not before assuring her that she need not get dirty doing such work. Calista glanced over her shoulder and gestured with a sharp nod that Phoenix should get his lazy ass over there and start helping.

Catching the hint, Phoenix removed his jacket, rolled up his shirtsleeves, and prepared to start hauling the ropes and nets. The sight of his shirt pulled tight across his chest caused a salacious smile to creep across Cali's face. Phoenix took note but dutifully helped drag the nets in, successfully keeping his hands to himself.

After they docked, Calista climbed into the all-terrain vehicle that was waiting for her, then leaned over and planted a chaste peck on Phoenix's cheek.

"What was that for?" he asked, brushing his sweat-dampened hair off his forehead. He looked like he just worked out.

"For helping," Calista replied.

"What do I have to do to get more than a peck on the cheek?" he murmured as he reached over the dividing console and planted an all-consuming kiss on Calista that he hoped would turn her insides into molten waves of anticipatory pleasure. Without thinking or caring who might catch a glimpse of them locked in the intimate moment, Calista ran her hand down the curves of his muscular chest, all the way to his belt buckle. She gave a sharp tug and was rewarded by Phoenix smiling against her lips.

"Frisky?" he asked.

Calista broke their kiss and composed herself as best as she could. The flush on her cheeks was all too satisfying for Phoenix to see. Knowing full well he was responsible for Cali's state of arousal, he settled back into his seat, though he left his hand resting on the slice of skin that the slit in her skirt revealed as she drove them back to Cerulean Palace.

When they arrived at the estate, Phoenix gathered his belongings and rounded the vehicle to stand beside Calista. He fought the overwhelmingly natural urge to reach for her hand and lead her through to her private terrace the way a pair of lovers might.

"You really don't care what your people see you do?" he asked as he followed her through the labyrinth of open-air halls and corridors that led them to her private suite of rooms. Although everyone and anyone was welcome to enter her suite, only very few people besides Luxx and the cleaning staff ever did.

"It's not that I don't care, but it's different here than when I'm in West Marra with you. There's so much surveillance everywhere, and those people always hanging around taking portraits with the flashing lights outside your place. I feel like I'm being watched, like I need to sneak around, and it's uncomfortable." Calista explained as she led the way deeper into the estate.

"The portrait people?" Phoenix muttered. "Oh, the photographers, yeah, they're annoying, but they're part of the security of Aterna. People assume that wherever they congregate, I must be there, or something is happening. They're useful to have around if I want to slip out of another exit unnoticed."

"That's just what I mean—so much secrecy and deception. Here there's none of that, but people do see things, and I don't want to fuel any gossip that could reach West Marra and, well, you." Calista pushed aside the curtains of her favourite terrace and, to her delight, found Luxx and someone else leaning on the balcony overlooking the landscape.

CHAPTER 26
Foursome
Calista

Calista and Phoenix exchanged the briefest of glances, indicating that neither of them knew who the large man standing beside Luxx was. Calista took a few steps closer to them and glanced over her shoulder toward Phoenix, gesturing with her eyes for him to walk with her and pleading with him to follow along with her half-baked plan to intrude on what looked like a very intimate conversation between Luxx and her mystery man. Luxx had her hand across his lower back, casually letting it drift to his gorgeous, toned backside.

In an exaggerated tone, Calista began speaking and widened her eyes at Phoenix as she spoke, urging him to follow her lead.

"The maps are down in the library," she said. "We can go find them after lunch."

"Yes, of course. Did you receive the ones I sent you?" Phoenix replied stiffly as he held his hands up in a "What did you expect?" kind of way. Their weird interaction was enough to announce their presence to the pair standing at the balcony.

"Hello, Calista," Luxx said, her voice tinged with amusement. She turned around, her companion following suit. They were smiling pleasantly and appeared very comfortable in each other's company. They were holding hands, and it did not escape Calista's notice that markings were peeking out on the back of his hand and up his arm that looked like his skin was embossed. It was like a tattoo but without colour.

Phoenix moved closer to Calista, positioning himself slightly ahead of her in a subtly protective stance, a gesture that didn't go unnoticed.

"Hello," Calista said. The awkwardness was tangible.

Unwilling to let the discomfort stretch out, Luxx stepped forward and bowed her head formally to Calista and Phoenix before making introductions. "Queen Calista, King Phoenix, it is my pleasure and honour for you to meet . . ." She paused and looked toward Lev before continuing. "Leviathan."

Lev stepped forward and kneeled before Calista and Phoenix, bowing his head. "It is my great honour to be presented before your majesties."

Luxx tapped Lev on the shoulder to indicate he needed to stand up. He turned his head to the side. "They must accept me first," he whispered.

Luxx looked at Calista and Phoenix and mouthed "I don't know" while shaking her head.

Phoenix cleared his throat and spoke with as much authority as he could summon under the strange circumstances of that meeting. "You may rise, good man." That did the trick, and Lev stood up, rejoining Luxx.

Calista stepped forward and extended her hand, smiling broadly. "It's a pleasure to meet you, Leviathan. In future you can call me Cali. We no longer observe such formalities in East Marra unless we're attending a formal occasion."

Lev nodded and nudged Luxx as if to say, "You could have said something earlier."

Phoenix also extended his hand and introduced himself. "Phoenix, Ruler of West Marra."

The awkwardness of the introductions began to dissipate as Calista guided them all toward the pillows placed around a low table in another area of the terrace. Once everyone was settled, Phoenix taking longer than everyone else, drinks were served.

"What are you doing?" Calista whispered to Phoenix, who looked very uncomfortable as he tried to find a dignified position to sit on the pillow.

"These pillows are weird, and my pants are too tight."

The four of them erupted into raucous laughter at Phoenix's expense. Then he finally let it go and relaxed, remembering that no one was watching or taking photos. The embarrassing moment would not be plastered across the daily news in West Marra. He laughed along with them and made a show of removing his belt and jacket, then sitting cross legged on the pillow. Lev, who was also wearing what looked like rather restrictive trousers, lifted the edge of his shirt to reveal that he too had undone the top button of his pants.

Lunch was a collection of finger foods, ranging from delicate sandwiches to more complicated confections and an arrangement of locally available fruits and vegetables. It was nothing as grand as what was on offer at a typical meal in West Marra, but it was delicious, nonetheless. Phoenix waited for everyone to serve themselves and take a bite of food before he attempted to do the same. Calista noticed but said nothing, realizing the depth of his mistrust. Food and wine eased the awkwardness of the situation considerably, and conversation began to flow more genuinely.

"I would love to say that I've heard wonderful things about you, Leviathan, but Luxx has been very reserved when it comes to her friends from the past." It was Calista's attempt to learn more about the man she now suspected was Luxx's mate.

"Please call me Lev, and while I realize you don't know much about me, I must thank you for everything you have done for my Ray." Lev glanced at Luxx and ran a finger down her cheek.

"Ray?" Phoenix asked as he flicked his gaze among the three of them.

"It's my nickname, Ray of Light, because of my hair," Luxx said shyly.

No one missed her uncharacteristic behaviour. She appeared softer and more content than Calista had ever seen her. It was profoundly affecting her own judgment on the situation she found herself in with Phoenix. She was feeling braver than she had ever felt about revealing their relationship, but she remained silent. The moment was not quite right. Not yet.

"I must be honest," Lev said. "I'm very unfamiliar with the customs of this place. Please accept my apologies for acting so formally before. Luxx and I have a history that is as dark as it is encouraging. I don't know what you know of our, well, Ray's past, but we are to remain together from now on. I hope these are terms that you can accept, Cali."

Calista remained silent for several moments, considering her response. Then she nodded. "Tell me more about yourself."

Lev cleared his throat and launched into the origins of his making. He revealed that he had met Luxx as an infant and that they became bonded by blood when her mother used Luxx's blood to pay the blood token to cross Siphon Lake. He also explained that his refusal to accept the token resulted in him being sentenced to become a falso-humanis gatekeeper. His blood bond with Luxx meant he was her protector under any circumstance. Invisible magical borders prevented him from leaving his land to go to her. As Luxx's life unfolded, she suffered, first at the hands of her mother and then at the hands of the renegades but never the man who led them. All the while Lev stood by. By the time Luxx had grown into a woman, she and

A World Divided

Lev recognized their bond ran deep, and they were, in fact, mates. When he and Luxx reconnected, Lev made his decision known to the counsel of water dragons and became fully mortal.

The decision to become mortal would have its consequences. Lev would age, suffer from illness, and eventually parish. Such consequences, however, do not outweigh the privilege and the overwhelming joy he felt to be with Luxx for as long as time would allow.

"That's quite the story." Phoenix, who had been listening quietly, appeared to be truly invested in Lev's life. "That scar over your eye," he said, nodding to it.

Lev reached his hand up to touch the faint line that was only visible because it parted the hair of his eyebrow. "This, oh, it's much better now. No matter displeased the counsel of water dragons was with my decision to renounce them, they still restored my vision in the eye that was destroyed, leaving me with this small scar as a reminder. Still, I have some unique abilities, including a heightened sense of vision and hearing, and I can smell things from a mile away."

Calista shifted uncomfortably for a moment as her gaze flicked to Luxx. A silent realization passed between them.

"If I may ask," Lev began, "what is the story between you two? How is it that you are opposing rulers who are known to despise one another, and yet your scents are mingled into a single aroma, a smell specific to a mated bond, no less?"

The air around them thickened with tension. Phoenix and Calista exchanged a loaded glance.

Calista turned to Luxx. "How long have you suspected?"

"I've suspected that you have been attracted to one another, but I wasn't sure until Lev confirmed it when he told me you were both on your way up to the terrace. I was explaining your love/hate dynamic when you arrived."

Phoenix's mind turned to brooding as he realized the others knew that he and Calista were bonded and could now be considered mates. "How many others will be able to detect our bond?" he asked Lev, his voice taking on an aggressive edge.

"Only me and perhaps some animals, but they generally can't speak, so unless I or present company share the information, your secret is safe."

"So it's true then." Luxx turned on Calista, her eyes wide. "Why didn't you tell me?" The pain in her expression tore a hole through Calista's heart.

"I wanted to tell you, but you and everyone else never missed a chance to remind me of how wrong it would be for us to be involved romantically." Calista moved toward Phoenix, who put his arm around her waist. He looked down at her and then looked up to address Luxx

"All our lives we have been coached to be wary of each other, to protect the interests of our respective lands and peoples. Yet, deep in the recesses of my soul, I've always felt an instinctive need to protect her."

Calista looked up at Phoenix as he spoke. He had never expressed himself in such a raw state of emotion. Stunned by his confession, she reached up to kiss him on the lips before pulling away. "I love you," she said in a breath that was softer than a whisper.

Phoenix brought her close and pressed his forehead to hers. Luxx and Lev looked on, touched by the pureness of the moment. The air around them was charged with the feeling that change was imminent. For the first time in living memory, the rulers of East and West Marra were bonded together as mates.

CHAPTER 27
The Safe
Phoenix

Phoenix returned to Aterna amidst a haze of emotions. Meeting Lev left him with an impression that he could not shake. He had a genuineness that gave Phoenix the confidence to trust him. This thought weighed heavily on him as he ruminated over the fallout he would have with Knoxx when he discovered that he and Calista were bonded—more than that, they were bonded mates.

Calista had been a bright spot in his life ever since they were children despite the fact that they had been coached to show pleasantries when being watched and to despise each other privately.

Phoenix found his way to his study where he poured himself a glass of whisky neat and then settled into the plush sofa facing a floor-to-ceiling window that overlooked the lush gardens. He ruminated for a few moments about his past and how Calista had always been a wonder to him. There was a feeling that ran deeper than trust, deeper than love, an intrinsic connection they shared that could only have been bestowed upon them by the Goddess. Only now did he realize that the comfort he had been seeking was Calista. Now more than ever, he wanted to preserve that feeling and figure out what was going on under his nose. No doubt more deception from Knoxx.

Phoenix set the glass of whisky on the floor beside the sofa and, with tendrils of memory guiding his thoughts, made his way to the safe, which was located in the back sitting room of his suite. He placed a palm on the scanner and leaned in for the retina scanner to confirm his identity. The door of the wall safe, which was as large as a regular door, swung open, accompanied by a feminine digital voice. "Access granted."

Phoenix scanned the objects on the shelves to the left and right, noting the usual items—heirloom jewels, money, and some select family photos he kept away from the prying eyes of those who wandered the halls of Aterna Estate. There was a photo of Calista as a young girl as well.

Phoenix had the key he found in the cage of the fountain tucked away in a corner of the top shelf. He took it down and inspected it. It seemed like a regular key, cool to the touch. He pocketed the key and then turned his attention to the other door. The back wall had another scanning pad that required both hands to gain access. After following the procedure, the door popped open, and it took some force to push out of the way. Behind the door was a wide hallway dimly lit by pot lights in the ceiling that were motion activated, turning on when he stepped within range and going out when he left. Lining the hallway were big, heavy metal-enforced doors. There were six cells, three on each side of the hall. Each door was solid except for a small opening at the bottom that could be opened by sliding the cover to the side and scanning the food trays assigned to that cell. There were no locks on the doors, only digital trackpads, so that only Phoenix could access them. He had made that adjustment when he became King of West Marra.

Just as he was about to leave the depressing dungeon, he heard a dull thudding sound coming from the last cell on the left. He approached cautiously and waited, listening for the sound again. *Thump! Thud!* it sounded as if a man was groaning.

There can't be anyone in here, Phoenix thought. *These cells haven't been used in years.* Hearing the thudding noise again, he approached the trackpad mounted in the centre of the door and scanned his left index finger. The door hissed and popped outward, allowing him to swing it out into the hallway and peer inside the room. The single dim pot light outside the cell provided enough light for Phoenix to see that a man was inside the cell. He was shirtless, and his pants were hanging loosely off his hips. His feet were bare, and he was filthy. He reeked of human waste and appeared to have it smeared all over his lanky, sickly body.

The moment the door opened, the man backed away, cowering in the corner of the cell. "Knoxx?" he rasped, followed by shallow, laboured breathing.

"Knoxx put you here?" Phoenix had barely asked the question when the man began slamming the back of his head against the wall.

Phoenix rushed into the putrid cell to stop the man from injuring himself but stopped short when the man took a run at the opposite wall and rammed his head into it. There was a sickening crunch, and the man staggered back, falling into a heap on the floor, blood draining from his ears and nose at an alarming rate.

Phoenix watched for several long moments, stunned at what he had just witnessed. He leaned forward to place two fingers at the man's neck and found no pulse.

Shocked by this morbid discovery, Phoenix closed the door and left. He shut the safe and sent Calista a message through their bond, telling her to bring Luxx and Lev.

CHAPTER 27
Teamwork

Phoenix

Phoenix met Calista, Luxx, and Lev in a popular social district near the bank of the Marra. He had been flying under the radar for some time, but Calista arriving in West Marra with company would start the rumour and conspiracy mill churning. He planned on using it as a diversion that would hopefully keep Knoxx busy enough to stay out of his way for a while. The photo opportunity would fuel gossip and create some chatter that would keep his people busy with speculation while he got down to the business of finding the other key and making his way to that damn waterfall.

As he waited on the dock, people all around him were bustling about. He took special notice of a family greeting each other with the customary touch of the forehead. The thought crossed his mind, and not for the first time, that this was never a custom he practiced in his own family or with close friends except for Calista. It did not escape his notice that Calista and Luxx greeted each other that way, and it seemed very natural.

As the three of them disembarked from the fishing vessel that had carried them across the Marra on short notice, Phoenix handed the vessel's captain a hefty package.

"What was that?" Calista asked as she watched the man open the large bag and smile before thanking Phoenix profusely.

"Just some practical things I thought might be useful and a little snack," he replied with a wink.

Calista looked over her shoulder as the man pulled out several pairs of heavy-duty gloves, a sturdy, non-digitized fishing net, and several bottles of wine. Acutely aware of her surroundings, Calista thanked Phoenix politely and resolved to *really* thank him with appropriate enthusiasm later.

The four of them climbed into Phoenix's large vehicle and made their way to Aterna in relative privacy, thanks to the tinted windows.

"I want one of these," Lev declared as they drove through the streets of the capital.

"You know how to drive?" Luxx asked.

"Drive, yeah sure. I'll figure it out," Lev said with a confidence that set the four of them laughing.

"I'll have the ATVs set up, and we can take a spin," Phoenix offered. The mood among the four of them was comfortable. Phoenix hated to end it by recounting the gruesome scene he had just witnessed.

Calista reached over and placed a hand on Phoenix's leg while they were stopped. His leg was bouncing and jittering enough to draw her attention. "Why did you need all of us here so urgently?" she prompted.

"I was in an area of the estate that I thought only I had access to," he said. "It's a secure holding area. I found a renegade locked in there. He looked like he had been there for a while. When I opened the door, he called out for Knoxx and then rammed his head into the wall and killed himself."

The silence among them was papabile. Phoenix realized his choice to trust them with this information could be damaging for him and his people, but it was no worse than the damage someone like Knoxx could cause with all the privileged information he had and all the secrets he'd been keeping. Knoxx couldn't be trusted. Big changes were on the horizon.

"I know none of you have anything to do with this mess," Phoenix continued, "but without a trusted advisor, I need the help of people I can trust. I've seen a little of how Cali and Luxx operate as a team, and now that Calista and I are bonded, I hope that I can trust you the same way." Phoenix's revelation of his trust in them was the most vulnerable he had ever allowed himself to be with anyone other than Calista. Anxiety churned in his gut as he hoped they would not reject him.

"Have you spoken to Knoxx yet?" Luxx asked, the edge in her voice indicating she was already plotting her attack plan, should one become necessary.

"No, not yet. There have been other incidents where I've found out after the fact that he has been keeping things from me. I've been cautious around him since the—well, since the explosion."

"Yes, I remember," Calista said, looking straight ahead.

"Knoxx knows nothing about . . ."

"He doesn't know about us," Calista said.

Phoenix nodded. "He suspects it, but I've never confirmed anything, and I don't want to. I can't trust him like I used to. I won't put you—any of you—at risk.

"Lev, I know we don't know each other well, but you were able to pick up that mine and Cali's scents were mingled from a distance. I need you to come with me to the cell and tell me if you pick up on anything," Phoenix said as he pulled the vehicle into the cavernous garage.

"OK," Lev replied.

"We can discuss compensation later "

"Compensation? What for?" Lev looked to Luxx for an explanation.

"Not many people have your abilities, and typically using them at someone else's request means they will pay you for it," Phoenix said.

"Phoenix, Your Highness, sir, no compensation is needed. If what I can do will help, that's enough for me."

The corner of Phoenix's mouth lifted slightly. He glanced at Calista before looking in his rear-view mirror at Lev. "Call me Nix."

CHAPTER 28
The Cell

Phoenix

Phoenix led Lev to the room containing the safe. Lev remained observant, his eyes taking in everything around him. Occasionally, he would inhale deeply as if he could sense something dangerous in the air. His large form was intimidating to behold. Standing only a few inches taller than Phoenix at six feet four inches, he was broader and definitely strong. Phoenix couldn't help but feel like Lev had a natural protective skill perhaps a ruminant of his centuries spent as a water dragon, that his bodyguards would benefit from if Lev were to train them.

"How many people have access to these rooms?" Lev asked as he walked around the sitting room and observed the door to the safe.

"Hardly anyone. The cleaning staff, me, and Knoxx but rarely," Phoenix said as he unlocked the safe.

"There are several scent tags in here. One smells like shit. It's strong. The other ones are male." He inhaled the air. "Human. And if I'm not mistaken, very recent, within days."

Phoenix opened the door to the safe and nodded for Lev to follow him inside. "The source of the shit smell will become obvious in a second," Phoenix said. "The other smells are probably my staff"

"Are your staff allowed inside the safe?"

Phoenix shot a glance at Lev, a sickening wave of comprehension washing over him. His suspicions about Knoxx having gained access to his safe were likely true. *What the fuck else is that bastard keeping from me?* Knoxx's secretive behaviours were increasingly annoying, and they needed to end.

"No one should have access beyond this door besides me."

Lev raised his scarred eyebrow. "Well, let's see what that smell is. It's disgusting."

Phoenix opened the cell door and revealed the man, who was covered in human waste and blood. Phoenix pulled his shirt up to cover his mouth and nose as Lev did the same. The smell had become even more rank in the few hours it had taken Lev and the others to arrive from East Marra.

"What fresh hell is this?" Lev asked as he inspected the heap on the floor from as close a distance as he could stand.

"He took a run at the wall, and I'm positive the crunching sound was his neck breaking. I have no idea how long he's been in here."

"You didn't put him in here?"

"No. For a few weeks I had been hearing weird noises, I just attributed it to staff moving around more than usual since the riot, but I never expected anyone would be in here because I refused to put anyone in here and no one except myself should have access." Phoenix backed away from the door to get some fresher air. "I know all too well what it's like to be in here. I can be cruel, but I'm not *this* cruel, to leave a man in here covered in his own mess."

Lev bent closer to the man for a moment before backing out of the cell. "He's a renegade. I recognize him. He was always causing crap up in Vulnari, chanting about the true King. If I'm being honest, I thought he was talking about you."

"I rarely go up to Vulnari. Knoxx takes care of all my business up there."

Lev and Phoenix exchanged a knowing look, the same thought occurring to both of them.

"Go meet the girls," Phoenix said. "They're in the library. I have to meet with my advisor."

Lev and Phoenix left the safe, Phoenix locking it behind them.

"Do you want a witness?" Lev asked tentatively. Phoenix dropped his head, humbled by the offer and sensing the sincerity of it.

"No. Thank you though. I can handle Knoxx."

Lev nodded and then made his way to the library, fumbling his way through the foreign halls of the grand estate.

CHAPTER 29
Catch up
Calista

Upon their arrival at Phoenix's estate, Calista and Luxx went straight to the library.

"Daisy, nice to see you here. What are you studying?" Calista asked as they entered the vaulted room, which was filled to bursting with books.

"Actually, I was just browsing the shelves here while I waited for . . . never mind," she said shyly.

"Who are you waiting for, Daisy?" Luxx prompted. "Don't be shy."

Daisy blushed, barely able to contain her excitement. "I'm waiting for Knoxx. We're kinda sort of together now."

Luxx raised an eyebrow at Calista, whose face was registering the same level of shock. Calista knew Daisy to be a sweet, smart, and very capable young lady, but clearly, growing up in West Marra had not taught her anything when it came to discerning between true romantic feelings and when she was being taken advantage of.

Daisy directed them toward the maps that were still spread out on the table in an effort to shift their attention away from her and Knoxx's relationship.

"These are interesting," Daisy said. "I've never seen such a complete version of LaMarra before. And here." She pointed to the base of Siphon Lake. "Some seriously rare plants grow there, and it looks like they knew about it even in ancient times."

Luxx and Calista exchanged a knowing look. Daisy has been studying the maps more acutely than anyone. Perhaps she knew more about the significance of the waterfall. Calista also thought Daisy could be a valuable asset as a healer if she chose to travel with them to the waterfall.

"You've been keeping busy since the Zenovia Ceremony," Luxx said, smiling.

Daisy nodded. "Yes. I started with the herbal tinctures and medicines, but recently I've discovered that there are absurdly strong healing properties associated with metal objects. I haven't figured out their connection yet, but I'm hoping to learn something when I visit the archives later today."

"Ah, well, please share your findings with us," Calista said. "I would be very interested."

"Absolutely. Of course I will," Daisy responded brightly.

"Daisy, how would you feel about maybe becoming a healer exclusive to the royals?" Calista asked. "That is, to me and King Phoenix?"

Daisy's jaw dropped as she absorbed the weight of the request. She blinked away her shock before she replied. "That is quite the honour, but I'm hardly as experienced as the centenary healers. Do you really think I could be of any use to you?"

"Daisy, you are smart, young, and capable. I'm sure you would be an asset to the royals. Plus, I think you would have an easier time keeping up with us on our travels than a centenary," Calista said, hoping to convince her to join her company and also to create distance between her and Knoxx. It was no secret that Calista disliked him, but those feelings ran far deeper now that she knew how little Phoenix trusted him.

Daisy smiled, clearly happy to be welcomed into Calista's inner circle. "I would be honoured. I can hardly believe it."

Calista smiled, pleased with her enthusiasm. Now would be a good time to bring Daisy up to speed on what they were doing. Maybe she could join them the next time they set out for the waterfall. Calista sent Luxx a quick glance, hoping she was picking up on her plan to bring Daisy along and to keep her as far away from Knoxx as possible.

"So far, Luxx, Phoenix, and I have noticed that there is a waterfall on every map, both ancient and relatively recent. There is also an image of a key on each map, but we haven't figured out the significance of that yet. It's interesting that you mentioned metals with healing properties. That could be something." Calista hesitated before continuing. "A while ago I was wearing a key as a piece of jewellery. As it turns out, Phoenix had a similar key on display in one of his fountains. I've since misplaced mine, but we think there is magic in those keys. They give off a hum of power, but we don't know much else about them. Do you think you can search the archives to see what these keys mean and why we don't know anything about them?"

Daisy drew her eyebrows together as she looked more closely at the maps, then nodded. "Hmm . . . yes, I see the keys. I'll look into it and let you know what I find."

"We'll probably be heading out to the waterfall today, if not tomorrow," Calista said with the faint hope Daisy would join them from the start.

"OK. I'll collect whatever information I can from the archives and will ask Knoxx to come with me to meet you. He's so smart, and he knows Gold Leaf Forest well, so I'm sure he'll have no trouble finding you guys." Daisy blushed, obviously smitten with Knoxx. Calista couldn't stand the sinking feeling in her gut. Daisy was too good for him.

Daisy looked at her watch and then jumped when she realized the time. "I'd better get going. He should be back by now, and he'll take me to the archives. I can't wait to tell him you've taken me on as your royal healer." With a bright smile that was filled with excitement, she disappeared down the hall toward Knoxx's private quarters.

Once they were alone in the library, Calista and Luxx exchanged a concerned look over Daisy's relationship with Knoxx, not that there was much they could do about it at the moment. Instead, they returned their attention to the maps, trying to figure out the significance of the waterfall and the best way to get there.

While examining various routes, their conversation turned toward the logistics of travelling together and how their group dynamics had evolved.

"Do you love him?" Luxx asked out of nowhere.

"What does that have to do with the maps, Luxx? What are you getting at?"

"Nothing. I just want to know. Phoenix is your bonded mate. I know what that feels like, and I can't imagine ever being without Lev again. Do you feel that way about Phoenix?"

Calista was silent for a time as she picked at a corner of the map. "I was never supposed to even like him. He represented everything I was told was wrong with the world. Yet I've known ever since we were kids that there was something about him that wasn't all that bad. Love doesn't even scratch the surface of what I feel for him. It's so much more than that."

Luxx smiled and wrapped her arm around Calista's shoulders, pulling her into a tight one-armed hug. "I couldn't have described it better myself. You two are just better together."

CHAPTER 30
Confrontational Truths

Knoxx

Knoxx shrugged out of his soiled and stinking clothing as he prepared to take a shower. *I'll check on the prisoner before I head out with Daisy,* he thought as he stood under the hot, luxurious spray. *I need to see what nonsense she's up to. That girl knows too much for her own good. She's obsessed with me though, so it will be easy enough to get her to tell me what she knows.*

When he was finished, he wrapped a towel around his waist, only to hear a gentle knock on the door.

"Damn it. Who the fuck—Daisy," he grunted as he yanked open the door.

Knoxx arranged his features into a mask of pleasant surprise as he opened the door, then yanked her inside with a firm grip on her upper arm.

"Hey, I got lonely waiting for you in the library," Daisy said, smiling as she took in his half-naked, freshly showered presence with great appreciation.

Knoxx leaned down to give her a quick peck on the cheek. "I'm almost ready. Then we'll head out to the archives."

He disappeared into his dressing room, Daisy following. She leaned against the dressing table as she watched him drop the towel and reach for a fresh suit.

"What's the hurry?" she asked shyly. She wore her emotions on her sleeve for all to see, so innocent. Knoxx does not miss it. He seized the opportunity to rope her deeper into her fantasy about her bad boy. *She has no idea the evil I'm capable of, but she will,* he thought. *I just need her to behave a little while longer.*

He turned to face her, oozing charm and feeding into her lustful imagination, not bothering to hide his naked form. As he approached Daisy, he realized she was blushing. She was so innocent, a virgin before Knoxx took an interest in her. He slipped his hands around her waist and gave her backside a playful if not slightly forceful smack. He encouraged her to stand on her toes, so he could kiss her deeply. A few weeks earlier she had been shy under such circumstances. Not so much now. He knew she trusted him completely. It was too easy for him. He had her swooning and warming his bed within hours of showing some interest in her. *Heartbreak is a part of life. She'll get over it,* he thought as he took a moment to unbutton her pants and push them down her hips, so he could have access to the warmth pooling between her thighs.

He broke their kiss but kept his mouth close to hers. "Always ready. Hmm . . . slick," he said in a low, rough tone. Daisy's breath hitched, and a moan escaped her throat as Knoxx teased her and then slid a finger into her and massaged her wanton flesh.

She strained her hips against his body as he continued his slow exploration of her insides. He dragged his finger out of her warmth and left her wanting as he pulled away from her and resumed getting dressed.

"Later," he said with a wink.

Daisy hardly had a chance to recover when a loud, urgent knock echoed through the room. Without a moment's consideration,

Knoxx shoved Daisy into his closet, then put a finger to his lips, motioning for her to stay quiet while he answered the door. Knoxx snatched a robe from a hook and then went to answer the door.

Phoenix's voice immediately filled the room. "Explain, now," he said with an edge that signalled to Knoxx that Phoenix had found the prisoner. "Tell me, why is there a man covered in shit and blood in the cells of my *private* safe?" Phoenix asked.

Knoxx pinched the bridge of his nose between his thumb and index finger and cursed under his breath. "Nix, can't this wait? I didn't even know you had returned."

In reply, Phoenix slammed his fist into the centre of Knoxx's chest, causing his Aquavass to fall off his neck. "Fuck no! This can't wait!" Phoenix shouted as he pushed his way into the room, forcing Knoxx back a few steps.

Knoxx was taken aback by the physical assault, the wheels in his head spinning wildly as he raced to come up with a story that would calm Phoenix down and buy him time.

"I didn't want you to find out this way," Knoxx began.

"Nope, try again," Phoenix said through gritted teeth.

Knoxx straightened his stance, squared his shoulders, and stood to his full height, toe to toe with Phoenix. The men were of a similar build, strong, tall, and muscular. Knoxx's chest tattoos were visible beyond the lapels of his robe, and his muscles were flexing. Phoenix took notice, realizing the conversation could come to blows at any moment.

"Phoenix, I was doing my job, protecting you."

"What threat would cause you to break into my private safe and leave a man in the cells to rot?"

Knoxx decided that sticking to his story was the best course of action. "During the commotion of the riot some rebels were wandering around. I didn't know where to put them. Before the security breach was fixed, I came across the cells behind the safe, so I shoved him in there as well as a few others. The one you found was particularly violent, so I left him in there to settle down after I released the others."

"He's dead, covered in shit, puke, blood, and everything else," Phoenix said, not allowing a stitch of emotion to bleed through his voice. "Fuck, Knoxx, the riot was months ago. Why didn't you tell me you had access to my safe?"

"I didn't want you to know. I was going to get rid of him before you found out anyone was in there."

Phoenix paced around the room, scrubbing his hand down his face and scratching at the short facial hair that he couldn't be bothered to shave. "I don't even know where to start," he said, frustration lacing his voice as he looked around the room. He didn't go into Knoxx's room often, but he took a cue from Lev, taking in every detail as discreetly as possible. His eyes landed on Knoxx's bar cart in the far corner of the room.

"Here, boss, let me get you a drink, and we can talk this over," Knoxx said, but he was stopped dead in his tracks when Phoenix raised a hand and picked up what was unmistakably the key that Calista had lost.

Phoenix held out the key so that it dangled from his index finger on the delicate chain that Calista used to wear the key around her neck. "Where did this come from?"

Knoxx was about to answer when Phoenix cut him off midsentence. If there was ever a time to pull rank, this was it. He was fed up with the lies, the deception, and everything else. "Never mind. I'll decide what to do with you later. Your behaviour will not go unpunished, even if you are my advisor. I am still your King, and you will do as I say."

The icy, authoritative tone that came over Phoenix was enough to silence Knoxx into momentary submission.

"Get rid of the body now. And clean the cell. I'll be recalibrating the security codes. You will be able to get out but not get back in. I am also revoking your master security clearance. You will have limited access to the main house, to the fleet of security vehicles, and your private chambers but nothing else."

With those words, Phoenix left Knoxx standing there, slightly stunned, slamming the door behind him.

Daisy peeked out of the closet as Knoxx approached her, his expression as hard as stone.

"What did you hear?" he asked, his eyes boring into hers.

"His Majesty sounded upset. I did what you wanted and stayed quiet," she said meekly.

"Well, now you know what the King is really like. I do my job to protect him and advise him. The spoiled, ungrateful brat that he is. Keep this to yourself if you know what's good for you."

Daisy nodded, her eyes wide, Knoxx disappeared into his dressing room and quickly put on a sharp-looking charcoal suit and crisp white shirt. He opted to leave the shirt opened to reveal the crest of his chest, which showed the hint of his tattoos.

"I thought you had to go clean up a . . . body." She hesitated on that last word.

"That's what the maids are for. I have a date with you and the archives."

Acutely aware that the dynamics of the situation were changing, Daisy remained silent and went along with Knoxx to the archives. Ultimately, knowledge is power, and that fact was never more important than it was at that moment.

CHAPTER 31
New Information
Phoenix

Phoenix quietly opened the double doors that led to the main chamber of the library. The beautifully vaulted ceilings created an echo that gave away his attempt at a stealthy entrance. He approached Calista as she turned to face him. He swept her hair over her shoulder as he clasped the necklace around her neck and arranged the key neatly on her chest in the void of space between her chin and the deep V of her Aquavass necklace.

"Where did you find it?" she asked as she held the key in her fist. She noticed it was warm, unusually so even though it had been in Phoenix's pocket.

"I found it in Knoxx's room," was all he supplied as an answer. He caught Lev's eye at the mention of Knoxx and, with a subtle nod, indicated that he would fill in the details later.

Calista launched into what she and Luxx had been discussing regarding the maps and their invitation to Daisy to be the royal healer, so she could travel with them.

"It's becoming very clear that we need to head out there," Luxx declared. "We need boots on the ground to see what's going on."

"Well, we sort of tried that, but it got a little derailed," Calista said, smirking in Phoenix's direction as she hinted at a private moment of deep significance between them. "Daisy mentioned she would be heading to the archives today. She also said something about metals having healing properties. I've asked her to let us know what she finds."

Calista straightened up from the table to peer into Phoenix's face. He appeared preoccupied, enough to cause her to question him. "What happened?" she asked.

"I need to recalibrate the security controls. I'll tell you after that. You can't trust anything around here," he said in a deflated tone. "Speaking of which, Knoxx isn't to be trusted with any sensitive information."

"Fine with me! He's a douchebag!"

Lev leaned in toward Luxx. "No, Knoxx is that bald guy, the advisor or whoever."

Luxx turned to face Lev, unable to contain her laughter. "I know who he is," she explained gently after taking a moment to compose herself. "A douchebag is an insult. It means he's a mean, nasty, deceitful person."

Lev blushed in embarrassment; however, the moment struck Phoenix deeply. The openness between them, the levity over a simple misunderstanding . . . he couldn't help but wonder if that was what it was like to be among loving and affectionate members of a family.

Phoenix looked over the map, taking in the separate versions of East and West Marra and the etching that Calista made of the map in the cave at Vulnari that showed the two lands united by a what he assumed was a large bridge over the River Marra and, of course, the waterfall. He sighed. "Let's gather some supplies and then head out to that waterfall."

All eyes turned to him. The air became charged with excitement and a feeling of something big about to happen. For the first time

A World Divided

in living history, the rulers of East Marra and West Marra would be working together to restore LaMarra to its original glory. Truths were going to be discovered.

After some preliminary planning, it was decided that Luxx and Calista would head back to East Marra to prepare for their journey through Gold Leaf Forest and on toward the base of the waterfall. It was decided that Lev would remain in West Marra to assist Phoenix. Phoenix supplied him with a set of battle leathers and some lessons on how to drive the ATV. Lev's senses were remarkable. His internal compass was spot on, and his hearing and sense of smell would be incredible assets—once his hand-eye coordination on the ATV caught up, of course.

"The girls know how to drive those things?" Lev asked over dinner as he and Phoenix ate an absurdly large amount of food. Phoenix was always hospitable, but having learned the details of Lev's origins, he pulled out all the stops and had a spread of food laid out for them it was truly outstanding. Lev's honest and gracious nature was so out of place in West Marra, and Phoenix felt it was his responsibility to protect him from the corruption that had corroded his land and his people.

Calista and Luxx joined Phoenix and Lev early the next morning when they set out. The drive to the edge of Gold Leaf Forest was short and pleasant. It only took a few minutes to unload the four ATVs. The foursome donned their helmets, battle leathers, and survival packs before departing with Phoenix in the lead, Calista and Luxx following, and Lev bringing up the rear.

By midday they stopped for lunch and to consult the etched map as well as the more detailed map of West Marra.

"What's so important about the waterfall?" Luxx inquired as she munched on an apple and plucked a piece off to feed to Amari. Luxx kept the little Savarra nearby all the time. Its skin was becoming a bright shade of purple with the ridges on its back taking on a slightly golden tinge. He ate the apple with a ferocity that nearly took off the tip of Luxx's finger.

"We should make the water's edge by nightfall," Phoenix announced as he stroked one finger along Amari's head and chewed a massive chunk of rosemary-and-garlic bread.

"Lev, you lived for centuries as a water dragon. Is there anything you know about the waterfall?" Calista asked as she drained the last of her water canteen.

"Well, there are legends, but as water dragons we patrolled Siphon Lake and collected blood tokens. We saw prisoners come and go. Speaking of which, Knoxx was responsible for collecting a good many of the ones released during my time as gatekeeper."

"Not surprising," Phoenix said, raising an eyebrow and shaking his head.

"I can tell you that the water dragons stay in Siphon Lake by preference. The legend states that the waterfall contains a magical border that can't be crossed by magical beast or man, but it's not true. At the time of the fall, the most ancient water dragons descended the waterfall and populated the River Marra. Some did battle with other magical creatures and bear the scars even now.

"The legend also mentions an immortal ancient beast known by many names over the ages. We called him Lusca, he lies in wait at the bottom of rivers and reveals himself in a variety of forms but usually with large tentacles in the hour of need to help the righteous claim victory—but not without securing payment, and for that, anything goes. It could be a life, a sum of money, or a precious element, anything. He's as helpful as he is vengeful.

"The legend also speaks of a deep-sea beast that drags humans of base moral characteristics to their watery demise. That's probably a myth though."

Lev's version of events caused a newfound weight to settle over them. Calista, who had been listening intently, couldn't help but speak up. "That's very interesting. None of this ever came up in my studies. Why would these legends be ignored?"

Phoenix confirmed that he had never learned anything about those stories either. In fact nothing about the fall was ever really detailed, other than it had happened because of a war between the two originating Queens and their different views on the chaos of magic.

"That's a lot to consider," Luxx murmured as she absentmindedly stroked the top of Amari's head.

"These waters are full of water creatures," Lev continued, "most of them dormant since the development of West Marra and the fall. No one has seen or heard from these beasts. There was a time though when some of them were a real problem."

"What kind of problem?" Phoenix prodded, needing to know exactly what he was getting into and making a mental note to ask Daisy about the creatures when he saw her.

"People would go missing often enough. The Rusalkas were usually to blame. Occasionally, when the people got spooked, a sacrificial offering was presented to the Goddess Marra to appease all the water creatures, both known and unknown."

"Wild times," Luxx said dryly. She placed Amari on a flat stone, then packed up to continue their trek. Lev poured some water over Amari's back and watched him frolic a little until the little Savarra began to go rigid, and the purple scales and skin on his back began to split, revealing gold skin shining beneath. They gathered around the little creature and watched as an aura began to build around his changing form.

"What kind of Savarra did you say this was, Cali?" Luxx asked, her eyes fixed on the small creature.

"I thought it was a little purple one," Calista replied, bewildered at what was unfolding before her.

"This is a Gold Savarra," Lev said, his voice full of wonder.

Phoenix approached the Savarra in complete awe of what was happening. "The prophetic kind . . ."

CHAPTER 32
The Prophecy
Phoenix

The aura surrounding the Savarra grew and became brighter and brighter as it stirred up the wind, which carried the golden leaves in swirls around the little creature. The aura expanded into an orb of translucent mist so large that it crested the tops of the trees.

The mist within the orb began to shift and form images. There was a vision of a large structure, tall and perched on a bridge made of arches. There were people . . . a family perhaps, standing before a crowd of other people. Below the castle were waves, large tumultuous swells crashing against the base of the bridge's arches, the arms of a strange beast poking through the surface. As suddenly as the images appeared, a whirlwind of leaves and smoke whipped the images into a frenzy, and the orb vanished, leaving in its wake the four of them stunned and staring at the clueless little Savarra, who stood there blinking up at them.

"Um . . . Amari?" Luxx leaned forward to tentatively touch her little pet. He crawled into the palm of her hand in his golden form and licked her as if nothing had happened.

"What did we just see?" Phoenix asked, wondering if everyone had seen the same thing. His sense of paranoia getting the better of him, he corralled everyone into motion and instructed them to follow him. His cabin was the only place he could be sure that no one would be listening in on them.

"Follow me," he said in a clipped tone. Everyone mounted their ATVs and followed without hesitation.

Within a half hour they were pulling up to the quaint little cabin that Phoenix had built. He and Calista exchanged knowing looks while Lev examined the cabin's structural integrity. Luxx was cradling Amari, still a little shocked that her little pet was a rare prophetic Savarra.

As everyone settled into the cabin, Lev explored the kitchen, pointing to the wood-burning stove. "This thing work?" Lev asked as he examined the cooking surface.

"Yeah, of course," Phoenix replied. He unloaded his bag, pulling out plates, glasses, cutlery, and cookware along with a small bag of dry foods. He even brought out a small stovetop espresso pot. Upon seeing the fancy coffee pot, Calista rolled her eyes in amusement.

"I see you came prepared this time."

"I did," Phoenix admitted through a smile. "We'll have more than almond butter and jam on crackers with wine this time."

Overhearing the pair, Luxx's ears perked up. "That sounds like a good snack."

"I'll put some coffee on," Phoenix announced as the others made themselves comfortable in the living room. Lev took it upon himself to start a roaring fire in the fireplace.

While the coffee brewed, Calista poked around in the cupboards and located the wine. She happily poured herself and Luxx a glass, in proper wine glasses this time, then offered some to Lev and Phoenix. Phoenix declined, Lev raised an eyebrow skeptically, unsure he would like the drink.

"Well, I can say with all honesty I never in my life thought I would be lucky enough to see a gold Savarra," Luxx said, still in awe of her pet. She sipped her wine and then passed the glass to Lev, who took a giant sip and then immediately started gagging and spluttering.

"What is this? Why does it burn?" he choked out, wiping the back of his hand across his mouth.

Luxx and Calista couldn't contain their laughter

"It's wine, basically aged grape juice," Calista explained.

"Who the hell drinks old grape juice? And why is it spicy?" Lev said with disgust as he moved toward the kitchen where Phoenix was pouring himself a ridiculously small cup of espresso.

"Hand me one of those," Lev said, pointing to Phoenix's coffee.

"Here you go," Phoenix said, an edge of humour in his tone as he handed Lev a small cup.

Lev took a sip and then shot Phoenix a look of pure contempt and disgust as he placed the cup on the counter. He continued scowling and muttered loud enough to be herd "I was a water dragon we drank water, not spicy water or tar water what's wrong with simple herb water?" as he reached for the kettle of hot water, then searched in his own pack for a sachet of herbal tea and poured himself a cup. "You can all keep your stupid spicy grape juice and tar coffee. I'll stick with my own drinks, thank you," he mumbled as he took up a space beside Luxx on the sofa. The four of them started discussing and analyzing the prophecy while reassessing their expedition to the waterfall.

"We can't be too careful," Phoenix cautioned. "We aren't certain anyone else saw the prophecy."

Calista pulled out the maps and spread them on the table. She labelled the etched map "Past" and the map of West Marra "Present."

"The structure isn't represented in either of these maps," she said, "which means it had either been destroyed or it hadn't been constructed yet. And the arches of the bridge it was on . . . hmm." She studied the maps and then pointed to the aqueduct system outlined on the West Marra map. "It could be here," she said, pointing.

Lev leaned forward and examined the map. "No, they're too weak and too recent. There's no way they could support a structure like the one we saw"

"Maybe that's just it," Luxx chimed in. "We need to do something to strengthen the aqueducts to support the castle, and we need to build it."

Phoenix contemplated Luxx's reasoning for a while before shaking his head. Deep down, something was nagging on him. He turned his attention to the etched map. "Look here." He pointed to the line representing a bridge over what they assumed was the River Marra. "What if this is where those arches were, and the water beneath is the River Marra?"

Calista zeroed in on the map, continuing his thought. "That makes sense. The water crashing may have destroyed it, or maybe whatever beast we saw in the water is responsible. Maybe this is a prophecy showing us the past rather than the future."

"The sea creature fits the legend of Lusca," Lev interjected, "A beast that has not been seen since ancient times."

"What are the chances this is a prophecy that is set to happen in the near future?" Phoenix wondered aloud. He was met with silence as they all considered what should happen next.

Calista looked to Luxx. "I wonder if Daisy has come across any of this. I hope she joins us soon."

CHAPTER 33
Life Interrupted
Knoxx

Daisy selected several volumes from the shelves at the archives as Knoxx sat at the table brooding. She pored over the various articles and manuscripts that detailed all manner of magical elements associated with metals. One article caught her eye. It included a drawing of what she recognized as the key that Calista showed her on the maps.

"Knoxx, come look at this," she said, remaining focused on the image and information in front of her.

"What is it?" he drawled, looking up impatiently. "It's a key. So what?"

"Don't you recognize it? I think Queen Calista has one," she said, skimming the text. "The metal used to make this key and its mate were forged by water, stone, and magic. They possess the power to heal almost anything, including resurrecting the dead, it seems. They can also transverse time. The owners must be chosen by the Goddess and blessed by the elements."

Sensing the power possessed by the keys, Knoxx was quick to dismiss their value in front of Daisy. He had suspected they were of value based on his interactions with the miners in Vulnari. After he snatched Calista's key and showed it to them, they confirmed that it was a rare metal. He needed to get those keys in his possession by any means necessary. If it was true that those keys had the ability to heal anything, including resurrecting the dead, and also move time, the power he could wield would be tremendous. He would be unstoppable. Immortal. He could own LaMarra.

"I need to tell Calista," Daisy said with determination. "She needs to know. Could you take me to her, please?"

"Yeah, sure. She's probably back at her own estate by now," he replied.

"Actually, I'm not sure," Daisy said. "She said something about going on an expedition through Gold Leaf Forest to the base of the waterfall. I was hoping you could track them for me and bring me to them."

Knoxx considered Daisy for a moment as he took in in this turn of events and tried to figure out how to work the circumstances to his advantage. He was now in possession of what he thought was privileged information. Phoenix had no idea of the power that those keys held, and Knoxx had no intention of letting him find out. With his limited access to Aterna, Knoxx was reliant on his water bond with Phoenix to figure out where he might be.

Knoxx excused himself to go to the restroom. He swept the room to ensure it was empty before he ran the tap in the skink and sent Phoenix a quick message. Several tense moments passed, and there was no response, no indication at all that Phoenix had even received his message. That only happened when he was in an area that could block magic. The cabin was the only place that sprang to mind. Knoxx reasoned that Phoenix was already on the way to the waterfall, and he certainly wouldn't be alone.

They both have the keys. There's no way I can let them find out the power they possess. Those idiots are out hiking to find a waterfall, and they have the answer right under their damned noses.

With his mind focused on getting the keys and taking control of West Marra, Knoxx saw his long-awaited plans finally coming to fruition. He had spent years grooming Phoenix, gaining his trust, and learning all the secrets of Aterna. Only recently things had gone off the rails when Phoenix and that bitch Queen started hooking up. Driven by blind ambition and lust for power, Knoxx decided that now was the time to act.

He returned to retrieve Daisy and rush her from the archives.

"So, are you just about done here?" he asked, not bothering to mask his irritation.

"Sure, just let me gather up my notes. Is everything OK? You seem rushed," Daisy asked as she hurried to collect her things.

"Hurry up!" he barked, causing her to hasten her pace. Knoxx registered the look of shock on her face, but he couldn't bring himself to care, her days were numbered. Daisy had outlived her usefulness.

As Knoxx practically dragged her from the archive building toward his vehicle, he wondered what Daisy might know about the keys. Dropping the terse attitude he had shown moments earlier, he decided to placate her, to get her talking as he drove them from the archives toward the river.

"Sorry about before. I get like that when I'm bored. Did you find anything interesting?" His question was as genuine as he could muster under the circumstances.

Daisy prattled on endlessly while Knoxx drove, reviewing the information she had gained and its implications. She was formulating theory after theory about the potential usefulness of those damn keys. She was obviously a smart girl. Having gained everything he needed from her, he wanted nothing more than for her to shut her up.

"Hey, love, did you remember to take your potion?" he asked. "We don't want any little brat—uh, kids—running around too soon," Knoxx said with an unsettling wink.

"Uh, actually, I did forget. Ha! Oops."

"Let's get that sorted out before you head out to meet Calista and the crew," he said. "One less thing to worry about."

Knoxx steered them toward the string of restaurants and shops in the social district on the bank overlooking the river. He dipped into the apothecary and within minutes emerged with two opaque takeaway beverage containers containing bright green liquid that was indicative of the potion commonly used to protect against the consequences of adult relationships.

Before getting back into the car, Knoxx discreetly dropped a lethal dose of powdered snakeweed into her cup. The liquid fizzed slightly. Then the drink turned a light purple colour.

"Drink up, love," he said once he was back in the car.

Daisy took the container and sipped. "Mmm . . . this tastes a bit funny."

"Every place makes it a little different. Go on, drink," he urged as he took large swigs of his own potion.

"What did you get? If I'm taking the potion, both of us are safe," Daisy said as innocently as ever.

"You can never be too sure, darling," Knoxx replied in a clipped tone, thinking about what an insufferable know-it-all she was. *I'll be glad to be rid of her.*

Daisy chose not to challenge Knoxx after his kindness that day, taking her to the archives and keeping her company as she worked and even looking out for her welfare by buying the potion.

As Knoxx started driving north along the coastal road, Daisy fell silent, looking aimlessly out the window. The snakeweed was clearly taking effect, he realized.

As she struggled to keep her eyes open, she turned to face Knoxx, suddenly realizing what had happened. With great effort she reached for her potion container, pulled the lid off, and saw that the contents were purple, not green. Knowing she had been poisoned she turned pleading eyes on Knoxx. He shoved her head away from him as he pulled up to the riverbank in a carved-out corner near King's Bar.

Knoxx hauled Daisy's limp, barely conscious body out of the car, slamming the back of her head against the edge of the car and the ground as he dragged her out by her ankles. He tied her legs to a large, heavy boulder at the water's edge.

The seedy surroundings were nothing short of terrifying for Daisy, who was paralyzed by fear and the drug. With no strength to fight, she widened her eyes in horror as Knoxx picked up the boulder and dragged her to the edge of the river. He took off his shoes, pants, and jacket and then dragged Daisy into the water. The water rose around her chest, then her neck, and then covered her face. Helpless, alone, and betrayed, she met her end.

Knoxx felt for the underwater cliff edge that gave way to deep water. Once he placed the stone on the edge, he checked to see if Daisy was still alive. Nothing would ruin his plans more than committing murder and being instantly whisked off to Blackstone. As long as she was alive when he threw her into the river, the river would kill her, not him. He grabbed a sturdy log and used it to shove the boulder over the edge, dragging Daisy with it into the dark depths of the river.

Out of breath and freezing from the water, Knoxx waded back to dry land, got dressed, and rewarded himself with a drink at King's before setting off to intercept Phoenix.

I'm getting those keys back.

Knoxx was known to have a taste for the finer things, and it wasn't often that he degraded himself to appear like the renegades he led. On that occasion, however, discretion was of utmost importance.

He changed out of his sleek suit in favour of the working man's attire he had stolen from a poor soul at King's a while ago. Then he went upstairs to the suites he is so fond of occupying with any of the women who regularly threw themselves at him.

Once changed and able to blend in, he set out on foot toward the northern edge of Gold Leaf Forest. Among his few possessions were his knives, some snakeweed capsules, and the papers with Daisy's notes. He was a thug, but he was far from dumb. The information that Daisy had collected would be invaluable when he retrieved those keys.

As night fell on West Marra, Knoxx set up camp near the northern part of Gold Leaf Forest a short distance from the base of the waterfall, where the forest met the river. There he lay in wait for Phoenix and company to arrive, planning to ambush them when they eventually figured out what the hell they were doing. Blinded by his own sinister ambitions, Knoxx resolved to take this mission on alone, no witnesses. Phoenix's time was up.

CHAPTER 34
The Waterfall
Calista

"Lev, you've had a long day of firsts," Calista said. "We'll need your senses sharp tomorrow. Go rest. You too, Luxx. We'll leave for the waterfall tomorrow at daybreak."

The finality in Calista's tone was enough to convince Luxx and Lev to take the first shift in the bedroom while she and Phoenix stayed awake—just in case.

The soft click of the bedroom door signalled that Calista and Phoenix were alone in the living area.

"Do you really think someone is out there?" Phoenix asked quietly

"I don't know, but I'm not about to challenge Lev's superhuman sense of hearing, are you?"

"Uh, no I'm not," Phoenix said, laughing. He reached into a side pocket in his leather pants and pulled out his key. Calista's eyes widened and then she smiled, pulling her own key from a hidden pocket in her chest plate. They laughed quietly.

"I guess great minds think alike after all," she said as she traced the details of her key with her finger. "This key is always warm, like, warmer than usual. Is yours the same?" Calista reached out to touch

Phoenix's key. To her surprise, it was warm. She picked it up and held them side by side in the palms of her hands and examined them. Phoenix looked over her shoulder, doing the same.

"They look like they might fit together, almost like a puzzle," he said. The deep-blue stones that traced the flat part of Calista's key, which was the smaller of the two, shimmered in the firelight. The outline of deep-red stones that decorated the flat part of Phoenix's key complemented Cali's key.

"What if . . ." Calista began as she laid her key on top of Phoenix's. Sure enough, they fit together perfectly and began vibrating, producing a visible form of energy that was so strong that Calista felt it in her bones. She tried to separate the keys, but they were tightly bound, as if attracted to each other by a magical force.

Phoenix placed his hand palm down over the key in Calista's hand, and they sprang apart, the humming and vibrating stopping instantly. They put the keys on the etched map and watched as they slid, propelled by some unknown force, to the point on the map that marked the base of the waterfall.

Phoenix and Calista exchanged glances, unsure of what to make of it but certain in the knowledge that they needed to find out what was at that waterfall.

CHAPTER 35
The Portal
Calista

As the rising sun warmed the bedroom where Phoenix and Calista spent the latter half of the night, they arose to the sounds of Lev and Luxx packing and preparing breakfast.

"I made you your tar crap," Lev said with a sneer, causing Phoenix to smile as he yanked on his battle leathers.

Lev and Luxx were already dressed and had eaten a substantial breakfast, saving some for Phoenix and Calista.

"Did you go hunting this morning?" Calista inquired around a mouthful of delicious grilled meat, some roasted root vegetables, and some of Phoenix's "tar coffee."

"It's nothing," Lev replied. "I went out early this morning to see if there was anyone nearby, and I smelled a few small animals. Luxx's deadly aim nailed them to a tree, and now we call them breakfast."

Phoenix choked around his last mouthful of food in response to Lev's description of what animal was sacrificed for the meal, but he smiled and thanked him, nonetheless.

"Remind me not to upset her," Lev added innocently, if not a little conspiratorially. "She's scary with that little blade."

"Let's move out!" Calista ordered, exuding regal confidence and leadership. The four of them abandoned the ATVs and continued the trek northwards on foot so as to attract as little attention as possible. They also wanted to avoid clouding Lev's senses with the vehicles' emissions. As they walked, Calista told Luxx and Lev what had happened with the keys and how they suspected there was a deep magic embedded in them. Lev inspected the keys and confirmed they were indeed imbued with an ancient and powerful magic, one he didn't think continued to exist after the war that divided east and west.

"Shhhh." Lev put a finger to his lips, indicating for everyone to be quiet as he listened keenly. "We're not alone," he said, his voice barely audible above the distant sound of the waterfall, which was perhaps a half kilometre away.

Phoenix glanced around but saw nothing amiss, nor did Calista or Luxx. On Lev's signal they advanced again, carefully and quietly. The cold air was frosting the tips of the leaves on the trees, an indication that they were near the northern bank of the River Marra. The trees and soft underbrush gave way to rocky terrain and fallen logs.

Calista climbed up on the rocks on the edge of the riverbank to admire the beauty of the waterfall. Curtains of water crashed down, sending up plumes of cold mist that obscured the base of the waterfall where it met the river. The inky black waters of Siphon Lake crested over the edge and came splashing down into the deep navy-blue waters of the River Marra. As the waters drifted southwards downriver, they became lighter and almost clear where they met international waters.

As Phoenix looked at Calista, his back facing a cluster of trees downriver, Knoxx emerged from his hiding place and, in one swift motion, wrapped his forearm around Phoenix's throat and put his blade against the base of his skull.

"Don't fucking move," Knoxx rasped, his voice harsh from breathing the cold air all night.

Lev, Luxx, and Calista, then froze in place in response to the scene of Phoenix being held hostage by Knoxx. He shoved Phoenix toward the edge of the rocky embankment. It was unlikely anyone would survive the violently churning waters if they fell in.

Luxx glanced at Lev, then crouched low and moved toward Calista, who was standing stock still on the rocks, watching the horror unfold as Knoxx moved Phoenix along the edge of the embankment toward her.

"If nobody moves, nobody dies!" Knoxx shouted over the roar of the waterfall.

Calista was now a few feet away from where Knoxx was holding Phoenix at knifepoint on the edge of a steep rock shelf. Lev was positioned behind Knoxx, and Luxx was zeroing in on Cali's position.

Suddenly, the three of them rushed in and converged on Knoxx. Using his height advantage, Lev reached over Knoxx's head and pressed his palm into Knoxx's nose while he put pressure on the base of his skull, causing him to jerk violently and release Phoenix, but not before kicking him over the edge of the rocks and into the river.

Calista shrieked in terror before attempting to launch herself into the frigid water, only to be caught at the last minute by Luxx, who grabbed her leg and hauled her back from the edge of the rocks. Calista's screams were shrill and frantic as she demanded that Luxx let her go, so she could go after Phoenix.

"Let me go, Luxx! He's going to die! Let me go!" she screamed as Luxx dragged her back.

"Follow me!" Luxx said as she yanked Calista to her feet and pulled her farther upriver toward the nearly vertical cliff face that the waterfall was crashing against.

Meanwhile, Lev was engaged in intense hand-to-hand combat with Knoxx. Lev leaped back as Knoxx pulled out a short Vulnari-steel blade he had tucked into his boot. He took wild swipes at Lev, his eyes bugging out of his head. He looked like a man possessed.

Lev was light on his feet and was able to dodge and avoid being seriously maimed. Shifting his gaze to the water, Lev sensed Knoxx had become unhinged. Before Knoxx could strike again, Lev dove into the water to search for Phoenix, leaving Knoxx bewildered on the edge of the water.

Knoxx raced toward the cliff where Luxx and Calista had taken shelter. Hearing him approach, Luxx launched herself at him and landed her knee directly in his groin, causing him to double over in pain. When his head was bowed, she planted her thumbs into his eye sockets and brought her knee up hard and fast into his face, causing a sickening crunching sound that could only be his nose breaking.

Knoxx staggered back, his eyes still wild as he took in Luxx and like a caged animal. He shifted his eyes toward Calista, who was also in a fighting stance. He lunged at her, but she sidestepped him, allowing him to crash into the wall behind her. Breathing hard, he rolled over, spitting blood.

"The key, you bitch. Hand it over."

Without a moment's thought, Calista raised her foot and stomped down with all her strength on his groin again. While he writhed in pain, Luxx planted her knee in the hollow of his throat, cutting off his air supply until he passed out. She reached into his pockets and felt his legs down to his boots, removing all his weapons, just in case he regained consciousness. Calista picked up the wad of papers and saw they were in Daisy's handwriting—her notes about the keys and magic. Luxx snatched the papers from Calista's hand.

"We can go over that later. Look." she pointed to the edge of the waterfall on the opposite side of the river. Lev had fished Phoenix out of the raging water and was dragging him up onto the rocks.

Calista ran as best as she could across the jagged rocks behind the waterfall, then pressed herself against the sheer cliff face as she inched along, desperate to get to the other side.

Once there she dropped to Phoenix's side, holding his face in her hands. Luxx gave Lev a look to communicate her feelings of deep gratitude for saving her best friend's mate. The reality of losing him struck Luxx deep in her soul. Losing one's mate is like losing half of one's soul. It was harder to survive than any other kind of separation, including death by natural causes.

"Nix, I'm here, wake up," Calista pleaded, shaking Phoenix's listless form.

"Lev, do something!" she shrieked in desperation. "Do something!"

Lev knelt on the other side of Phoenix and raised his head. Phoenix started to cough and spit water as he slowly opened his eyes and took great gasping gulps of air. Relief washed over Calista as she threw herself over his chest and hugged him tightly.

"You scared the life out of me," she murmured against his throat as he continued to cough.

"It was a close one," he rasped.

As he sat up to take in his surroundings, Phoenix turned to Lev. "Thank you," he said. "I owe you my—" He stopped when Lev held up a hand to silenced him, shaking his head

"Don't thank me. I wasn't going to let the river swallow you."

Phoenix smiled and allowed Lev to help him stand. He was a little unsteady at first but eventually he made it to his feet with Calista and Lev helping him balance himself.

"Let's get you back to the cabin," Calista said. "We've had enough excitement for one day." She made her way back to the ledge that she had inched along to get across the waterfall. "Follow me. We can use this ledge to get back across the river behind the waterfall, but be careful; it's slippery." In single file, with Calista in the lead, the others hugged the wall behind the waterfall, using the small ledge to inch their way back across to the west bank.

Still a little unsteady, Phoenix slipped a few times, but Calista took no chances in losing him to the river twice in one day, holding onto one of the loops of his chest plate. Tucked into the loop she felt the shape of his key. She realized he had tied it on before they left that morning. As she felt its warmth, she became aware of her own key around her neck, which was also warming.

"It's narrow here, Nix. Slow and steady. Nix!"

He slipped off the narrow edge, pulling Calista after him into the waterfall's dark, icy, churning depths.

Calista flailed about under the water, still holding onto Phoenix for dear life when she felt an unmistakable heat well up around her throat. As if being pulled by a magnetic force too strong to fight, she was drawn toward Phoenix. A flash of bioluminescence exploded from the collar of her battle leathers and from where she was holding Phoenix. The keys were alight with energy. Vibrating and exploding with bioluminescence, threads of water weaved together, becoming thick like ropes and forming a beacon of energy made of ancient, powerful magic until the beacons connected. With the water swirling around them, Phoenix and Calista held onto each other as they were pulled down into the depths of a whirlpool of magic until they vanished.

CHAPTER 36
What Now?
Luxx

"Calista!!" Luxx shouted at the water's surface, searching frantically for her head to pop up. The force of the waterfall churning the water made it difficult for her to see where the current may have carried them off. She turned toward Lev, her eyes wide with panic. "Go in! See if you can find them!" Her voice was caught somewhere between pleading and panic.

Lev pulled her back from the water's edge, holding her tightly against his body to prevent her from diving into the churning waters. "Shhhhh," he said, trying to soothe her. "They're gone. They've vanished."

Luxx stared up at him in disbelief. "How could you possibly know that?"

Lev released her, and she sat heavily on the rocky bank, a safer distance from the waterfall but not far enough away for Lev to leave her side. He sat beside her and spoke as gently as he could manage while still being heard over the rushing water. "I heard them struggle underwater. Then I heard it, the sound of a portal opening."

Luxx looked at him in confusion. "Portal?" Lev had never seen such a look on her face before, a mixture of incredulity and disbelief. Luxx shook her head to clear her thoughts. "What portal?" she asked. "What do you mean you heard it open? What do you know about a portal?" Her rapid-fire questions revealed the mounting anxiety that was twisting her insides.

"I could hear them underwater," Lev explained. "I could hear their heartbeats, their bodies moving, kicking, and trying to swim to the surface. Then I heard this deep and powerful blast of energy. There was a brief flash—I don't know if you could see it from where you were standing on the bank. Then there was silence. They're gone." Lev paused for a moment to allow Luxx to calm down before he continued. "Ages ago, when I was a young water dragon, the elders spoke of a force at the base of the waterfall. We were forbidden to descend over the waterfall and cautioned against the force. I think that force must be a portal that is connected to the magic of Siphon Lake. I think Cali and Nix have fallen into the portal, and I don't know where they've ended up."

As Luxx stared up at Lev, tears streamed down her cheeks. "You never thought to mention this before now?" she asked in bewilderment.

"I didn't think it was true. Especially since the water dragons were able to descend the waterfall into the river to help in the war, I thought it was just a way to keep us in line. I'm sorry; I had no idea it was real."

Luxx believed he didn't know. She could feel his anguish as he admitted how he had misinterpreted the force. "Do you think they're alive?" she asked.

Lev brought Luxx into a tight hug. "I don't know," he said, his lips pressed into the top of her head.

Luxx allowed herself a few moments to feel the acute pain of losing Calista. Then she let out a howl as she expressed the depths of her grief.

After some time she tried to pull herself together. With tremendous effort she collected her thoughts. She was drained emotionally and physically. The day's events had taken their toll. Lev watched as Luxx stood up and went to the water's edge. Clutching her Aquavass in her fist, she turned toward Lev, who was ready to pull her back from the edge if she tried to jump. Luxx could sense his anxiety as he anticipated her next movements.

"Lev, Calista is gone, and so is Phoenix. There are no heirs for East Marr or West Marra. I was—am—I don't know." As Luxx stumbled over her words Lev reached for her hand. She took it and squeezed it tightly before continuing. "I'm her second in command, the royal advisor to the Queen of East Marra. With Calista gone and no heir to take the throne, I'm the interim ruler of East Marra." Luxx sighed deeply as the weight of her new position bore down on her. "If this is the case for East Marra, then that means Knoxx the interim ruler of West Marra." Speaking the words aloud to Lev sounded absurd, but she knew it was their new reality. Lev dropped to one knee and bowed his head before Luxx.

"My Queen."

EPILOGUE

Knoxx lay in a bloody, battered heap against the rocks. His body was aching, but he was conscious. Unable to move, his vision drifting in and out of focus, he remained still. In the stillness he listened to the thoughts formulating in his mind. Through the haze of confusion, he hoped Phoenix had died in the river, but he couldn't have hoped for the good fortune to have Calista fall into the water as well. There was no way they survived. The realization that Phoenix and Calista were gone elated him to his core. He was the new King of West Marra. His sinister thoughts didn't end there. With Calista gone, he quickly re-evaluated his ambitions. He decided there and then in his depleted state that death would not claim him. He would rise up as the King of all LaMarra.

ABOUT THE AUTHOR

Emily Stone & Diana Bloom were born to Italian immigrants who traversed the Atlantic from Italy to Toronto in the 1950s and 1960s. They both reside in Toronto, Canada, and have a passion for travel, crafts, fashion, makeup artistry, and literature. Writing has always been an important creative outlet, and they hope to help readers escape the mundane. *A World Divided* is their first novel.

Printed in the USA
CPSIA information can be obtained
at www.ICGtesting.com
LVHW092303160924
791252LV00005B/398

9 781039 149649